TECHWITCH BOOK TWO

WICKED WORDS

M.J. SCOTT

Free Short Story

Sign up to my newsletter and I'll send you
TO CATCH A WITCH
an exclusive short story set in the Techwitch
universe, plus you'll get all the news on upcoming
releases and sales.

Sign up at www.mjscott.net.

*For all the writers, artists, musicians, and other creative
peeps who gave us places to escape over the last year.*

Chapter One

I'D NEVER EXPECTED MAGIC.

Never wanted it.

My mother showed me magic's darker side when I was a child. Having a demon hunt me once I'd found my power as an adult hadn't done much to change my mind about the chaos and trouble magic trailed in its wake.

But now mine had vanished.

I hadn't wanted magic, but the fact that it had gone AWOL hadn't improved my life. In fact, I was coming to the rapid conclusion that, if I couldn't get my powers back, I was totally screwed.

The lines of code on my monitor started to blur, and I blinked reluctantly, pushing away from the desk and standing to stretch and give my eyes a break. But looser muscles didn't help. When I sat down again, the code remained seemingly flawless. If there was a glitch somewhere, I couldn't spot it.

Which was a problem because spotting impossible-to-spot glitches was what I did. Or had done.

Before.

Nope. Don't think about before.

I leaned closer to the monitor as though proximity might improve my chances of figuring out the problem. Which got me nothing but an urge to squint and lower the brightness on the screen.

It didn't matter which way I studied and analyzed the various codes, routines, sub-routines, and databases. As far as I could determine, there was no reason why the eye-wateringly expensive computer system running this state-of-the-art, cost-the-client-a-fortune manufacturing facility was suddenly refusing to talk to the similarly state-of-the-art computer system running logistics or the one in the design department.

There had to be one, of course. The not-so-state-of-the-art messes rolling off my client's production line in all the wrong quantities, and at all the wrong times, were compelling evidence that something had gone seriously wrong.

The company's own tech gurus had tried to fix it.

They'd failed.

Then they'd called me.

Normally I'd be able to find out what the problem was.

That's what I do. I'm the TechWitch. (Yes, I named my company before I knew I had magic. The universe, it seems, has a sense of irony.) Show me a computer or a program that's sulking, misbehaving, or generally causing havoc, and I can always find the problem, even when legions of programmers insisted there couldn't possibly be one.

Maggie Lachlan. Computer whisperer.

Solving unsolvable tech problems had provided me with a nice little living before my life was thrown into chaos by demons and magic and death. It had taken me nine months since I'd fought a demon to even think about returning to work.

Nine months of hiding out, trying to cope with the death of my best friend and the rapid departure —stage left—of Damon Riley, the man I'd foolishly let myself fall for. Nine months in which the only real bright spots had been the fact that nothing had tried to kill me, I'd grown a lot more proficient using power tools, I knew a lot more about California's post-quake building codes, and I hadn't had to use any magic. But I couldn't hide forever—I didn't have a bottomless bank account—and I'd taken this job after a number of increasingly hard-to-resist offers.

Piece of cake, I'd told myself. *Make a quick*

chunk of change, then go back to hiding out for a few more months.

I'm sure they say something in songs about the problems with making assumptions and counting your chickens, too.

Because whatever it was that let me find the things no one else found lurking in obscure recesses of code, it seemed to have left the building. I never made any promises to my clients about how long it would take me to solve their issues, but I figured they'd notice eventually if I continued to suck this hard.

A computer whisperer who could no longer whisper was about as useful as square wheels on a bicycle.

I'd been trying to pedal forward on right angles for two weeks now, making about as much progress as you'd expect. Last night it had finally occurred to me that this was the first time I'd tried to do my job since I'd tangled with a demon. So maybe my inability to find the answer had something to do with that...with my magic

I hadn't tried to use magic since the day I'd buried my best friend. Last night I'd tried one of the most basic exercises I'd been taught—lighting a candle. I'd failed. Several times.

Nothing. My magic was gone. And I didn't think it was just that I was out of practice. Or that I didn't know a lot about magic in the first place. Yes, I'd only just found my power when the demon had thrown my life into chaos, and yes, I'd barely had time to learn the basics before I'd decided magic wasn't for me. But magic isn't something that vanishes on its own. I had chosen not to use it since Nat had died but even if I'd forgotten the knack of it, I should have been able to feel something when I tried. I knew how my power felt.

I knew I couldn't feel it now.

The realization had led me to a night of tossing and turning. Lack of sleep only increased my frustration with the system I was trying to diagnose. If this job dragged out much longer, my client would start to get antsy. My contracts included a flat rate I earned no matter the result of the job, but if I couldn't show some progress, the client wouldn't want to keep paying my hourly rate over and above that. I kind of needed that money. I needed to get my shit together.

I glared at the screen one last time. Time to shut down for the night. It was already after eight. On a Friday. Sometimes its better to sleep on things and try again in the morning.

The blank screen seemed to stare at me accusingly as I packed up my stuff. I ignored it. I'd do some more analysis at home over the weekend, but I didn't have to face my client again until Monday. I did, however, have to face facts. I wasn't getting anywhere. I needed to woman up when I got home and ask my accidental housemate, Lizzie Reagan, for advice.

I might be the TechWitch, but Lizzie was an actual witch. One who was in full control of her powers and fully immersed in the magical world I'd been so desperately avoiding. In fact, she was the youngest member of the Cestis. You didn't get much more magical than the USA's ruling council of witches. Police, judge, and jury all in one. Not to be messed with. Which was why I was hoping Lizzie might have a solution that would keep me from having to deal with them in any official capacity again.

I was the reason they were only four instead of five. Antony, one of their members, had tried to help me rescue Nat, my best friend, from a demon. We'd failed. Nat and Antony had died. I really didn't want to face the others. The fact that they, apart from Lizzie, had left me mostly alone for nine months seemed to indicate the feeling was mutual.

My anxiety over asking Lizzie for help only grew on my trip home. The elderly electric car I'd bought when I'd moved back to Berkeley groaned up the hill toward Tilden Park, the artificial hum of its engine underscored with noises that didn't sound good. I really needed to get it checked out. I'd picked it up for a bargain price, and it had done well enough when I wasn't straying far from Berkley, but in the last few weeks it had started showing its age.

My grandparents' house—mine now—was located in the North Berkeley Hills. Before the Big One, it had been one of the most expensive areas in town. But high real estate values hadn't spared it from damage in the quake, though it had fared better than the areas down by the beach. The streets were now a mix of brand-new mansions rebuilt fast by those who could afford it, vacant blocks that hadn't sold after the owners had decided California was no longer the place to be post-quake, and half-wrecked works in progress like mine, slowly being put back together as cash became available.

My house was in a quiet area, close to the park, and when my grandparents bought it, it had definitely been the worst house on the street. Grandpa had done it up lovingly over the years, but it had still been one of the most modest places in the neighborhood. I was trying to restore it to a little of its former glory. But rebuilding was expensive these days. There were exacting new standards for quake safety to be met, not to mention the environmental requirements. I probably would have qualified for one of the grants the city gave out for reestablishment, but I figured there were people who needed it more than me. I could do it on my own.

As long as I was working. My bank account was beginning to look very lean after my time off. Hence not wanting to drop chunks of cash on a new car. I just had to hope my mechanic could work a miracle to keep me on the road.

Much like I hoped Lizzie might work a miracle and help me get my mojo back.

But when I pulled into the drive, the house was dark, other than the automatic porch light blinking on as the motion sensors caught the car. I watched as I killed the engine, but apart from the front hall light flaring as the housecomp started its "somebody is home" sequence, there was definitely no other sign of life. Just the house, the latest ramshackle pile of renovation rubbish on the front lawn, and the geraniums growing on the porch, as usual.

I didn't know whether I was relieved or disappointed. To distract myself while I pondered how exactly to tell Lizzie, I wandered into the kitchen to investigate dinner options. Lizzie was more of a cook than me, but she wasn't Nat's level of domestically obsessed. She usually left me something if she'd cooked before I got home, but clearly she'd been out all day. There was no message on my datapad, so whatever she was doing, she hadn't let me know.

That wasn't unusual. When she moved in, I'd

made my stance on avoiding magic clear, so she tended to be cagey about her movements when she was doing something involving the Cestis or her witch life. The only thing she'd put her foot down about was the silver bracelet that currently circled my right wrist. It was somehow connected to the wards Lizzie had laced the house with. I hadn't asked for details, just followed her instructions that I was to wear it. I only took it off to shower or if I was doing something on the house involving the kinds of tools it wasn't safe to wear jewelry around.

I blasted a frozen burrito, added a handful of baby carrots and some arugula to fool myself that it was vaguely healthy, smothered them in enough dressing to cancel out the vitamins, and carried it all into the living room. My home office was still unfinished, so I'd set up a temporary desk in there.

We'd had the weather screens installed downstairs a few weeks earlier so that the living room, kitchen, and our temporary bedrooms were pleasantly cool despite the warm night. Spring had brought decent rainfall, but the weather was heating up fast, as it did these days. We had to hope the rain and the continued re-greening projects would keep the fire season from being like the bad old days. I avoided my business email as I chewed, distracting myself with newslinks and general web nonsense.

I was too hungry to eat slowly, and fifteen minutes later, I was back in the kitchen, washing my plate and silverware and wondering whether I should find something to stream or just attempt to go to bed. Without Lizzie in the house, I knew I wouldn't fall asleep easily. I trusted her wards, but having a demon invade your dreams for years didn't make for easy sleeping, and even though my demon was gone, the insomnia that had plagued me since my teens still paid frequent visits.

So streaming it was. Lizzie and I were working our way through the many series of our current retro binge, but I couldn't do an episode without her. Instead I called up a real oldie—one of the ancient Hollywood musicals my gran had loved—and put it on while I tried to settle on the sofa.

I got about halfway through before I decided that not even fabulous frocks, sequins, and elaborate dance sequences were holding my focus. Maybe an hour of hanging drywall in the upstairs hall might wear me out enough to sleep? But I only got as far as the kitchen when the housecomp chimed, then announced I had an incoming call from Cassandra's Cauldron.

A shiver ran down my spine. What the hell was Cassandra Tallant doing calling me at nearly midnight? She was the Cestis's oldest member, and I hadn't spoken to her in months. I doubted she'd suddenly been seized by the urge to call me for a casual chat.

"Answer. Voice only," I said to the comp, leaning against the counter and wrapping my arms around myself.

"Maggie?" Cassandra's crisp voice came out of the speakers, clear as a bell tolling a warning. "Can you come to the store and get Lizzie? She's hurt."

Chapter Two

IT WAS AMAZING how fast my car could go when I was driving in a blind panic. Cassandra had hung up before I could ask for any details, and I hadn't wanted to waste any time calling her back. By the time I got back across the bay to the edges of the Tenderloin and lucked into a parking spot right outside Cassandra's store, I'd half convinced myself Lizzie must be dying. My therapist—before I'd stopped seeing her—had warned me that I might be triggered by any danger to people I was close to in the wake of Nat's death. It seemed she'd been right.

I pounded on the door to the panicked beat of my heart. A light flicked on inside, and I almost lost my mind in the time it took for Cassandra to unlock the door. She took one look at my face and said,

"Goodness, child. She's not dying. Come upstairs and I'll make you some tea. You look worse than she does."

I didn't completely believe her until I reached the top of the creaking wooden staircase to the small private quarters above the store and found Lizzie sitting on Cassandra's elderly purple sofa, sipping tea. Her left arm was cradled in a dark blue sling, and her freckles stood out against skin that was too pale.

"What happened?" I demanded.

Lizzie grimaced. "Long story."

I took that to mean "Cestis business you don't want to know about."

But apparently Cassandra, unlike Lizzie, wasn't going to spare my feelings. "She tangled with an imp," she said bluntly. "She fell and fractured her arm. Radha has done some work on it, but it will need a week or so to heal completely." Radha Morgan was the Cestis's chief healer. She was nowhere to be seen, which was something of a relief. I'd only met the woman a few times. She'd never seemed to warm to me much. But Cassandra was more intimidating than Radha could ever be.

"An imp? Why was there an imp?" Imps were lesser demons. Kind of magical attack dogs. Sent by the bigger ones from their world to ours through cracks in the energy fields too small for demons themselves to fit. Or they accompanied the demons who did manage to break through. But that was rare, and we'd dispatched the last one who had— my demon—back to its own plane. Or at least I thought we had.

"We're still cleaning up strays from your demon. Among other things," Cassandra said, her gold-brown eyes stern. "It's been keeping us busy. And now we're even more shorthanded with Lizzie sidelined."

"I can still help," Lizzie protested, but she snapped her mouth closed when Cassandra turned the disapproving look her way.

"Maggie can do her share." Maggie *would* do her share, the tone suggested.

Maggie kind of wanted to run back down the stairs and hide somewhere the Cestis wouldn't be able to find her. But I wasn't in the habit of abandoning my friends.

"Maggie doesn't want to do magic," Lizzie said, lifting her chin. Her hair was messy, the long blue bangs falling in her brown eyes. She blew them out of the way with an impatient breath.

"We don't always get what we want," Cassandra said. She turned back to me. "You're strong, Maggie. Untrained, yes, and we've respected your wishes and left you alone to lick your wounds. But right now, we could use some help. I think you owe us that much, don't you?"

I froze. Damn it, she was right. I did owe them a

debt. But I didn't want to pay up. "Even if I wanted to, I couldn't," I blurted before I could think. "I can't do magic."

Lizzie dropped her teacup.

Ten minutes later, I'd cleaned up the mess while trying to answer a rapid-fire series of questions from Cassandra about what I meant by "couldn't." Apparently my answers didn't convince her that my magic had vanished.

We'd moved to the tiny kitchen, and I was staring at the candle Cassandra had placed in front of me like it might bite me. Lizzie sat opposite me, looking pale and nibbling on a cookie. She'd tried to get a few questions in herself but had eventually ceded the floor to Cassandra.

"Light the candle," Cassandra said, fixing me with the sort of gaze that brooked no argument. How someone who looked basically like Mrs. Claus —all round cheeks, silvery hair tied back in a fat bun, and curves—managed to be so goddamn intimidating at times was a mystery I'd yet to solve.

I stared at the slim white taper. "It won't work. I haven't done magic since—" I clenched my teeth. I still couldn't let myself remember too much about that day. Because all I saw was my best friend lying in a pool of blood.

Dead.

I straightened on my stool to hide the shiver that skulked down my spine, stealing the moisture in my mouth and leaving me unable to complete my sentence.

"Maggie Diana Lachlan, you called lightning to kill a demon. You can do this." Cassandra pointed at the candle. "So do it."

Lizzie smiled encouragingly, giving me a sneaky thumbs-up with her good hand. I ignored her and stared at the virgin white wick. I knew the theory. See the energy fields, change the energy fields, and, hey presto, flame.

But the white candle was only white. I saw wax, not energy. Just like I had the night before.

"Breathing will help," Cassandra said in a slightly kinder tone.

I took a deep breath and closed my eyes, trying to remember what it felt like to use magic. Trying to find that spark within, that sense of energy surrounding me. But there was only darkness behind my eyes, and all I felt was an echoing coldness.

Empty.

I opened my eyes and nothing had changed. The candle was still just a boring white cylinder. No slight shimmering colors to show me the energy field. I couldn't even see auras around Cassandra or Lizzie, and they were two of the four strongest witches in the country. My shoulders slumped. "This isn't going to work."

"Have a cookie," Lizzie said, shoving a plate of

Cassandra's oatmeal cranberry toward me. "Maybe you need a sugar fix."

"It would have to be one hell of a fix," I said, but I took one anyway. Cassandra might be terrifying when she chose to be, but she made damn fine cookies.

"You've really done no magic at all for nine months?" Cassandra asked as I chewed. The Cestis didn't take magic lightly, and neither Cassandra nor Lizzie would use magic for anything completely frivolous, but I could tell she couldn't imagine not doing anything with your power for so long.

I shook my head, then swallowed. "No. Didn't try. Didn't want to. Ask Lizzie."

Lizzie nodded in agreement but didn't add anything, avoiding getting dragged into the mess by taking another cookie. The sugar fix seemed to be doing her more good than me. Her skin was starting to show a hint of color again.

Cassandra frowned. "And you didn't use your —" She waved a hand in the air vaguely. "—whatever it is you do for your job?"

"No, I took a break from working. As I'm sure Lizzie told you."

Lizzie was the only member of the Cestis I'd spoken to since Nat's funeral. Mainly because she'd refused to take "no" for an answer. She found me after I moved out of the apartment Nat and I had shared in SoMa, kept checking up on me, and then eventually moved herself in once I'd begun working on the house. I figured she was reporting back to the others, but I'd needed the company. Someone to distract me from the gaping hole in my life where Nat—and, as much as I hated to admit it, Damon Riley—should've been.

Someone who could understand what I'd faced. Someone who knew the creatures who haunted my dreams were real, not just nightmares.

Lizzie had apparently decided I needed supervision. Or a friend. Or both. Whichever it was, it was hard to get rid of a witch who didn't want to be gotten rid of. Lizzie was young, but she had stubborn for centuries.

Cassandra frowned at the candle. I tried to look like I was concentrating on it.

"And now you're working again but having trouble? Are you sure you're not just out of practice?"

I reached for another cookie, shaking my head. "I've always been able to fix computer stuff. My gran used to have this ancient datapad she refused to upgrade. I kept it running. My friends all had me tweak their systems. I kept my grandad's tech, which wasn't much better than Gran's, running, too. I aced every computer-related class I ever took. But now I just can't seem to get a fix on the problem like I used to." I bit into the cookie again, focusing on sugar and cranberry tang. The taste took my mind off the unsettling incense-oil-wax smell that permeated Cassandra's store, even here in her tiny upstairs rooms. The smell of magic.

"How long have you been back at work?"

"Almost two weeks."

Cassandra's frown deepened. "Well, if you're telling the truth and your magic is blocked, you could well have bigger problems than not being able to do your job."

Suddenly the cookie tasted like dust. "Such as?"

"Without your magic, you're vulnerable."

My skin went cold. "Define 'vulnerable.'" I put down what was left of the cookie, hoping my hands wouldn't start shaking. I'd asked the question, but I had a pretty good idea what the answer might be.

"It depends on what's causing your block. You could be shut down tight, or you could just be blocking access to your power for yourself. Which would leave it wide open to anybody else. Have you noticed anything strange happening lately?"

I knew what "strange" was code for. Demons. My hands clenched. "Wait a minute, you think I could be possessed? By what, a carpentry demon?"

Lizzie snorted. "That would be chill. Also, handy. Though you'd think a carpentry demon would improve your skills."

I relaxed a little at that. If she thought I might be possessed, she wouldn't be making jokes.

"I'm not the one who hammers her own thumb with alarming regularity," I retorted. Not that I hadn't, too, in the beginning. I'd occasionally helped Grandad around the house, but teen Maggie had been far more fixated on computers than hand tools. I'd only remembered the barest basics when I'd started renovating. But I had a reasonable idea what I was doing now. Mostly.

Sure, I hired contractors for the complicated things, but putting in hours on the house myself saved both my money and my sanity. Without the renovation to focus on, I wasn't sure I would have survived the first few months after Nat had died.

I'd ignored the house for a long time. I still had trouble thinking of it as mine, not my grandparents'. But turns out that renovating the house I'd grown up in—despite all the memories of Gran and Granddad and the still sharp flashes of grief for them—was less painful than dealing with my guilt about Nat.

I was sure that Lizzie's initial motivation for stepping in to help me had solely been her worrying I might do something stupid. But while she worked hard, she wasn't naturally gifted in DIY. But the two of us muddled through, and nothing we'd built had fallen down. Yet.

Cassandra scowled at both of us, holding up a

hand. "This isn't a joke. Maggie was bound to a demon for years without anyone knowing about it."

"She killed the demon," Lizzie protested.

"She killed its physical manifestation. I'm sure it's alive and well back in the demon realm."

What? My throat tightened, and my stomach flipped. I clapped a hand to my mouth, not sure I wasn't going to throw up. That was a tidbit of information that no one had bothered to tell me. The demon that had once had my power to feed on was alive? Alive and well and probably pissed at me?

I shivered as the demon with its bloodstained aura and dead eyes floated into my head. I could smell its screwed-up scent, choking with rot and filth as though it stood before me. Lizzie was the one who had to deal with garbage in our house because even the faintest whiff of decay could make me gag these days.

I had to swallow hard and do some of the deep breathing my therapist taught me before I could talk. "I can't be bound. There's been no ritual. Definitely no mysterious illnesses with memory loss."

As near as the Cestis had been able to determine, it seemed Sara—my late unlamented mother —had bound me to the demon just before my thirteenth birthday, before my powers had a chance to make themselves known. At least, we assumed it was her. She'd also done her best to make sure I had no memory of the ritual. Her best had been very, very good.

If only her morals had been, too.

Unfortunately she died not long after I turned thirteen, and I never knew what she'd done until a series of weird events last year led to the binding being broken and the demon expressing its displeasure about that.

Which had led to where I was now.

Screwed again.

"Demons aren't the only threat you might face," Cassandra said calmly. She held up a hand as I opened my mouth to protest. "I'm not saying you've been bound again, I'm saying that, if you can't defend yourself, someone with your power is a tempting target. And you don't have to be bound if the demon can just possess you. You know they find it easier to get through the barriers of anyone who is...not themselves."

She meant depressed or otherwise mentally ill. I didn't know if I'd have met the definition of clinical depression over the last nine months, but I'd definitely been to some dark places.

Knowing that a demon could have been waiting for me in one of them made me want to puke all over again. The fact that I hadn't seen any sign of a demon didn't matter. If my powers had gone, perhaps I wouldn't. After all, demons preyed on humans when they could. It was rare for one to make it through to our world from whatever hell realm it was they came from, but even from there they used their influence to spread misery and pain here. Had one of them gotten to me again? "How do we know one hasn't?"

Cassandra and Lizzie exchanged a look. One that made me uneasy.

"We have the house well warded," Lizzie said eventually.

"Very well warded," Cassandra agreed.

"I know that," I said. "Wait, what do you mean by 'we'?" I'd assumed Lizzie was keeping the Cestis informed about how I was doing. I didn't think any of them had been near my house.

"You were tangled up with a demon," Cassandra said. "You didn't think we were just going to wave goodbye and leave you on your own, did you?"

"You've been to my house?" I asked Cassandra.

"Early on," she said. "Lizzie thought it might be easier if we kept out of sight. One of us comes by now and then to check nothing has frayed if Lizzie wants a hand. And I live in Berkeley, after all."

I'd forgotten that. Or chosen not to think about it, maybe. I turned back to Lizzie. "And you never thought to tell me any of this?"

She shrugged. "You never asked. You've been fairly clear that you didn't want to hear about magic."

"But if the house is warded, how could anything have gotten to me?"

"The *house* is warded. You're not," Lizzie said. "At least not completely. The bracelet is a shield of sorts, but it's not a full ward. It was easier at first when you didn't go anywhere much without me. But you do now. Nothing has pinged any of the wards at the house. That's a good sign. That's what we were worried about in the beginning."

I suppressed a shiver, not wanting to think about exactly what might have come after me. "Wouldn't I have noticed if someone had put the whammy on me at the hardware store or shopping for groceries?" I hadn't really been venturing far from home until I'd started working with this new client. But they made titanium custom parts for manufacturing machinery that I couldn't imagine a demon could use to possess someone. Their systems were fancy, but they weren't based on the kind of virtual reality tech the demon had exploited last time.

"Maybe not. Not if it was something subtle," Cassandra said. "One would hope that a direct attack wouldn't have passed you by. After all, you know what imps look like."

"You haven't been out wreaking havoc nightly," Lizzie said, her tone cheerful. "Another good sign."

"But you can't know for sure? You didn't set wards to check if I'd been possessed?"

The two of them exchanged another look.

"It's not really possible," Cassandra said. "The wards protect you and keep things out. But they wouldn't register if you were being...influenced."

I didn't like where this was heading. "So what are my options?"

Lizzie's mouth twisted. "You know the drill."

I did. Two choices. Let one of the Cestis try and read me and see if they could spot the signs of me having a demon running my brain, or stick my hand in a bowl of demon stone.

Both options made my skin crawl. Demon stone was partly responsible for Nat's death. And after having a hidden demon passenger tucked away in my head for years, knowing my thoughts and feelings and secrets, I liked keeping my mind to myself.

"Can't I just jump in a baptismal font or something? Dowse myself in holy water?"

"That's vampires, dear," Cassandra said. "And it only works in stories."

I stared at her, hoping like hell she meant vampires only existed in stories rather than that they existed and holy water did nothing to stop them. But it was entirely possible she meant vampires were real. The sum total of what I knew about the magical world was probably about a trillionth of what Cassandra held in her head.

What I did know scared me silly. Anything was possible. Including all the bad things.

Which meant I could have a demon inside me. I was beginning to regret the cookies, the food sitting uneasily in a stomach turning rapidly to acid.

"You could just let me read you," Lizzie said.

"That's not necessarily a wise idea," Cassandra replied. "Not if Maggie has a passenger. Safer to let Radha do it with the rest of us shielding."

Passenger. Aka demon. I ducked my head, trying not to let them see how freaked out I was.

Which left me staring at my fingernails. When I'd taken the job, I'd filed them short and painted them a neutral pale pink to hide the fact that they'd been neglected for months. A blood blister bloomed on my thumb where I'd dropped a brick on it several days earlier, and my fingers sported calluses and fading scars from various renovation mishaps. All in all, my hands looked pretty beaten up. Which matched how I felt. What I wanted right now was to disappear, lie down somewhere soft, and not think about anything until I stopped feeling like I was the universe's favorite whipping girl. I didn't care how long it took.

Sadly, I couldn't afford that option. I wouldn't be able to afford many options at all if I couldn't sort out my work problems. I needed to know why my magic had disappeared. But I wasn't ready to leap straight down the path of "a demon is eating your magic again, Maggie." Especially if that meant facing demon stone.

I lifted my head and met Cassandra's gaze. "I'm not possessed. I'd know it."

Sympathy flashed in her gold-brown eyes, but her expression was stern. "I'm sorry, Maggie, but we can't just take your word for it."

I swallowed hard. Tried to sound calm. "Surely Lizzie would've noticed something?"

"Not if the creature has been biding its time. And we might not have sensed it with everything else going on. There's a lot of noise right now."

Noise. Magical noise, I had to assume. Stuff that had been happening since I'd killed the demon? That they hadn't been telling me about?

"What exactly has been happening?" Time to woman up and face the full extent of the catastrophe I'd caused. People were getting hurt again. As Lizzie's sling attested to. I might have been able to ignore the fact that she'd been very busy with secret witch business on and off during the time we'd been roomies, but I couldn't stick my head in the sand forever. I probably owed Lizzie an apology for not asking her what had been happening before now. But damn it, I didn't want all the complication the magical world seemed to bring with it. I wanted to be normal. The trouble was, I wasn't.

Lizzie sighed. "The quick version is that when the demon fried, all its bonds to the world—to the people it had been feeding from other than you and to whatever imps and afrits and lesserkind it was controlling—snapped and recoiled and caused some havoc. Plus all those imps and afrits were set free to do whatever they wanted. What they mostly want to do is destroy, eat, kill. So we've been tracking them down. We're mostly done."

"That sounds...bad." I'd tangled with imps a couple of times, but then I'd leveled straight up to facing a demon. There hadn't been much time for learning about demonkind other than how to try to defeat the one who was after me. If I was remembering correctly from the basic information Cassandra had given me back then, afrits were smaller and less problematic than imps. Lesserkind were more of a problem. They were smarter and more powerful. But also, I thought, maybe they were uncommon?

"It's not great but not terrible. We've been busier than usual. That happens sometimes," Lizzie said. "Luckily, it's mostly been imps and such. If there were any lesserkind hanging with your demon, then there's been no sign of them. Which is good."

Cassandra's lips pursed. She didn't seem to agree with Lizzie's assessment. "It would be easier if we weren't shorthanded. We have help, of course, but Antony was a loss."

I winced.

"I'm sorry, Maggie. Nobody blames you, but he is missed," Cassandra said, her tone gentler.

I blamed me. And I was sure that, on some level, the others did, too. I stared down at my hands for a moment, fighting off a wave of guilt and regret. "What are you saying?"

"It would be useful if you could help, as I said earlier. But for that you need access to your magic. So. We need to find out. Soon. Now, if I can arrange it." Cassandra reached for her datapad.

I had little doubt she could. It might be early in the morning, but for this, the members of the Cestis would come.

I, on the other hand, wanted nothing more than to be safe in my bed where I could yank the covers up over my head and pretend none of this was happening.

I definitely did not want to find out I was tainted with demonkind in some way. Or face the Cestis. But that had to be weighed against the trifling matter of my need to be able to do my job and continue to eat. Also my desire to never have a demon —or anyone or anything else—have a magical hold over me again.

Hello, rock, meet hard place. I needed a third option. "What if I can light the candle? Get my power back?"

"Then we would be more likely to assume that everything is okay," Cassandra said.

"More likely" wasn't the same as "would." If the Cestis wanted to test me, I had no illusions that they would. But I could worry about that if and when it happened. "Right. So how about I take Lizzie home and she can help me practice in the morning? She's hurt, and she needs to sleep. If a demon hasn't eaten me up yet, then I doubt it will change its mind in the next few hours. If I can't light the candle, then tomorrow night we'll do it the hard way."

Cassandra didn't look convinced. I shot Lizzie a pleading look.

Apparently she had more faith in me than Cassandra. "I really don't feel that great," she said. "I'll be more help in a test if I can get some sleep."

Cassandra pursed her lips, then nodded. "I can live with that. But I want you at Ian's at eight tomorrow night if you don't light the candle." She stood and bustled over to the desk standing in one corner of the room, pulling out the drawer. She came back and handed me a leather-bound notebook. "Here. This might help."

"What is it?"

"Notes on magical basics. Enough to get you started again."

If I could manage to find my powers. But this wasn't the time to argue the point. I had a reprieve. I was going to take it, and Lizzie, and run.

Chapter Three

"NOT EVEN A FLICKER?" Lizzie asked the next morning. She cradled her syncaf, looking as bleary-eyed as I felt. I'd insisted she go straight to bed when we'd gotten home around two. I'd tried to sleep myself but only managed a few hours before I'd given up and dragged myself out of bed and into the kitchen. I'd eaten a silent breakfast of cold cereal and milk, not wanting to wake Lizzie, and then unearthed a candle and candlestick from one of the cabinets.

I'd been sitting at the kitchen table, alternating between staring at the candle and reading bits of the book Cassandra gave me since about six. It was now closer to ten. The candle remained unlit. I'd gained a bit more information about some of the basics of magic. Fire and wards and psychic shields. The kinds of things that would come in handy if I had to deal with imps or demons again. None of which would do me any good if I couldn't access my powers.

Lizzie, still wearing her pjs with a light cotton robe festooned with otters dancing with robots draped over her shoulders, had joined me only a few minutes ago. Blue hair rumpled and squinting slightly, she slurped from her mug and studied me over its rim.

I shoved the book across the table. "Cassandra could give me the entire Encyclopedia Witchtannica and I still couldn't light that candle," I said, trying to ignore my urge to drown myself in a vat of syncaf. Having access to real coffee when I'd dated Damon had spoiled me. I couldn't afford it myself, and I missed it. Syncaf tasted nothing like the real thing. But it did, at least, contain caffeine.

Maybe not enough for my current level of tired. Trying to do magic was exhausting. Or maybe it was just the complete failure that had drained me of energy. I'd tried everything I could think of to jolt my powers into action, staring at the damned candle until I was dizzy. "Maybe I need to accept that it's gone."

Lizzie's mug thumped onto the table. "Magic doesn't just disappear." She tapped the book with her good hand. "Try again."

I scowled. Honestly, if it wasn't for my work

problem and the unwelcome knowledge that there was a threat of demons taking me over again, I'd be perfectly fine with not having magic. I'd spent twenty-nine years without it and my life had been happier for it. Mostly.

"Maybe mine never really had time to take hold. After all, the demon had it bound for over half my life."

"It was yours to begin with. Nothing can change that."

The book was clear on that. Powers could be blocked or bound away but not removed. "So everyone keeps telling me. Yet I can't light candles, I can't see the energy fields, and if an imp tried to attack us right now, the only thing I'd be good for would be running away screaming. And now I have to worry about demons again." And demon stone. "You could have warned me that was a risk."

She shrugged. "You weren't ready to hear it. And we took precautions. There's been no sign of demons or lesserkind or anything remotely magical anywhere near here."

Just elsewhere. Wherever they'd been hunting down imps and afrits and whatever. "And yet, if I can't light this damned candle, the rest of your Cestis friends are going to either want to rummage through my mind or use demon stone on me." The thought of letting demon stone touch me again made me regret my breakfast.

Lizzie grimaced. "Don't worry about tonight. No one is going to hurt you. Despite what you think, we want to help you. I think this is all in your head. It'll come back. You just need to get over what happened."

Easier said than done. Nat was dead. How was I supposed to get over that?

Not to mention the man I'd loved had walked away, unable to handle the fact that I was a witch. Both things still hurt every day. And, if I was completely honest, part of me hoped the magic would stay away and somehow that would bring him back to me. Which only meant that part of me was stupidly over optimistic.

"Next you'll be suggesting I see a therapist again."

"I already did suggest it," Lizzie pointed out. "You refused."

The Cestis, via Lizzie, had offered to hook me up with a therapist who was also a witch to help me immediately after Nat died. I'd refused. I'd eventually tried one of the regular kind but had skirted around the issues of exactly what happened to her. "It didn't help."

"You tried a normal therapist. You need one who understands magic," Lizzie said. "And before you say anything about not having enough time, let me just add that you can do virtual therapy. All from the comfort of your own sofa or car or wherever."

As if doing it virtually made the prospect any more appealing. I hadn't set foot in a VR environment since my encounter with the demon. I looked down to the barely visible scar on my left wrist. There was no longer an interface chip beneath my skin. I didn't miss it, even though I couldn't deny that code wrangling had been easier with the chip. But easier wasn't enough to overcome the fact that the chip had also started my demon problem. "Me and my sofa are fine, thanks."

Lizzie looked at the candle and raised her eyebrows.

I pushed back my chair. I needed a break. Lizzie needed breakfast.

"What do you feel like eating?" I asked. My mind was blank as to what there was in the fridge. I hadn't paid attention last night when I grabbed dinner.

Lizzie squinted at me and then looked down at the sling. "Maybe just toast. I can eat that one-handed."

"Toast isn't exactly nutritious," I said.

"It'll do for now," she said. "I'm not super hungry. I'll have more later."

I pulled bread and jelly out of the fridge. Found plates and peanut butter. I held up the two jars. "Which do you want?" Lizzie didn't believe in PB and J. One or the other only. Given everything she'd put up with from me, I could indulge her breakfast quirks.

"Peanut butter," she said. "Am I imagining it, or did Cassandra give you a bag of cookies when we left?"

"She did," I said. "I'm not sure cookies are breakfast." I sounded like Nat. Who would laugh herself stupid if she heard me lecturing someone else on eating healthy. She'd had to nag me to not subsist entirely on takeout when we'd lived together.

"Oatmeal. Cranberries. Those are things people eat at breakfast." She pushed her chair back.

"Sit down," I said, sliding the bread into the toaster. What the hell. She was a grown-ass woman. She could eat cookies for breakfast when-ever she wanted. I might join her. Sugar might help with the exhaustion.

Lizzie sat, fidgeting with the sling a moment, looking cranky.

"Is it hurting?" I asked.

"No, not really. But it's itching like mad."

Itchy was better than painful. Itchy meant it was healing and whatever Radha had done to help her injury along was working. "Don't fuss with it."

"I'm not twelve," she said.

I fished in the cabinets, found the bag of cook-ies, and poured them into my Nano Kitty cookie jar.

I carried the whole jar over to Lizzie. "Sure. Eat your adult cookie breakfast."

I took one for myself, scarfing it down as I wandered back over to the counter to wait for the toast. "Are you sure your arm isn't hurting?" The last thing I needed was Cassandra on the warpath if Lizzie developed a complication.

"Yep." She yawned, then nibbled at her cookie. "You know, I've been thinking about your work thing more. Maybe until we get this sorted out, you need someone to help you." The swift change of subject made it clear she wasn't going to be talking any more about her injury.

I raised an eyebrow. "I work alone." Primarily because no one else did what I did. Sure, I'd used virtual assistants on and off to handle admin when I was busiest, but I couldn't exactly delegate the actual TechWitch part. By the time clients came to me, they'd usually already tried conventional IT consultants. My job was a weird little niche I'd fallen into by accident. I wouldn't know how to train someone to do it. Especially not if it turned out that my intuition for computers was somehow related to my magic.

"Yes. But if you can't work, then no money for Maggie. Or Maggie's house. It would be nice to finish the rebuild sometime this decade."

She had me there. "I take it you have someone in mind?"

Her enthusiastic nod made me wonder if she'd had this idea even before she knew about my problems.

"Someone who can do what I do?"

She shrugged. "I don't know exactly how you do what you do. But he's a very fast learner. He's ice when it comes to tech, that's for sure. He does all kinds of things."

"White hat kinds of things or black hat kinds of things?" There were all sorts of options open to someone who was good with tech. Some of them involved activities ranging from faintly shady to out-right criminal. In my line of work, I couldn't afford to be associated with anyone who operated in the murkier shades of the web.

"White hat," Lizzie said. "Trust me, I've poked around in his background. Unless he hides his tracks very, very well, he's one of the good guys."

"Being able to hide your tracks very, very well is pretty much the job description for the wrong sort of hacker," I said.

Lizzie rolled her eyes. "When you do what I do, you get an instinct about people. So the question becomes whether you trust me."

Trust wasn't something I did easily. My child-hood with my mother—who'd been the magical equivalent of a grifter and had taught me more about hightailing it out of town under cover of dark-ness than normality—had left scars.

I stared out the window.

Lizzie was right. I needed cash. Which meant I needed to work. And Lizzie was one of the people who I could trust. After all, she'd stuck by me so far, for no good reason other than she thought I'd needed a friend, as far as I could tell. "Let me think about it. Maybe I could give him a trial."

"Chill. Just let me know." She looked satisfied, then sniffed the air. "Toast's about to pop."

It was, and it did. I made two platefuls of toast and peanut butter, then let Lizzie eat in silence.

I finished my toast before her, hungrier than I should be given I'd eaten breakfast earlier, but I knew I needed the fuel to keep trying to light the candle, let alone face the consequences if I failed. I pushed my plate away and pulled out my datapad, pretending to check my mail. Lizzie nibbled and looked at her own datapad, alternating bites with swiping with her good hand. I couldn't help noticing she kept glancing at me. By the time she'd finished her breakfast and started chewing her lip instead, I got the message.

"There's something else, isn't there?" I asked.

Her gaze stayed fixed firmly on her datapad as her mouth twisted slightly

"Spill," I said when she didn't start talking.

"I'm not sure you're going to like it," she said. She looked up slowly, nose wrinkling.

My stomach squirmed again, but I was apparently becoming a proponent of the just-rip-the-Band-Aid-off-because-it's-going-to-hurt-either-way school of communication. "Just tell me."

She pushed her datapad across the table. "Have you seen this?"

I leaned closer, trying to make out the image. Then froze as I recognized the logo hovering in the corner of the screen. Riley Arts.

An ad. For a new game. Feathery letters—creamy white on a summer-sky blue background—spelled out "Archangel." The game Damon's company had been developing when I'd worked for him. When I'd fallen for him. When I'd found out I had magic.

The game previously infested with a demon.

With an effort, I sat back, shrugging as though my heart wasn't jumping around in my chest like a mad rabbit. "Well, he had to release something new sooner or later. Good for him." Guilt warred with a jumble of other emotions I didn't want to examine too closely. Because of me and my demon, Riley Arts had recalled a lot of games. One of the biggest recalls in gaming history. It could have broken the company.

I'd tried to avoid the news, but it had been hard to miss the fact that Riley's stock price had plummeted, people had been screaming for him to resign as CEO, and there'd been calls for criminal charges.

And, okay, it wasn't my fault, but that was how it felt.

Somehow Damon had survived it. Fixed the problems, made amends, put in the hard work. Now, it seemed, he was back in the game. No pun intended.

"That's all you're going to say?"

"What more is there? I don't game anymore. And—"

Lizzie made a disgusted sound, face scrunched with displeasure. "You're going to give me the 'Damon Riley walked away and that's that' speech again, aren't you?"

"Nothing's changed, so what else is there?"

She pushed the datapad closer. "I think you should watch the whole ad."

I stared down at the screen. I'd rather have held a ticking bomb in my hands. The walls I'd managed to scrape together around my beaten-up heart were thin and shaky. It wouldn't take much to blow them to smithereens, leaving me hurting and battered all over again.

Damon had caused part of that damage, even if, logically, I couldn't blame him for walking away. But it seemed I hadn't learned the lesson yet, because even while my brain screamed not to, I lifted the datapad and looked at the ad.

The feathery letters fluttered slowly on the screen, looping around each other slowly before settling back into formation. Like everything Riley Arts did, it was beautiful, breathtakingly real work. Light seemed to reflect off the letters as they floated as though touched by the lightest of breezes. All I had to do was touch the screen and the ad would play.

No doubt it would be just as beautiful.

But beautiful didn't mean it wouldn't hurt.

"I don't think this is a good idea." My voice shook.

"Trust me."

Now it was me chewing my lip. Luckily I wouldn't be ruining my lip gloss. I wasn't wearing any.

To watch or not to watch, that was the question.

"You're going to see it sooner or later," Lizzie said gently.

"I'm good with later," I muttered. But she was right. Damon had made it through. He'd stood his ground and kept his company afloat. The fact that he was now launching his first new game since his problems would generate even more press than the recall had. There wouldn't be a billboard or netflash or newslink that wasn't covering the return of Righteous, as the gamers called Riley Arts.

This ad, and Damon's face, were going to be everywhere.

In order to stick to my "just rip it off" theory, I

needed to just watch the damn ad and see whatever it was Lizzie thought I should see.

Still, I would've preferred the ticking bomb and having to reach down and cut the red wire or the blue one over having to tap the screen and start watching something I knew would have Damon's stamp all over it.

I tapped anyway. And held my breath as the screen bloomed to life.

The feathers dissolved into black, which then shimmered back into a familiar landscape.

An alien planet, heavily forested, the trees a thousand moody shades of green. It looked very real, and the memory of standing in that landscape, plugged into the VR via the interface chip I no longer had, smelling the remarkable recreation of that world, rushed over me. I stopped the memory in its tracks. Before it could turn to pain and filth and demons.

My pulse started to hammer in my ears. I told myself to breathe. I was safe. There was no chip. No demon. It was just video on a screen.

The ad took off at high speed. Winged characters battling monsters, epic landscapes, day and night and life and death cut together in a montage that made me wish I could play. And I'd never been a total game head.

Like everything Righteous did, it was a brilliantly executed piece of marketing. The snippets of scenes set up the fragments of an intriguing quest. A search to save the Archangel, cruelly imprisoned. To free her so she could save everyone else. Which sounded simplistic, but the world that unfolded in the images was anything but.

The ad finished with a swooping shot that started long before zooming in on a tower that looked like something out of a fairy tale on speed. Narrowed down to the shape of the window, then moved through it to settle on a steady shot of a spotlighted winged figure, viewed from the back. The feathers of those glorious wings shone with the same glowing white light as the original letters. This, I assumed, was the Archangel, the object of the quest.

And when she turned around, there were my green eyes glowing in the golden skin of her face.

Chapter Four

MAGIC CAN DO MANY THINGS. Heal a wound. Start a fire. Shield a mind.

One thing it can't do is mend a broken heart. Magic or no magic I was stuck with the good old-fashioned way of dealing with heartbreak.

Lots of angry-girl rock, ice cream binges, and wearing myself out with manual labor so I could sleep had been my go-to after Damon left me.

In the hours since I'd seen the Archangel ad, I'd almost blown out my earbuds trying to drown out the whirl of "Does it mean anything? It can't mean anything. Maybe it does mean something? Don't be an idiot" that had been ricocheting around my brain since I'd seen my eyes staring back at me from my datapad.

My eyes and my long brown hair.

In the face of the angel—who, while not exactly me, could possibly be recognized as my younger, more beautiful sister or cousin or something—who needed rescuing.

What the fuck was that supposed to mean?

Thunk.

The bite of iron into wood didn't help. I probably shouldn't have been operating a nail gun angry, but heaven help me, it was punch nails into wood or start breaking things.

Thunk.

Squinting through my protective goggles, I aimed the gun again and again and again.

Thunk. Thunk. Thunk.

Thunk.

The last nail shot into its place along the beam and I straightened, feeling each vertebra click in protest as I examined the line of nail heads. They gleamed silvery against the wood, straight and true.

Unlike Damon Riley and his electronic mind games.

Think about something else.

I stowed the nail gun, goggles, and the ear protectors I wore over the earbuds away, then wiped my sweaty palms on my jeans before reaching for a rag to wipe my face. It was warm again, and upstairs had no enviro-system yet. It made for sweaty work. Particularly when I was in a mood and didn't stop to take a break. I stretched, grimacing.

One day this house would be a techno geek's dream. My dream.

But until I got the cash flowing again, any more work would be done by Lizzie and me. For now I had a damned good security setup—something I'd never skimp on—and my old office system, resenting the tweaks I'd given it to make it play nice as a housecomp. It found subtle ways to protest, like throwing the odd As-Pop ballad into my preprogrammed list of Rock-to-hammer-to and randomly making my shower freezing cold halfway through the programmed cycle. Never let anyone tell you that machines can't sulk. Lizzie never got the icicle treatment.

I planted my hands on either side of the comp panel and pushed back, trying not to groan at the pull in my shoulders.

I needed to be Maggie Lachlan, computer whisperer, not Maggie Lachlan, face of VR game character.

Which meant I needed to stop thinking about Damon freaking Riley and start working out how to get my magic back. Starting with going back downstairs and letting Lizzie try to coach me through lighting the damned candle.

I eased out of the stretch and turned. Then jumped, an involuntary shriek escaping my lips as my pulse redlined.

Lizzie stood in the doorway.

I yanked the earbuds from my ears.

She grinned at me, raising her hands. "I come in peace."

"I didn't hear you," I said defensively. I'd never liked people sneaking up on me, and a brush with demonkind hadn't improved my jitters. "What's up?"

"Someone at the door."

The system should have killed the music and told me about that. Bitchy damn thing. My hand twitched. Where was that nail gun when I needed it? But I couldn't afford a replacement if I succumbed to the urge to see if a nail to the processor might deal with the problem, so I just had to live with electronic attitude until I could spend some time reworking the setup. Come to think of it, maybe that would be easier if I got my magic back, too.

"Can't you deal with them? I'm not exactly fit for company." I swept a hand down my body, indicating my outfit and general state of grime. I hadn't even showered.

Lizzie was a genius with contractors, and nobody else tended to come to our door unless we ordered takeout. She went out to socialize. As for me, nobody—well, mostly nobody—knew where I lived now. Which was exactly how I liked it anyway. Even if I'd been feeling social, I was wearing my oldest jeans, an even older band tee, and my hair twisted up into a bun that had to be a sweaty mess now. Not exactly dressed for company.

"You have to deal with this one yourself," Lizzie said with a shake of her head.

I wiped my forehead with the back of my hand, wishing I could wipe away the crappy day as easily. But Lizzie had her "I mean it" face on. Grudgingly, I traipsed downstairs, brushing the worst of the dust and dirt from my clothes. When I saw who was standing in my front hall, I kind of wished I hadn't left the nail gun upstairs.

Damon Riley.

The man I hadn't seen for nine months.

A big chunk of the memories that haunted me.

"What are you doing here?" I said stupidly. Nine months. You can create a whole new life in that time, but I hadn't even managed to put my old one back together.

"We need to talk." His voice was tight and low. Hardly the reunion I'd pictured all those times I'd lain awake and imagined how things could have worked out differently between us. In my stupid head, he'd looked sad. Regretful. Heartbroken. And his opening line was always some variation on "I'm sorry, Maggie. I was an idiot," followed by suitably abject groveling.

But it seemed I was the real idiot. Because Damon didn't look remotely sad.

Tired, yes.

Different, yes.

Older somehow. And harder, his dark hair cropped close and new lines arrowing the edges of his brilliant blue eyes.

Some of those lines were probably my fault. But there were a few lines on my face that he could take the blame for, too.

"Nine months is a long time to wait to talk," I said, blocking the doorway.

"I don't have time for games, Maggie. Let me in."

Ah. His I-am-lord-of-the-universe tone. Familiar. I'd found it amusing once I'd gotten to know him. Pity I wasn't in the mood to play the grateful serf today. I didn't owe him anything, and besides, this was my turf, not his. "I don't think that's a good idea, do you?"

"Damn it, Maggie," he growled. "This is serious."

My stomach sank.

Of course. He hadn't changed his mind. He hadn't seen the error of his ways and decided he just had to see me.

Damon wasn't the sort of man who had sudden changes of heart. The Archangel looking like me might mean anything. It was probably Benji or Eli— the two Righteous programmers I'd hung out with the most—who'd designed her anyway. They probably hadn't even made the connection as to where they'd gotten the inspiration for her face. The only reason Damon was here was because he needed something.

Disappointment—stupid, pathetic, useless—soured my tongue, and I was suddenly too tired to argue. "Fine." I stepped back to let him in. "Just remember this was your idea."

"Hardly," he muttered as he stalked into my house, eyes scanning everything, no doubt locking away the location of every unfinished paint job and empty doorframe in his brain. Not one to miss the details, Damon. You didn't get to where he had by missing details.

I closed the door, wondering where to take him. Upstairs was a jumble of unfinished rooms and building supplies. Downstairs was the kitchen—but he didn't seem to be here for a cozy chat over syncaf—and the living areas, including what would eventually be a study but was currently my makeshift bedroom. No way was Damon Riley getting near a bedroom of mine again. And no way was I letting him see the single futon mattress that screamed the fact that no one else had been getting near my bedroom either.

The garden, then. Maybe I could put him to work clearing up the contractor's mess and trying to disentangle Gran's favorite stubborn tea roses from the weeds doing their best to choke them. I ducked past him, trying not to let myself breathe in his all-too-familiar scent.

"I'd offer you a drink, but you'd have to take my word for it that no magic was involved," I said when we reached the kitchen, then kicked myself mentally for how sharp my tone was. Indifferent was what I was going for. Not upset.

In my imagination, when I'd opened my door to see Damon standing there all remorseful, I'd been gracious and forgiving, taking the moral high ground. Of course, in my imagination, he'd been there to beg me to forgive him. And I hadn't been dressed in my oldest clothes and covered in sweat. My imagination was a dope. But apparently nicer than me in real life.

"I'm not thirsty."

I got another faint whiff of cotton and soap and spice that spiked my pulse. He was close. Too close.

I started moving again. Away from him. I didn't need a cascade of pointless Damon memories.

"Fine," I said for the second time as we reached the back door. I stepped out into the late afternoon sunshine and started down the steps to the one mostly clear patch of grass. What would eventually be vegetable beds and garden again was almost all covered in weeds or building junk. "You want to tell me what this is about?" I asked, watching where I was going and trying to remember if it was the fifth or sixth step that was loose.

"You need to stop," he said, still in that weird tight voice.

Stop? Stop walking? Somehow, I didn't think that was what he meant. Confused, I turned to face him. He loomed over me. I wasn't short, but he had about five inches on me plus a two-step height advantage. Still, I held my ground. "Stop what?"

He leaned forward, a frown slashing a crease between his eyebrows. "The messages."

He'd not only lost me, he'd dumped me in the middle of a forest with no map. What the hell was he talking about? "What messages?"

To my surprise, he looked almost relieved by my question.

"What messages?" I repeated.

He shook his head, scrubbing a hand over his jaw in a familiar gesture of frustration. "I told them it wasn't you, but they insisted."

"Told who?" Not only was there no map, but I was starting to feel like I'd dropped into a conversation that had started long before he'd arrived on my doorstep.

Damon didn't answer. Instead, he turned on his heel, as though he intended to walk right back out of my life again.

Before I knew what I was doing, I lunged up the stairs between us and grabbed his arm. "Oh hell no.

You can't just waltz in here, say a few cryptic sentences, and waltz out again without explaining what's going on."

He stopped, and we both looked down to where my hand was wrinkling his very expensive blue shirt. My palm tingled. It took a lot not to curl my fingers deeper into the comforting strength of his bicep. Instead, I pulled my hand back as though it didn't feel like it might just burst into flames. Thankfully Damon didn't immediately retreat.

I backed up as far as the width of the porch steps would allow, resisting the urge to rub my palm on my jeans and remove that tingling awareness.

What were we talking about again? Messages. Right. Something about me and messages.

Not good messages presumably if they were enough to bring Damon to my doorstep after he'd made no attempt at contact since the day of Nat's funeral.

My payment for services rendered had arrived in my bank account the next day. I hadn't even had a chance to send an invoice. The deposit was accompanied by a very impersonal message from the Riley Arts legal department stating that my contract was considered complete, that my payment had been made, that Riley Arts would be happy to provide a testimonial should I require one for future clients, that all my access to the Riley Arts campus and systems had been revoked, that they would be sending someone to collect my security pass and scan my system for proprietary information per the contract, and ending with a stern reminder of just how watertight the nondisclosure agreement I had signed as part of that contract was.

That had been it. Nothing from Damon himself.

I didn't know if he'd thought he'd been making things easier for both of us, but at the time, it had felt more like a boot to my stomach after I'd already been knocked to the ground and run over.

After a farewell so precisely calculated to let me know that I no longer had any place in his world, I had to assume that only something really bad could have brought him back to my door.

Just what I needed, another freaking problem. Irritation and apprehension surged through me, burning away the confused jitters of my hormones. "What messages? And what makes you think they're from me?"

Damon put his hands on his hips. The movement made his loosely rolled cuff move higher on his arm, and I caught the glint of the gold and silver circuitry embedded in the skin of his left wrist. His interface chip. Key to the most realistic virtual reality experiences anyone had yet invented. "Because my cybersecurity department traced them back to your system. Which wasn't easy."

"Apparently not, given they came to the wrong

conclusion." I tore my eyes from his wrist and fought the urge to rub the scar on my own. I'd had a chip once. Not for long. Because it turned out getting it installed had broken a magic binding I hadn't known about and set a demon on the warpath. Not to mention giving me seizures as a nice little bonus.

I hadn't been tempted to get a new one. After learning earlier that lack of magic could equal vulnerability, I could only think that was a good thing. But that didn't mean that I didn't sometimes remember just how amazing the experience of being in a virtual world enabled by one had been.

Or how much easier it had made my job, letting me visualize and search the acres of code and data I waded through in ways that just weren't possible without it.

I stomped down the stairs, hoping he'd follow me to level ground. Staring up at him gave my neck and shoulders even more reason to protest. "So, perhaps you come down here and explain what the hell is going on?"

He descended the stairs and joined me. My patch of scruffy grass felt way too small for the both of us. Even over the garden smells of rose and grass and dirt and wood, his scent made my heart clench with remembrance. But I wasn't going to give him the satisfaction of seeing that I wanted to back away from him.

"You sure you need an explanation?" he asked.

I tilted my head, staring up at him. There wasn't a flicker of anything approachable in his eyes. They were the blue of storm clouds and frost, not the brilliant summer sky shade I remembered so well. "Trust me, if I was sending you hate mail, you'd know it was from me."

A dimple flicked to life in his left cheek as his mouth quirked. "That's what I told them, but they didn't believe me." The dimple disappeared again as he straightened his shoulders.

Nice to know he had some scrap of faith in me. Didn't make up for him dumping me, of course. "Aren't you the boss? Don't they have to believe you?"

"Not according to my head of security. That was our agreement when I hired him. That he'd push back when things needed pushing. I told him he was wrong about this. But he's pushing back."

"I think this conversation might be easier for both of us if you tell me exactly what's going on. Start at the beginning."

Out of the corner of my eye, I saw Lizzie drift past the back door, hovering just inside. She raised a brow inquiringly. I gave a tiny head shake. No rescue required. Not yet, at least. Lizzie nodded and disappeared again. Not that being out of sight meant she was necessarily out of earshot.

"The beginning is, you know, where the problem

started," I prompted when Damon didn't immediately start speaking.

His frown reappeared. "It's complicated."

"I gathered that much the second you turned up on my doorstep."

The frown deepened. The problem was that on him, after nine months of not seeing his face, even a frown looked good.

Curse my stupid hormones. And curse his stupidly handsome face.

"We could try small talk," I suggested. "Start with something easy. Like 'So, Damon, what have you been up to lately?'"

The frown smoothed from his face like chalk under an eraser, wiped clean by a flatly unreadable facade.

Score one to me. I knew perfectly well what he'd been up to.

Riding out a media shit-storm the likes of which had rarely been seen since the aftermath of the Big One when he'd revealed that a demon had been using technology developed by Righteous to harvest enough energy to break out of its realm and into our world. Clawing back his reputation and his company's viability inch by inch.

He had scars, too.

So what? My inner voice sounded petty asking the question. Maybe rightly so. Why should I care about his scars when he didn't care about me? "I shouldn't" seemed to be the obvious answer.

The more complicated one was that part of me did. The part of me that now watched his face and tried not to hold its breath, trying to read what lay behind the careful mask he wore.

"I could ask you the same question."

My breath caught as my stomach clenched. Apparently he hadn't bothered checking up on me. The fact that the newslinks didn't write stories about me the way they did about him wasn't an excuse. With the resources he had at his fingertips, he could find out almost anything about anyone, anytime, anywhere. If he hadn't, it meant he hadn't wanted to. Hadn't cared enough to.

Didn't care enough about *me*.

Even though I'd known that already, such blatant proof felt much like being stabbed in the heart, the pain just as sharp as the day we'd said goodbye. I bent and tugged a few weeds from the edge of the nearest bed, determined to make sure he couldn't see my face until I regained control of my emotions. Even then, I didn't want to face him. But I didn't think he was just going to stand there silently while I weeded. I straightened and lifted my chin. "Or we could just get to the point. What messages?"

Damon met my gaze for a long moment, then

parked his denim-clad butt on a stack of bricks. I stayed standing.

"I've received some strange emails."

"What kind of strange?"

"Threats."

"And obviously threats must come from me? Gee, thanks."

The look he gave me had a distinct flavor of "Don't be an idiot" about it.

"Maggie, I get threats all the time. But these tripped more than the usual red flags. My cybersecurity team traced the emails back to your system. Mitch wanted to bring in the cops. I told them no. I wanted to speak to you first."

Mitch, I assumed, was his pushy head of security. "And now you're speaking to me. I didn't do it."

"The proof says otherwise."

"Then you need better cybersecurity guys." But unless the fallout from his recall had been a lot worse than I'd gathered from the newslinks, he already had the best money could buy.

"If it's not you, then it's someone pretending to be you. Maybe *you* need better cybersecurity guys."

I didn't have cybersecurity guys. I had me. Well, I had friends who were no slouch with security and had given me advice when I'd bought the system. But I'd tweaked and refined and rebuilt it so often that it was fully customized. And as near impregnable as I could make it. Certainly it had never failed me before.

My stomach sank as the implications finally hit me. He was right. If someone was managing to clone my system and make it look like messages were coming from me skillfully enough to fool Damon's team, I needed help. Not that I was going to tell him that. "I don't have cybersecurity guys. You know that."

"No, because you're one of the best. So how did someone hack your system without you knowing about it?"

Because apparently part of my ability came from my power. But I'd rip my tongue out before confessing that to Damon. Or telling him I seemed to have lost my magic.

He'd broken up with me over my powers. I didn't want to know what was possible if he thought I no longer had any. If it didn't change his mind—and really, that seemed a very distant possibility—it would be awful. And if it did, well, I could hardly take him back anyway. What if it came back? "My system is secure."

"'As far as you know' isn't going to cut it. These messages are the real deal, Maggie. My guys will give what they have to the police soon. If you're not doing this, you need to prove it fast, or you'll be proving it to them."

Prove it? Track down a hacker so good he'd gotten around my systems?

Nine months ago I would've laughed at Damon for suggesting someone could hack me. I would have bet good money my systems were rock solid. But that was when I'd been on top of things. Had something gone wrong? Something I hadn't noticed because my intuition, or whatever it was, was shot to hell?

And if it had, how was I going to find it?

"How long do I have?" I asked.

"I can hold them off a little longer. Forty-eight hours at most."

Shit. And other very bad words. "Fine. I'll have your proof before then."

He stood. "Good."

There was an awkward pause while I tried to figure out what to say next. The things we probably should talk about, I had no intention of discussing. And he didn't seem in the mood for small talk. But a stupid part of me didn't want him to leave yet. "Why are you doing this?"

His brows lifted. "Doing what?"

I gestured between us. "This. Why did you come to see me? You could've just let your guys throw me to the lions. That demon almost killed your company." My demon, I meant.

He looked insulted. "That was the demon. That

wasn't you. I broke up with you. That doesn't mean I think you're a lunatic who'd make death threats."

What *did* he think of me?

I bit my tongue. That was another thing I'd rather die than ask. Suddenly tears stung my eyes. It didn't matter if I didn't want him to go. He needed to leave. Before I made an idiot of myself. I needed to remind both of us that there was no point prolonging things. "No, not a lunatic. Just a witch," I said. "Nothing's changed about that. So I guess we both know where we stand. Thanks for stopping by, but you'll appreciate that I have a lot to do." I looked past him, at the house where Lizzie was hovering by the back door again. "Lizzie will show you out."

"Mag—"

"Don't," I cut him off. "I can't. You don't do witches. I get that. But that means I can't do this." I waved a hand between us. "Send me what your team thinks they have. I'll look into it. You'll have an answer in the next two days. Then you can go back to pretending you never knew me at all."

He winced, and for a horrible moment, I thought he was going to move closer and touch me. I stepped back. Damon shook his head and turned to climb the steps. I turned in the opposite direction, staring at the mass of Gran's tangled roses—something else in as bad shape as I was—until I heard the screen door creak open, then click closed.

The garden felt very big and empty without Damon in it. I hugged my arms around myself and breathed hard, determined not to cry. I didn't have time for a meltdown. I had forty-eight hours to prove I wasn't harassing Damon—presuming, of course, that I didn't turn out to be possessed by a demon later tonight.

I ignored the little voice inside that whispered that death threats were the sort of things demons would love. And could make me not remember doing.

A demon I couldn't do anything about right now. Finding out whether my systems had been hijacked, maybe I could.

Presuming Lizzie's mystery tech guy was as good as she thought he was.

Chapter Five

IT TOOK some time for Lizzie to get hold of her mystery man. Long enough for me to calm down and shower. Sawdust and sweat swirled down the drain and vanished. Unfortunately soap and water didn't work the same way on my lingering confusion over seeing Damon.

Nor did it ease my nerves. I'd told Lizzie to call Cassandra after Damon had left. It didn't matter how much I tried, I knew the damned candle wasn't going to light. Better to know where I stood. Especially now that I also apparently needed to find out who the hell was pretending to be me and threatening Damon if I didn't want a whole bunch of legal trouble or worse.

I debated whether to wear something fancy to face the Cestis but decided that if I'd be finding out that I was possessed by a demon later, I might as well be comfortable. When I emerged, armored in jeans, boots and an old Chill Sugar concert tee, Lizzie was still making calls on her datapad. While she typed one-handed and talked furiously, I prowled the kitchen, then poured myself a syncaf.

I always drank too much syncaf these days. Too much, too fast. Wanting not to taste it and remember the real thing. Damon had given me a taste for things I couldn't afford.

Real coffee being the least of them.

Lizzie finally ended the call as I was finishing a second cup.

"Everything's set?" I asked.

She grinned, more than a touch of smug lurking around the edges of her expression. "Yes. We've just got time to go meet Yoshi before we have to be at Ian's."

"Meet him where?" I asked, suspicion flaring as I took in what she was wearing. She'd applied blue lip gloss that matched her hair. Somehow, she'd managed to pull it up into a rough bun one-handed. Impressive. Her clothes continued a blue, silver, and black theme, mixed with leather and studs that looked more like she was planning to go out dancing than meeting with her fellow witchy overlords. There weren't that many places in San Francisco these days where tech-heads-for-hire and places where Lizzie's dress code might be appropriate occupied the same zip code.

"Dockside," Lizzie said, her voice a shade too casual.

Oh crap.

The closer we got to Dockside, the more my body tried to make me change my mind and just go home. My mouth dried, my stomach churned, and my spine started to feel like it was made of sparking steel, electric jitters skittering up and down it. By the time our ride-share let us out on the outskirts of the precinct, I was close to panic.

The last time I'd been to Dockside, I'd been hunted by an imp and accidentally fried it in self-defense. That was how I'd discovered I had magic. It was also one of the last places I'd been with Nat. I'd never liked Dockside much to begin with, and it carried nothing but the memories of terror and pain and fire and loss.

My footsteps slowed as Lizzie led the way across cracked pavement, heading toward the water. I wasn't sure I could do it. The wind blowing in from the bay carried the sounds of voices and music and the creaks and groans of the decaying buildings that lined the battered docks.

Quite a lot of the bay's altered shoreline had

been rebuilt after the Big One. Dockside was left to rot when the city decided this portion of the piers wasn't a restoration priority. Then the seedy side of town moved in. Now it was home to a mix of sleazy nightclubs, game rooms, gambling halls, and other businesses that preferred to operate from the shade. The paths along the docks themselves that led to all these dens of not-so-delight were lined with makeshift booths housing all sorts of businesses. Fences, gray-side nano wear, knock-off tech, street food, and souvenirs designed to appeal to the type of tourist who came down here seeking a thrill.

I was seeking to keep my shit together. I sucked in a breath that must have been a shade too loud.

Lizzie stopped and turned back to me. "It will be okay," she said encouragingly. Apart from the sling, her outfit blended in well with the others who were out and about in Dockside this early. The clubs wouldn't really get going until much later. Fine with me. I was happy not to tangle with any more Docksiders than necessary.

I moved closer to Lizzie, trying to will my pulse back to normal. "This from the girl who might make me stick my hand in a bowl of demon stone later on."

"Only if necessary. It's not like I want to. And that will be okay, too." She tipped her head in the direction we'd been headed. "C'mon, this will be fun. I'll buy you a hot dog."

Like I would ever eat anything sold by a Dockside food cart.

"Explain to me why this guy hangs out down here," I said as we picked our way along the broken hypercrete sidewalk. Time hadn't improved Dockside's charms any, merely layered on another nine months' rust and dirt to the abandoned buildings, another nine months' rotting sea stench to the shattered shoreline, and another nine months' garbage to the alleys and abandoned spaces. I clenched my teeth as my stomach rolled uneasily with each waft of rot and ruin.

"Rent on the booths is cheap." Lizzie kept walking.

Well, yes, it would be. Though given the kind of people who now controlled Dockside, I'd imagine cheap rent came with some catches.

Life was cheap down here, too.

And no one was going to save you. To get within shouting distance of any regular police presence, you had to go farther around the Embarcadero, where it was still a street. There they'd actually made an effort to get some of the piers operational again so the hover ferries could run, and freight could be shifted and tourists could be shipped out to see the tumbled ruins of Alcatraz, which hadn't faired any better in the quake than Dockside.

Fisherman's Wharf and Pier 39 were distant happy memories.

Dockside was a nightmare.

Some clubs had guards, but they were more interested in keeping the peace inside the walls belonging to whoever employed them than they were in interfering if anything happened outside.

We were essentially walking into no-man's-land.

Which didn't greatly raise my confidence that Lizzie's Yoshi would live up to the press she'd been giving him. There were other ways to get cheap rent while hustling for money, after all.

"I thought you said he was a deck jockey. Shouldn't he be hanging out at the clubs?" Deck jockeys fixed VR and other game systems. Game clubs were their natural habitat. Most of those were in nicer parts of town. Not all. But if this guy was any good, he didn't need to be trawling for work in Dockside clubs.

"He does. But he also comes down here to fix other stuff for people who need it and can't afford other places. Chill, Mags. He's a good kid. He knows his shit. And he needs a break."

We'd reached the edge of the cleared areas where the street booths clustered. The eau-de-rotting-garbage lessened somewhat, though the various perfumes of hot dogs, fries, marijuana,

Sandman, and greasy canvas weren't really any better. I shivered as we passed a nano-tatt stall, decorated with all the cheap electro-flash your heart could desire.

I'd passed that same stall when Nat brought me down here to Unquiet to play. That was the night I'd first realized something was wrong with her.

The night I used magic for the first time.

I'd rather have gone for the nano-tatt since and risked septicemia and nanowrack. I hugged my arms around my waist, suddenly cold.

Lizzie must have seen me shiver. She moved closer, linked her arm through mine. "It's just down here." We left the

tattoos behind and headed farther into the forest of booths.

"This is it." She stopped next to a narrow stall crammed between a knock-off game vendor and an open grill BBQ that proclaimed to offer genuine South Carolina-style hog. The smell of it might have been tempting if my stomach had been more set-tled, but as it was, the grease and smoke and tang just added to my queasiness. I avoided looking too closely at the meat itself. The canvas sheltering the stall might have originally been red but had faded to something closer to rust in the weird light cast by the combination of the BBQ's glowing coals and the flashing solar glows running around the edges of our destination.

"Hey, Yosh," Lizzie said, leaning over the skinny slab of banged-up steel that barred the stall's entrance. "You home?"

I didn't know what I'd been expecting, but the figure who rose out of the dim interior of the stall wasn't it.

Short, skinny, and baby-faced. Lizzie had told me Yoshi was nineteen, but he looked younger. I hoped she was right. I couldn't use him if he wasn't legally able to sign a contract. Straight black hair hit his shoulders, chunky tortoiseshell glasses framed his eyes, and he was wearing an outfit that looked like it could've come from the pages of one of the ancient golfing magazines my grandfather used to collect.

Plaid, plaid, and plaid. In a color clash that was so bad it almost had to be deliberate.

Nothing like the stuff I was used to seeing the gamers wear in the clubs. Of course, I hadn't been in a game club for months, so maybe I was just out of touch.

"Lizzie R. How are you?" he said in a curiously deep voice. It didn't fit his body but gave me some comfort he was as old as Lizzie thought.

"I'm good, Yosh," she said with a grin. She jerked her head in my direction. "This is Maggie. The one I've been telling you about."

The glasses swiveled in my direction. It was hard to see what color his eyes were in the crazy light reflecting off the lenses. Not dark like his hair suggested. His expression was curious. "You're the TechWitch?"

I nodded. "That's me."

He smiled, flashing white teeth. "Chill. Lizzie tells me you're ice."

"Yeah? And what do your sources tell you?" If he was worth his salt, he wouldn't be taking Lizzie's word for it about my abilities. If she was right and he had his hooks into the game world, then he wouldn't lack for opportunities to check me out. If I was right and he dabbled elsewhere, then he should have even more ways to find out what it was I did.

"Word is also ice. Though word also says you're not around much lately." His head tilted as he looked from me to Lizzie. "Lizzie R here ain't talking."

I was beginning to feel like I was the one being sized up instead of vice versa. Which was true, in a way. If Yoshi lived up to Lizzie's press, I needed him more than he needed me right now. If he was good, he should be making a reasonable living doing what he did. Good gamers looked after their tech. And they paid well.

"I've been busy," I said. "Now I'm back. Lizzie tells me you've got some skills."

"What're you looking for?"

"You know what I do?"

He swept his hand in front of his body, palm down. "You work the mojo for those big-ass companies. Get the systems sweet. Like me and game gear." As he pulled his hand back, I saw the glint of a chip at his wrist. Well, that solved one problem. He could go where I couldn't at the moment. My current client didn't have interface chip tech, but Righteous did. I might need that access to clear my name from whatever bullshit was going on there.

"The systems I work with aren't exactly big on VR."

He shrugged. "Code is code."

I couldn't argue with that. He clearly knew his stuff if he could afford a chip. Unless someone else had paid for it. But kids with rich parents didn't often work Dockside stalls as a side gig. And Lizzie had said Yoshi needed a break. "So I'm told. How are you with security protocols?"

"Be right there, Drey." He looked past me, nodded at someone I couldn't see.

I turned instinctively. A tall black guy with bright yellow dreads stood behind us, keeping his distance.

"No problem, Yosh," he said, holding up his hands in an "I'll wait" gesture. Customers who were willing to wait, that was another good sign.

Yoshi's gaze turned back to me. "You need a hack?"

I had to give him credit—he looked young, but he had balls beyond his years. "Hardly," I said.

Beside me I saw Lizzie glance at her datapad. Traffic had been slow on our way here. We were cutting it fine if we were going to make it to Ian's on time.

It said something that I would have chosen—if offered the choice—to stay here in Dockside rather than face demon stone again, but I wasn't being offered the choice.

So. I needed to make a decision so we could go. Being late wouldn't sway the Cestis in my favor. I looked at Yoshi for a moment, considering. He had Lizzie's recommendation. That was a plus.

And he hadn't set off my freak radar in the last few minutes. Unique, definitely, but he didn't seem weird in a bad way. I'd spent enough time in game clubs to be able to pick the ones who had crossed the line from quirky-odd to dangerous-odd. Yoshi wasn't ringing that bell.

So, Lizzie said he had the skills, and right now, I needed help to get out of the Riley Arts security team's bad books. I'd be stupid not to give Yoshi a chance.

"What time do you finish up tonight?" Game clubs run late. He wasn't going to be any good to me if he couldn't front for work at normal people hours.

"Got a club gig later, but I'll be done by two or so."

By which point I might be locked up by the Cestis for having demon taint. Or worse. If I didn't die, then I really needed some sleep. Fatigue fogged the edges of my brain despite the overload of syncaf.

"Tell you what. You come by my place about ten tomorrow. We'll see what you can do." I waited to see his reaction. Ten was early enough to be an inconvenience if he was only going to bed at two. He could blow me off if he wasn't keen.

But he had no hesitation. Another grin spread over his face for a moment before he wrestled it back into a neutral expression. Definitely young, I thought, watching the sparkle in his eyes that betrayed his excitement.

"Chill. Lizzie's got my tag. Send me your info."

I nodded. "Tomorrow, then."

"You got it, TechWitch."

I restrained myself from rolling my eyes. I wondered what Lizzie had told him about magic. For that matter, I needed to know if he had power. But that conversation could wait. He had a paying customer waiting, and I had to go see if the Cestis were going to make me put my hand in a bowl of magic goo that could potentially kill me.

Chapter Six

THE JOURNEY from Dockside to Nob Hill took less time than I would have liked. My anxiety didn't subside as we put distance between us and the harbor. Instead, I just swapped my anxiety about Dockside for my fear of demon stone, my stress ramping up as each minute took us closer to Ian Carmichael's apartment. By the time we stepped through his front door, I was clammy and once again feeling like I might lose my lunch.

Ian's apartment still looked like what you might get if a very expensive nineteenth-century Parisian brothel mated with Aladdin's cave. Ian himself looked older than he had nine months ago, his dark hair newly speckled with gray and the lines of his face sharper.

Regardless of whether I might be responsible

for some of that gray, the man had flawless man-
ners, and he automatically started to make polite
small talk as he led Lizzie and me to the living room
where Cassandra waited with Radha Morgan, the
fourth surviving member of the Cestis.

Radha nodded hello to me, blue eyes cool, but
immediately turned her attention to Lizzie, leading
her over to one of the silk brocade sofas. She gestured at Lizzie's arm, the champagne beaded earrings she wore glinting against her dark skin as she
bent closer and then asked a question I couldn't
hear.

I joined Cassandra. The room was unchanged
from my last visit. Enormous fireplace. Expensive
art. Elegant rugs. Furniture that was older than
anyone in the room. Its centerpiece was the immac-
ulately polished round walnut table.

But my focus was drawn not by the artistry of
the table but by the glowing white ceramic bowl
sitting on it. Like the room, it was all too familiar. I
knew exactly what it held beneath its warded lid.

Demon stone.

Very rare, very expensive, and requiring magical
containment. Deadly to demons or those deeply
infected with demon taint. Capable of eating
through wood, steel, or even hypercrete in a matter
of seconds and just keeping on from there. Only
magic kept it from devouring the flesh of humans
being tested by it or the vessels used to contain it.

Not the sort of thing to accidentally let loose in a city the size of San Francisco. It would do more damage than any earthquake. Definitely not the sort of thing I wanted anything to do with.

Because, if a demon was in any way responsible for my magical problems, it might just kill me.

My vision blurred as I stared at the table, and I blinked furiously. Demon stone had killed Nat in the end. Cassandra and Lizzie had tried to tell me it was the demon, not the demon stone, but I knew better.

I'd stabbed my best friend with a demon-stone-primed dagger to break her free of possession. It had killed her.

I had killed her.

I'd gotten not thinking about that fact too often down to a fine art. But much as it had been when Damon appeared on my doorstep, avoiding it here was kind of impossible. Last time I'd been given the choice between one of the Cestis reading my mind for demon taint or demon stone, I'd chosen demon stone. This time, I didn't think I could.

The others, at least, gave me the grace of silence as I took several shaky breaths, trying to regain control. When I felt sure I could talk without choking on the words, I turned back to Ian. "Let's start with that reading me thing this time."

One of his bushy eyebrows lifted. "Are you sure?"

"Yes." I tried not to shudder at the thought of the bowl behind me.

"Very well," Cassandra said. "Take a seat. Radha, will you do the honors, please?"

I pulled out the nearest chair. Radha moved to stand behind me. Lizzie came with her and rested my hand on her good one. "It's okay, I can shield you. She won't see anything you don't want her to see."

I didn't want her to see anything at all. But that wasn't going to get me anywhere. Radha was better than demon stone.

"Are you ready, Maggie?" Radha asked.

No. But I nodded anyway, closing my eyes. Putting it off wasn't going to make it any easier.

Radha's hands settled at my temples. The perfume she wore, warm and floral, drifted around me. "Just relax," she said.

Easier said than done. Part of me was braced for an invasion. Part of me was trying to see if I could sense anything of what she was doing, like I had the first time Cassandra taught me to feel the energy fields. But there was nothing. No tingle of energy. No sense of warmth. Just the same dark nothing I'd felt every time I'd tried to light the candle.

Fuck. What if I *was* possessed?

My jaw started to tic. I clenched my teeth harder and tried conjuring up imaginary sheep to frolic across the darkness while the seconds dragged past.

I got to about fifty of them before Radha said, "She's clear."

That should have been good news, but I just felt numb. And I was beginning to shiver. I pulled my feet up onto the chair, hoping Ian would forgive my abuse of his antiques, and hugged my arms around my knees.

"When did she eat last?" Cassandra asked Lizzie.

"Lunchtime, maybe?" Lizzie said.

"Does that mean you didn't eat dinner either?" Cassandra said, looking exasperated. "You can't heal if you don't eat."

Damn. I'd forgotten to feed Lizzie. Though there was food she could manage one-handed in the fridge at home.

"I had a protein shake," Lizzie said. "I'm fine."

"I'll send for tea," Ian said. "Then we can talk." He walked across the room and pressed a bell. His assistant/butler/partner—I'd never quite figured out which—stepped into the room, then vanished back out the door after a murmured conversation.

"No demon taint is good," Lizzie said. She patted my shoulder as she stood.

"It is," Radha agreed, coming out from behind me, "but it doesn't leave us any wiser about why Maggie can't access her powers." She tugged at one of her earrings, leaning down to peer at my face. "What have you done to yourself?"

"Don't you know now?" I managed to say through teeth that only chattered slightly.

"I wasn't looking for that," Radha said. "You didn't give me permission."

The thought of letting her try again made me shiver again. Dumb when I hadn't felt a thing.

"You're cold," Lizzie said. "Let me grab you a blanket." She took a couple of steps toward the nearest sofa before she swayed and nearly stumbled. Ian caught her before she could actually fall.

"Lizzie!" I said.

Ian scooped her up and deposited her onto one of the sofas as Radha crossed the room in three quick steps.

Cassandra gestured for me to stay put. "She overdid it, but she'll be okay."

Was that a hint of guilt in her voice? Well, she could join the club. It was hard not to feel like I'd caused this again.

Radha was hovering over Lizzie, blocking my view.

"What's going on?" I asked.

"She'll be fine," Cassandra said as Ian's assistant came back into the room pushing a trolley laden with a china tea service and trays of snacks.

Cassandra helped him serve tea, ladling sugar into each cup with a heavy hand, as Radha did whatever she was doing to Lizzie. When she finally stepped back, Lizzie was sitting straighter and sipping tea, looking no worse for wear than when we'd arrived.

Radha accepted a cup, her expression assessing as she watched Lizzie.

But Lizzie was apparently in no mood to be fussed over. She let Cassandra pass her a plate of small sandwiches and Ian put a napkin across her lap but then shooed them away irritably with a flap of her good hand.

Ian said something I didn't quite catch, which made Lizzie first roll her eyes and then smile reluctantly. He settled on the sofa beside her. Cassandra and Radha headed back to me, hemming me in.

"Now that we know it's not a demon," Cassandra said, "we need to determine what exactly is stopping you from using your magic."

I knew she was right, but I just wanted to crawl into bed and sleep.

"Can we talk about it tomorrow?" I said. "I've had a work issue come up. I have a busy day to get through. And I need to get Lizzie home to bed. She obviously still needs to rest."

"How do you intend to deal with a work problem if you can't do what you do?" Cassandra said.

"It's not that kind of problem," I said, unwilling to elaborate. I'd asked Lizzie not to mention Damon's visit to the others. Not yet, at least. He didn't need a team of Cestis-approved investigators descending to make sure his issue wasn't related to another demon. Especially not when it seemed my issue wasn't.

His code had given my demon a way through, so it was likely that any hints of more problems at Riley Arts would spike their interest. I doubted he'd appreciate that. I'd dragged enough trouble into his life so far; I should, at least, attempt not to bring more in my wake now. "Not difficult but very time sensitive."

The last part was true. I hoped that it wouldn't actually take me long to prove the messages weren't coming from me. Not if Yoshi was as good as Lizzie said.

"It would still be good to work out a plan to fix you," Cassandra said. "As I said, we could use the help."

An expression I didn't quite like flickered over Radha's face at that pronouncement.

"I think it's a mental block," Lizzie called from the sofa. "She needs to want it back badly enough instead of being scared."

I grimaced at her. "Aren't you supposed to be replenishing your blood sugar or something?"

She stuck out her tongue, which eased my worry a little.

"I can replenish and talk about you. I have skills." She saluted me with her teacup.

"A mental block isn't unheard of," Radha mused. "Maybe we could look at her energy meridians, see where—"

"I'm sure my energy meridians—whatever the hell they are—can wait another day," I said. I'd had my fill of mystical weirdness for one night.

"Well, there's always the old-fashioned way," Ian said with an evil grin.

"The old-fashioned way?" I asked.

"We could summon an imp, see if you can fry it again before it eats you."

I really hoped that was an attempt at humor. But there was an edge to his words—faint but there—that made me think that maybe Ian, like Radha, wasn't someone I could currently call one of my biggest fans.

So if two out of the four Cestis members didn't like me, why was Cassandra pushing to get me involved? "Hard pass."

"No one's summoning anything," Cassandra said crisply. "We have enough going on with without adding to our problems. Lizzie and I will keep working with Maggie."

I flinched; I couldn't help it. I knew I needed to try, but the thought of magic lessons—particularly ones I failed at—was about as appealing as sticking my hand in the demon stone. "Sure. We can work on that after I sort out this other thing."

"Wouldn't it make your life easier to fix the magic first?" Cassandra said.

"I have no idea," I muttered. That much was true. "Besides, I'm hiring an assistant. That'll get me through for a while."

"An assistant?" Cassandra said. "You didn't say anything about that this afternoon."

"It was Lizzie's idea," I said, hoping that would stop the other three from interrogating me about Yoshi. "It's just a trial." I wasn't renowned for playing nice with others. It was part of the reason I started my own firm rather than working for one of the big consultancies. I liked things better when I got some say in the rules. Maybe it was a legacy of thirteen years with a mother who was definitely in the my-way-or-get-out camp.

"Having someone else do the work for you is hardly an incentive for you to solve your problems," Cassandra pointed out.

"Maybe he'll be really annoying and drive me to it in self-defense."

"Yoshi's not annoying," Lizzie said.

"Yoshi Liebfield?" Radha's brows arched.

"You know him?" I asked.

"I've met him a few times. He's a good kid."

Well, that figured. The foundation Lizzie worked for did something with troubled teens. She'd mentioned once that Radha sometimes helped out in the kitchen there. That made sense. Radha struck me as the earth mother type. Feeding Lizzie's strays would be right up her alley.

Pity she didn't count me as one of Lizzie's strays. She might have liked me more. Then again, I understood why Ian and Radha had their reservations about me. Every time they met me, there were demons and disaster not far behind. In their place, I probably wouldn't like me much either.

"Yoshi's awfully young," Radha continued.

"He's good," Lizzie said. "Besides, a job with Maggie is better than a Dockside stall."

"True," I agreed. "Which is why we need to get home and sleep. We need to be awake when he arrives tomorrow."

Chapter Seven

Compared to me, Yoshi looked ridiculously chipper at ten in the morning. I should have known Lizzie would try and foist another morning person on me —if only so she could have company while I staggered around like a zombie trying to wake up. This morning was worse than normal. I didn't know if it was the late night or the two—okay, three—shots of scotch I'd had when I'd gotten home to calm my lingering panic, but I felt distinctly hung over. Just as well that I wasn't heading into work today.

At least Yoshi wasn't wearing another eye-popping plaid combo, just battered jeans paired with a pinstriped jacket and a button-down shirt. Of course, the jacket was a sludgy green and the shirt was a pale purple, so it wasn't exactly a tame ensemble.

Or normal for a nineteen-year-old. Then again, I knew nothing about what teenagers were wearing. I'd been holed up in my house for most of a year.

"This house is chill," he said, swiveling his head from side to side to scope everything out as I ushered him into the kitchen. The chunky glasses were nowhere to be seen, and in the daylight, his eyes were a pale blue-gray that stood out against his dark hair and gold-tinged skin.

They could be colored contacts, of course, given the lack of glasses—or even a more expensive eye tint—but somehow I didn't think so.

"It will be when it's finished." Where exactly was he living that my part building site, part wreck of a house seemed cool?

"It's still chill. I don't get out of the city much." He peered out the kitchen window, which looked over the back garden but also over all the gardens of the other houses that spilled down the hill from where mine perched. "That's a lot of green." He blinked a few times and leaned closer to the window as though snared by the view.

I frowned at that. Downtown San Francisco was redeveloped, and there'd been a lot of emphasis on making both the streets and the buildings greener. There were small parks, rooftop farms, and green spaces wherever room could be found. If those weren't enough, there was always Golden Gate Park. Only the nastier areas like Dockside were devoid of any vegetation. Note to self: Ask Lizzie where Yoshi lives. "Do you like gardens?"

"They look pretty," he said. "And growing your own food seems chill. Don't know much about plants though."

Note to self: Also ask Lizzie what his school situation had been. Even during my high school days, there'd been an emphasis on planting urban gardens and sustainable small crop methods in biology and home sciences.

"Do you want something to drink? Syncaf or something?"

"Do you have soda?"

I nodded toward the fridge. Lizzie usually stocked a variety of carbonated things with or without caffeine, vitamins, lurid coloring, and other ingredients. I stuck to syncaf, water, and juice.

Yoshi took the invitation to rummage and emerged with something in an acid-green bottle. "So, I guess you want to give me some sort of test?" He cracked open the drink.

"I guess." I'd spent the morning wondering if I was doing the right thing.

Maybe it would be smarter to call in a proper security expert. I knew a few. But confiding in any of them risked word getting out that I was losing my touch. My field was niche, but no one was going to pay me if I couldn't do the job. My reputation was what won me work. And reputations could be tanked easily. Of course, Yoshi could rat me out, too. But Lizzie trusted him, so I could at least give him a shot. Because he was here, and available, and I was rapidly running out of time. So, I'd give him a trial and then lock him down with a confidentiality agreement.

He had seemed eager last night. I hoped it was "I'm not going to screw up a gig" eager rather than "poking around in the TechWitch's systems will be a good story at the game clubs" eager.

I nodded at the comp panel at the wall. "Did Lizzie tell you I don't have an office right now? So this is my home system. Used to be my office system, so it's solid and has more grunt than your average bear. I've set you up an account. We just need to verify."

"Chill." Yoshi slurped soda, then went to the control panel on the wall and put his palm on the glass. I stayed quiet while the computer ran through its security routines, adding his voice and palm prints to the system.

His access was locked down tight, I'd made sure of that, but it still made me nervous to let a virtual—no pun intended—stranger into my system.

Something I needed to get over fast given I was about to drop the kid in the deep end. I'd considered dummying up something to test him with, but I didn't really have time with Damon's deadline ticking away.

I'd already spent more time analyzing the data in my logs this morning before Yoshi arrived. Unsurprisingly, I'd found nothing. My system still insisted it hadn't sent anything to Riley Arts since the day I'd submitted my final invoice—for the amount they'd already paid me a few weeks after Nat's funeral.

So whoever was sending those damn messages to Damon had either done an immaculate job of hiding their hack job, or they were spoofing my system elsewhere.

Hopefully Yoshi could confirm the first option by finding the sucker. If my system had been cloned at some point, that would be harder still to figure out. My security had always been as tight as I could make it. For someone to clone it meant skills of the very-expensive-pay-grade hacker. The black hat kind. Nothing I wanted to tangle with.

So I was clinging to the hope that I'd missed something and Yoshi could find it. Right after I made him sign a nondisclosure agreement. I'd stolen a lot of the content of that agreement from the one Damon had made me sign, so I was fairly certain it was watertight.

Once Yoshi signed, I explained the problem. At the first mention of Riley Arts, Yoshi's eyes lit up. I'd been hoping he wouldn't be a worshipper at the cult of Righteous, but I'd known the chances were slim given he was a deck jockey.

"You want me to find out if your system is sending messages to Righteous?" He was actually bouncing in place, rising up and down on his toes, reminding me just how young he was.

"I want you to try," I said gently. "It's not going to be easy. I've already gone over everything several times and found nothing." I braced myself for what would likely be the inevitable next question if he was a true game freak. Aka how did I know Damon Riley well enough to be sending him email in the first place?

Yoshi went still, expression turning serious. "If there's something there to find, I'll find it."

Ah, to be young and supremely confident again. But his lack of nosiness—or at least his restraint if he *was* feeling nosy—was a definite point in his favor.

"We'll see."

He just shrugged at me and pulled a terminal deck out of his backpack. "Do you mind if I use this?"

Given the alternative was him using the screen and keyboard in my makeshift office or doing everything verbally, I didn't. But I made him hand the deck over and ran it through my security scans before I let him connect. No red flags, so I gave him access and tried not to let my discomfort with him poking around my system show.

I busied myself making another cup of syncaf

and rummaging in the cabinets for snacks while Yoshi logged himself in and set to work. The screen on the wall showed me what he was doing, but I figured watching over his shoulder wasn't going to be helpful for either of us. I needed to know if he could do it on his own.

I put a plate of food in front of him—if Yoshi was sailing close to the wind financially, the least I could do was feed him while he helped me out.

Judging by the speed at which the food started disappearing, I'd been right about his appetite. I left him alone to fuel up and get to work and curled up on the sofa with Cassandra's book. Lizzie was still asleep. I didn't want to wake her. Sleep would help her heal. And if she was sleeping, she couldn't nag me into more magic practice. Still, even without nagging, I needed to read up.

I shot a glance at Yoshi, intent on his deck. How much did he know about Lizzie? I'd asked her, and she'd said he wasn't a witch as far as she knew, but I hadn't thought to ask what he knew about her and that part of her life. Not that magic was high on my list of topics I planned to talk to him about. It shouldn't come up if this all went smoothly.

Ian and Cassandra and Radha had given me another version of the "you need protection until you get your powers back" speech before they'd let us go last night. Cassandra had added something to whatever it was Lizzie's bracelet did. Lizzie, in turn, had refused to go to bed until I found the black tourmaline and amethyst pendant Cassandra had given me when I'd first found out I had powers. I'd stopped wearing it after Nat died, but I hadn't thrown it away.

I was sure if they'd known I'd lost my magic, they would have insisted on it before now. But the possibility obviously had never occurred to any of them. Which made sense. All four of them were deep in the magic world. You didn't become one of the Cestis by being half-assed about magic and power and all the benefits and dangers that came with it. Not that I had any idea how you did become a member of the Cestis. They certainly hadn't replaced Antony yet, which suggested there weren't that many suitable candidates around.

They were clearly shorthanded if Cassandra thought even someone as clueless-newbie as me would ease their load. As much as I wanted to pretend otherwise, I owed them. So I would do my homework so I might have some idea what to do if my magic came back.

"Have you played the new game yet?" Yoshi asked after about an hour of him typing away at the speed of light and me switching between reading about magic and trying to figure out some different approaches for my client's problem when I got too freaked out.

"Game?" I was deep in an inventory selection subroutine, not really paying attention.

"Archangel."

My head jerked up. Crap. Had he seen that stupid ad? "I don't game." I hoped my tone would make "let's not go there" perfectly clear.

He frowned. "But you worked on that project, yeah?"

Either he was crap at reading my tone or he was curious enough not to worry about annoying me.

I frowned, wondering how the hell he'd learned that I had worked on Archangel. I hadn't seen a mention of my name in any article about the game in the weeks after the recall. Not that many people at Riley Arts had known what I was doing there. Clearly someone had talked though. Maybe I should report *that* to Damon. Give his security team something to worry about other than me. "I did some consulting for Riley last year. I wasn't there to play games."

"So you never played it at all?"

I sighed. Gamers were all the same where Righteous was concerned. Endlessly eager for any intel they could gather. Any tiny inside tidbit was to be treasured. But if Yoshi was going to work for me, he had to learn the rules. "I saw a couple of snippets of early versions. And I signed an NDA that makes that one I just got you to sign look puny, so let's not talk about it. Have you found anything yet?"

Those pale eyes blinked, then narrowed. I got the feeling he was making a mental note to read his NDA more carefully. He should have thought of that before he signed. But I hadn't tied him up in any legalese that was anything I wouldn't have signed myself. I had signed it—or versions of it—many times. But I'd vetted first. Yoshi was young, but if he was running his own business, he needed to learn to look after himself.

"Not so far. It's all clean."

Which could either mean he wasn't as good as he thought or that there really was nothing to find. I needed to know which before I made any more decisions. I switched seats to sit beside him. "Tell me what you've tried."

Twenty minutes later, I had my answer. Yoshi knew his stuff. He'd come up with a few things I hadn't thought of and created a genius sniffer program on the fly that I would have been happy to call my own. That didn't change the fact that we'd still come up blank. I chewed my lip as I stared at Yoshi's deck, trying to figure out yet another angle. Problem was, we'd already done the full three hundred and sixty degrees and were right back where we started.

With a big ball of nothing.

"There's just not anything here," Yoshi said after we'd rerun his program for the third time.

"Tell me something I don't know."

"You're looking in the wrong place."

"Pardon?"

He waved a hand at his deck. "There's nothing here. But these messages that have Righteous all jacked up are coming from somewhere, right?"

That had been the obvious option B. Someone was cloning my system somehow. "Right. Which only leaves us with several billion possible suspects."

"Nah," Yoshi said. "Make like that old detective dude. You know, Sherlock Holmes." He snapped his fingers. "Consider the impossible. What's the least likely place you can think of for those messages to come from, apart from here?"

My heart sank. I knew exactly where his train of thought was headed, and I didn't like it one little bit. "Righteous."

Chapter Eight

THE SMILE on Cat Delaney's face had passed frosty and was skating toward arctic. She'd always been coolly polite to me. She was coolly polite to just about everyone other than Damon. But her voice, as she directed me to wait while she checked if Mr. Riley was available, was several degrees below zero.

Maybe Damon didn't blame me for the fallout from the recall, but it was clear Cat did. Unfair. The Righteous static filter had been partly to blame, too, but I didn't think making that point was likely to change her mind. Particularly if she knew all the ins and outs of what happened. Easier to assume she did. Damon trusted her, and a good assistant had to know more about their boss's life than almost anybody else if they were going to keep it running smoothly. Cat would know where all the bodies were buried, so to speak.

I kept my own expression politely neutral. I understood. I'd never really figured out how much Damon's employees knew about our relationship. It had happened fast and ended fast, and I, for one, hadn't tried to advertise it, but if anyone was going to have known, it would be Cat. So potentially, to her I was both wrecker-of-company-she-lived-for and breaker-of-boss-man's-heart. Apparently two strikes and I was out.

"You can go in now," Cat said after several long minutes of silence while I tried to pretend I was reading something on my datapad.

As she spoke the words, I realized that staying exactly where I was, soaking up the nuclear eat-shit-and-die vibes rolling off Cat, was actually more appealing than going in and facing Damon.

But wimping out wasn't an option. I pasted an "I'm perfectly fine" expression on my face, said, "Thank you," to Cat, and walked the twenty feet or so to Damon's door.

Damon's office was the same. Ridiculously huge, the walls all curves and sweeping glass. Built to reinforce that here sat the man in charge of the whole shebang. Still, that impression was softened a bit—as it had been the first time I'd ever set foot in the room—by some of the quirkier touches. Old surfboards still lined one wall. A giant screen domi-

nated another, currently only showing the reflec-
tions of the arc of screaming-red leather recliners
arrayed around it. They were game chairs, though
you wouldn't have known it at first glance, their
high-tech nature artfully disguised. *Expensively* disguised. But money was no object to Damon. Even
with the hit Righteous had taken from the recall, he
was rich in a way I would never be. That most
people on the planet would never be.

At least he tried to do good with that money.
Riley Arts had been instrumental in getting the city
redeveloped by declaring they were rebuilding their
campus downtown, and they did a load of charity
work. More of it since the recall, though they'd
taken flak for that, too, some calling it a cynical PR
move.

Maybe it was, but that didn't change the out-
come. The money went to people who needed it.
And Damon had never been a corporate asshole.
Much as it would be easier to hate him if he was.
So no, not much in the room had changed.

Just me. Or maybe both of us.

Damon rose from his chair, but he made no immediate move to venture out from behind his desk.
He stood there, looking far too good in a light blue
shirt and darker jeans. Damn him. He knew he
looked good in blue.

Though why I thought he might care how he
looked in what he wore for a meeting with me was

beyond me. I stopped well before I reached the desk. Safety in distance and all that.

For a moment we just stared at each other, no less awkward than we had been in my yard. I clearly didn't know how to do casual chat with this man. And it was better not to think too hard about why he might not be able to come up with something to say to me. I'd never been this awkward with an ex-lover before. Maybe because I'd never let one break my heart.

Another train of thought I didn't want to jump aboard.

I pulled a datachip from my purse, advanced a few steps until I was only a couple of feet away, and tossed it onto his desk. "My systems are clean."

His jaw tightened. "Hello to you, too."

I narrowed my eyes, then shrugged, going for "I couldn't care less" rather than "I really hate seeing you again." That emotion was something I was keeping to myself. "You're the one who put a time-frame on this. That chip has detailed diagnostics run by me and by an independent expert. All the traffic logs and every other kind of log your security team could want." "Independent expert" sounded better than nineteen-year-old uber-nerd with a plaid fetish. Yoshi had practically begged to come along, but I had refused. Seeing Damon was hard enough without the added complication of babysitting Yoshi and trying to make him behave himself in what was pretty much geek nirvana. "There's no evidence of any messages coming from my system."

"That you can find."

"It's a bit late for you to start questioning my competence, isn't it?"

"Maybe." He popped the chip into the reader on his desk and pulled up a terminal. I stood, silent, as he scanned through the reports.

"Well?" I asked when he finally looked up.

"Mitch would say this could be doctored." His tone was as flat and unrevealing as mine.

Apparently if I was going to do too cool for school, so was he. "Your head of security can say a lot of things. I'll say this. You have a choice to make. You said you didn't believe it was me. You either trust me or not. If you don't, well, let your security do their worst. They can come look at my system themselves. Believe me, they're not going to find anything."

"You could be using a different system."

I only just stopped myself from telling him to bite me. "You saw my house. Did that look to you like I have money to throw around to maintain secret hidden computer setups smart enough to beat whatever you're throwing at them?"

He frowned. Was he about to ask me why I didn't have the money? That was something I wanted to talk to him about even less than making chitchat.

"You said you believed they weren't from me. Your guys thought the messages were coming from my system, and I've just given you the proof that they're not."

"Which leaves me right back at square one."

"Not exactly," I said.

The frown deepened. "What does that mean?"

"Well, if it's not me, then it's someone who knows you and I had a relationship—a business relationship, at least. There aren't that many people who knew about the work I did here, are there? And even fewer outside Righteous, I hope. Unless you think one of the Cestis has a grudge against you."

He shook his head at that suggestion. "No, they've been nothing but helpful."

They had *what*? No. Focus. I wasn't here to talk about the Cestis. I was here to clear my name and get Damon Riley back out of my life.

"Right. So you need people who knew about you and me. Either them or someone they blabbed to. That's the logical place to start."

"You think someone in my own company is sending me death threats?"

I shrugged. "Well, you didn't suck too much as a client, but maybe you do as a boss." I knew it wasn't true. I'd seen him in action with his staff, and the whole Riley campus was a testament to a company that cared about its employees. Riley had a reputation as a great place to work that wasn't just driven by its success and it being on the cutting edge for anyone who wanted to work in virtual reality and game design. But even the best kind of boss made enemies over the course of doing business. Righteous must have its share of disgruntled ex-employees same as any other corporation.

"Gee, thanks," he said.

I held up my hands. "Don't shoot the messenger. Has your team looked at anyone else?"

"I don't know." He had the grace to look sheepish. "They were investigating whether or not it was you. I'm not sure how far the 'not' part got."

"Then I guess it's time you give them the order to try a little harder in that department."

He tapped the datachip. "My guys aren't going to necessarily take this at face value."

I folded my arms, suddenly wondering if I'd been suckered. "What does that mean? You know, if you've just hauled me in here for some weird revenge thing and there are a bunch of cops waiting to take me away, then I'm changing my mind. You *do* suck."

"Why would I have come to you if I intended to involve the police?"

"I don't know, Damon. I gave up guessing about your motivations about nine months ago."

He winced. "Maggie—"

"No. We did this at the house. Nothing to talk about. So." I pointed at the datachip. "This boils down to you versus your cyber dudes. You're the boss, no matter how much of a hardass this Mitch guy is. So, do you trust me? Or do I need to call a lawyer?" I couldn't afford a lawyer.

Damon picked up the chip, slid it into his pocket. "I trust you."

"Good. Because you know, if I wanted to do something to you, I wouldn't need email. And I wouldn't be stupid enough to leave a trail." I stepped back. "If there's nothing else, I should get going."

"Wait." His mouth twisted. "I'd like to hear more about your theory. About who else it could be."

I arched an eyebrow at him. "Damon, you have a cybersecurity team. Who are part of your overall security team. I'm guessing they can come up with a suspect profile in about thirty seconds flat if you tell them to look elsewhere."

"Just a few minutes," he said. "I'll get Cat to bring us some coffee."

That was playing dirty. He knew how much I loved the real stuff. I hesitated. I should get out while I could. While my exposure to him was limited and my emotions couldn't confuse themselves all over again. But as he leaned over to press a button on his system to call Cat and I got a waft of his damned clean cotton, spice, man scent, my feet seemed stuck to the floor.

"Coffee and one of those amazing cheese Danishes from the cafeteria in Building Two," I countered.

"You got it." He smiled at me and gave the order to Cat.

Damn it. I didn't want him to smile at me. Didn't want to feel the silly little rush it gave me. God. Hormones were the worst.

I lowered myself into the chair. Talk or do awkward silence. Talking seemed the lesser of two evils. "So what did you want to know?"

"What makes you think it's someone here?"

I shrugged. "Simplest explanation. Guys like you—"

"What the hell does that mean?"

I rolled my eyes. "Don't make me say it. You know what I mean." I meant rich powerful corporate kings. "You make enemies. Business rivals, who hopefully are too smart to email threats. People you've pissed off in life generally—there has to be some of those. And then game heads and employees have to be the biggest pool of possible nutters. Like I said, not that many people knew I worked for you. Fewer still knew that we...." I trailed off. That was another thing I didn't want to spell out.

"Anyway, it seems more likely that an employee would know enough about me to want to try and set me up for whatever this is." It was my turn to lift an eyebrow. "Maybe if you told me more about the messages, I could be more help."

Damon opened his mouth to answer just as the office door opened inward and Cat marched in bearing a tray. She set down two coffees—mine was black, the way I liked it; she might not be on Team Maggie, but she was too good an assistant to get that wrong—and a plate of Danishes.

"Anything else?" she asked.

"No, thanks, Cat." Damon smiled at her and picked up his coffee.

I waited until she'd closed the door again before I reached for mine. Then paused. "Should I assume this is safe to drink?"

Damon's eyes widened, and he swallowed his mouthful fast. Too fast perhaps. He coughed slightly. "Are you suggesting Cat would do something to your coffee?"

"Well, she isn't exactly one of my top fans," I said. "She did a good imitation of an iceberg while I was waiting for you." I shrugged and blew on my coffee. "I don't blame her. She's protective of you. And I caused trouble. I get it."

He frowned. "She doesn't dislike you."

"Oh, you've asked her that, have you? Do you think she'd tell you if she did?"

"She's never been shy about stating her opinion. But she wouldn't poison you."

I snorted. "I was thinking of something less

drastic." I inhaled the divine scent of genuine coffee beans and decided I didn't care. "But what the hell. Why waste the good stuff, right?" I took a reverent mouthful and closed my eyes to enjoy it.

When I opened them again, Damon was looking at me strangely. "What?" I said.

Was I imagining things, or was there a faint flush of color in his cheeks? And if there was, why exactly? That seemed to fall under the topic of things that shouldn't be discussed either. I put the cup down and grabbed a Danish, wanting to make the coffee last. It could be a long time before I got to taste it again. "So, are you going to tell me what these messages that have your team so up in arms are? Threats?"

"So they tell me."

"You haven't read them?"

"I read the first couple. Then security stepped in."

"How long has this been going on? "

"Two weeks perhaps?" He wrinkled his forehead as though he was trying to remember.

"Two weeks? Why did it take you so long to tell me?"

"I didn't believe it was you," he said. "But the team started digging. The last month has been a bit of a blur leading up to the launch. Last week, in particular, was madness. I've barely had time to come up for air. Mitch waited until launch day and then insisted we needed to do something. I still didn't think it was you, so that's when I came to see you."

I didn't know whether to be pleased that he trusted me or annoyed that me supposedly giving him death threats was obviously low on his list of priorities. "Launch?" I said, hoping like hell I sounded like I had no idea what he was talking about. I was in no way ready to talk about why the main character in his new game looked like me.

"New game," he said. "The first one since the recall."

Either he had bought my act or he was doing me the courtesy of pretending he had. Still, I wasn't quite sure what to say next. We were straying into dangerous waters again. There seemed to be a lot of them around. But when in doubt, return to a safer subject. If threats supposedly coming from me could be considered safer.

"Interesting timing. Did the messages say anything about the launch? Tell you to delay it or anything like that?" That could narrow it down to someone who'd been affected by the recall.

"No. They didn't make any demands. It isn't blackmail or extortion. At least not yet."

"Just threats. To do what?"

"Well, the ones I read involved me and various painful fates that await me." His mouth flattened. "I'm told they haven't improved."

If that was the case, I couldn't blame him for not wanting to read them. "And how many were there?"

"About ten that first day. There have been batches most days since then."

Batches? How many emails exactly did it take to get your point across if you were making death threats? "Any patterns?"

"I'd have to ask. But I would have thought they'd have looked into it if they'd identified any-thing. They haven't told me if they did."

"Okay. Just a thought," I said, sipping coffee. I was trying to make it last, I realized, and I had no desire to think too hard about why that was. I didn't really think I could add much to help Damon out that his own teams couldn't already.

He was staring at his own mug as if the black liquid might hold the answers he was looking for. Then he looked up and our eyes locked.

Blue. So goddamn blue.

"Do you think this could be connected to what happened?" he asked.

I almost choked on my coffee. Did he mean the demon? "Honestly? I have no idea."

"Is it possible?"

"I think you need to ask someone who knows more about that stuff than I do," I said. "Is there a reason you think it might be?

"Just trying to cover my bases."

I didn't believe him. He wouldn't be raising the

subject of magic with me unless he had something specific to talk about. "Has anything else happened besides the emails?"

"Nothing specific. Cassandra sent someone after...it happened, and apparently there was no sign of anything lingering then."

My eyebrows flew up. That was what he meant by the Cestis being helpful? Mr. I-don't-do-magic had let the witches check things out? "Who did she send?"

He looked vaguely guilty, and I realized it must have been Lizzie. She was no slouch with tech. She gamed, and she'd helped me install our system. She wasn't as good as me or Yoshi—after all, it wasn't her job—but I figured she'd know enough to do whatever the Cestis needed to do to make sure the demon hadn't left any nasty surprises at Righteous. "It was Lizzie, wasn't it?"

"Yes, her and another guy. Not someone from the Cestis. They checked out my house as well. And recommended some healers to work with the beta testers."

I filed that tidbit of information under "things Lizzie had neglected to tell me." But I couldn't blame her. After she'd started randomly checking up on me in those early days after Nat's funeral, I'd made it very clear that Damon Riley was strictly off-topic. In her place, I wouldn't have mentioned him either if I'd been trying to make friends with someone who just wanted to be left alone.

"I can ask them to take another look if you like," I offered.

"Can't you do it?" he asked.

"I wouldn't know where to start. I'm hardly an expert in that...kind of thing."

"I thought you might have studied up after what happened."

"I had a few other priorities," I said. Like avoiding magic as much as possible. Not something I'd admit to him. "You're not the only one who had fallout to deal with."

He grimaced. "I'm sorry. The last nine months have been...not pleasant. Then, yes, please. I would appreciate it if you could talk to Lizzie. My team can look into the employees, the betas, and whoever else they can come up with, but they don't know about magic."

"You didn't tell them exactly what happened?"

"About what was behind it? No. The Cestis said not to. As far as the vast majority knows, there was an unforeseen complication from the static code that adversely affected some users. Which we've fixed now. Mitch knows that magic was involved, but even he doesn't know about the...."

He didn't want to say "demon." I couldn't blame him. "I see." I wondered if the Cestis had signed off on the new version of the game. But it didn't surprise me that they'd covered things up. They'd covered up Nat's cause of death, too.

I sighed.

So much for getting Damon out of my life.

Hopefully the Cestis would either know what was going on or declare nothing magical was involved. "It will be easier for me to talk to Lizzie if we have the details of the messages."

He nodded and hit his datapad again. "Mitch? I need a complete dump of the emails you've been looking into and any analysis your team has done. Send it to my personal server." He slid the datachip back into the slot in his desk. "And I'll be sending you an analysis of Maggie Lachlan's system. It's clean. And before you start arguing, yes, I trust the source. You need to start looking at other possibilities. Maggie is in the clear."

He disconnected the call. Apparently no arguments were going to be entered into. So that was a relief. Though I wasn't entirely in the clear. I'd been hoping to get in and out with minimal contact, yet I'd already agreed to do the man another favor. I needed to get out of there before I did anything else stupid.

I stood abruptly. "Send that stuff to me. Or send me a datachip. I'll talk to Lizzie."

Chapter Nine

"WHAT DO you think he wants us to do?" Lizzie asked me about two hours later. When I'd first arrived home, she'd been napping. Yoshi had left me a message on the house comp saying he'd had to go to another gig and to keep him posted.

I changed out of my "visiting the billionaire ex" outfit that I'd been telling myself I hadn't spent way too much time choosing and wandered out to the kitchen to make myself syncaf—ugh—and then do some planning. But Lizzie had joined me. So I started making grilled cheese and talking instead.

She perched on a stool near the counter and yawned as I told her what had happened. Until I got to the part about him wanting the Cestis to check things out for him.

Then she got focused fast. Hence the question.

"I don't know," I said, poking the grilled cheese with a spatula to see if it was ready. "I guess whatever it was you did for him last time." I raised my eyebrows at her as I flipped the sandwich out onto the waiting plate.

Lizzie pulled it toward her. "Don't wriggle your eyebrows at me. You were very clear that you wanted nothing to do with Damon or Cestis business at the time. If I'd told you about it, you would have gone through the roof. Besides, I was just doing my job. It didn't take very long. It wasn't as though I was hanging out with the guy."

No. Because she'd been busy hanging out with me in those first few weeks after Nat died and Damon bailed. Yes, she'd disappeared for "work" a few times, but I'd been a mess huddled on my sofa watching mindless old movies and trying to remember how to breathe.

"I didn't say anything," I muttered.

"Good. I won't apologize for doing my job. Or for choosing your peace of mind over total honesty." She bit into the sandwich as I put the one I was making for myself into the skillet.

"You don't have to," I said. I sighed. "I owe you an apology though. I'm pretty sure I was an asshole most of the time when you first moved in."

"You had your moments," Lizzie agreed. "But grief sucks, and you had good reason to be off your game. You still do. So apology accepted." She wiped sandwich grease off her fingers. "Did he say why he thinks there's something magical going on?"

"No, he just said he wanted to cover all bases."

"Did you believe him?"

I hesitated, prodding the sandwich again. "I'm not sure. I'd like to think he wouldn't lie to me, but who knows? Or he might not be lying. He might just not be able to admit to himself that something has him spooked."

"Sounds like someone else I know," Lizzie said.

"I told him you were hurt and that he'd have to wait a few days."

"And he was okay with that?"

"They have other avenues to pursue," I said. I flipped the sandwich over. "And he's in the middle of a launch. Things must be crazy right now."

"I guess. Archangel is number one on all the charts, so it seems to be going well." She fixed me with a curious look. "Did you ask him about it?"

"Did I ask my ex-boyfriend who hates magic about why there's a character in his new game who looks like me? No. I'm not a masochist. I don't want to know."

"Liar, liar, pants on fire," Lizzie chanted softly.

"Shut up and eat your sandwich." I tipped mine onto the plate and put the skillet in the sink, too hungry to stop and clean it. The few bites of Danish felt like a long time ago, and my appetite was back now that I was over the nerves about meeting Damon.

We both ate in silence for a while. Lizzie looked better than she had yesterday, but she was still pale. Whatever it was Damon needed, he could definitely wait. She needed to rest for a few days. And refuel. Magical healing burned lots of calories. She was already wiping the last crumbs of her sandwich off her plate with a finger.

"Do you want another—" I broke off as the housecomp began to chime. I frowned toward it. "Are we expecting anyone?" I asked Lizzie.

"No. Yoshi said he'd check back later, but I assumed he meant he'd call."

"Identify," I said to the housecomp.

"Cassandra Tallant," the electronic voice came back, sounding somewhat bored.

I looked at Lizzie. "Been adding to the guest list, have we?"

She shrugged. "I didn't want any of them triggering an alarm when they came to help with the wards."

"Is that why she's here now?"

"I don't know," Lizzie said. "Probably checking up on me." She sounded irritated. "Better go let her in. She doesn't like to be kept waiting."

There didn't seem to be an alternative. I'd asked for a day or two to sort out my issue with Damon before we got back to the issue of where my magic had gone. It seemed I wasn't going to get it.

"Hi," I said, trying to sound enthusiastic as I opened the door.

"Hello, Maggie." Cassandra handed me a plate of something wrapped in a daisy-patterned sil-wrap. From the smell wafting up from it, I'd have to guess it was chocolate chip cookies. If Cassandra kept this up, I'd be 95 percent cookie before all this was over.

"I was in the neighborhood," she said.

That might have been true, but I doubted this was a casual visit. "You want to see Lizzie? She's in the kitchen." I waved behind me, indicating the general direction. Was this going to be life now that I'd broken my "no contact with the Cestis" rule?

"And how is whatever problem it was you had to deal with?" Cassandra said as I caught up with her.

Her tone suggested that she definitely didn't think I should take too long to find a solution. But I wasn't ready to just hand myself over so she could put me through my magical paces until something cracked and my magic came back.

"I'm heading in the right direction," I said, hedging. It might be easier to let Lizzie tell her Damon had asked for help. I pushed open the kitchen door, relieved to see Lizzie still at the table, calmly peeling an orange. "Cassandra brought cookies," I said, holding up the plate.

Lizzie smiled at that. "Cookies are good." She glanced at Cassandra. "Let me guess, you were just in the neighborhood?"

"Exactly. And now that I'm here, you can tell me how you're feeling."

"You could have just called." Lizzie rolled her eyes.

"I can't see your energy field on a call," Cassandra said. "Which means I can't tell if you're lying to me."

"I'm fine," Lizzie said. "No need to lie. My arm's still sore, and I'm definitely going to take another nap this afternoon, but I'm fine. It was only a fracture. You should all chill."

Cassandra watched her closely as she spoke, her big golden brown eyes narrowed. But apparently whatever she saw in Lizzie's energy field didn't contradict what Lizzie was saying, because she just nodded after a few moments and said, "That's good. We need you back up and running."

"More importantly, I need to get back to work. It's one of our busy times."

Cassandra wrinkled her nose. "Evie understands what you do for us."

"Yes she does," Lizzie agreed. "But I also understand what she does for the kids out there. So I don't want to leave her in the lurch right now."

Evie London, I knew, was Lizzie's boss. I hadn't known she knew about Lizzie's other job. Did that mean she was a witch, too? I was still hazy on exactly what the foundation Evie ran did. I knew it involved teenagers, and that Lizzie worked in "philanthropy management". That seemed to be a fancy name for fundraising. Obviously the Cestis took up a chunk of her time, too. I'd never been brave enough to ask if that was a paid position. I imagined it had to be. Ian was the only one whose lifestyle confirmed him to be actually rich. Though, to be fair, I hadn't actually seen Cassandra's house, just the store.

Radha worked as a healer, though, from what I'd gathered, that could be a vocation for witches as well as a job. The sort of thing you did even if you didn't need the money.

Lizzie contributed her half of the bills and groceries every month without complaint. I didn't charge her rent. I owned the house, even if it was a wreck, and the help she was giving me with the rebuild was worth more to me than a rent check would be.

I didn't know if there was a third job in there somewhere, but she didn't seem to lack for money. Though I was starting to feel bad for not knowing. Sure, I'd had a lot on my mind for the nine months, but exactly how self-absorbed had I been that Lizzie and I had never really talked about her job?

She and Cassandra were watching each other silently across the table. It was a little disconcerting to see them at odds. Usually Lizzie was easygoing. She wasn't a doormat, and she spoke up when she wanted to, but in the Cestis, Cassandra ran things. Maybe being injured made her cranky.

"Speaking of work," Lizzie said just as I was starting to rack my brain for something to say before the silence got too weird, "Damon Riley has asked us to do another sweep."

Cassandra turned to me. "When did you see Damon?"

"Why do you assume it was me? Lizzie did whatever a sweep is for him last time, didn't she?"

"Was it Lizzie?" Cassandra asked.

I grimaced. "No. He came to the house yesterday."

"Does that happen often?"

"I haven't seen him since Nat's funeral. As I'm sure Lizzie has told you."

Cassandra pursed her lips. "I think you overestimate our interest in your love life."

"I don't have a love life. And if I did, it wouldn't be with Damon Riley."

"Then why did he come see you instead of just asking Lizzie for help?"

"Because his initial problem was something that involved me."

"This is the same problem you mentioned last

night? The reason you couldn't work on your magic today?"

Gah! "Yes."

"And you didn't want to tell us that?" She peered at me over her glasses.

Cassandra would have made an excellent high school principal. I wanted to squirm. I resisted. She wasn't, despite what she might think, the boss of me. "Since when does the Cestis deal with fake emails?" I said grumpily.

Cassandra looked confused. "Fake emails? Whose fake emails?"

"Damon was getting some threats. His security team insisted it was coming from me. I proved otherwise. I went to see him to tell him so. Told him to look elsewhere. That's when he mentioned Lizzie."

"Did he say why he thought we should take a look?"

"No. He said he was just being thorough. If he has another reason, he didn't tell me."

"But he asked you about the emails?"

"Because it looked like they were coming from me. He wanted to give me a chance to clear my name."

"I see." She turned back to Lizzie. "I know you gave him the all clear last time, but this isn't some-thing we can ignore. Do you think you have time to help him? I can ask someone else."

Lizzie shook her head. "It'll be faster if I do it. I know what's involved."

"All right. Maggie can help you."

"What?" I squawked.

"Lizzie needed a hand with the technology aspects last time. You know more about computers— and Damon's company—than anybody else we have. It makes sense."

"What if he doesn't want me there?" Okay, I had officially turned back into a whiny teenager. I gave myself a mental slap and straightened my shoulders.

"Well, if he wants our help, he can just suck it up," Cassandra said. She smiled smugly. "Besides, if Radha and Lizzie are right and your magic has something to do with trauma from the demon, then he's part of that. Maybe spending some time with him might shake something loose for you."

"Man, you really believe in tough love, don't you?" I muttered. "Damon and I...it's hard for me to see him."

"I appreciate that. And I made you cookies, so you can wallow with those if you want to," Cassandra said. "But I'm not going to coddle you about your magic. You need it back or we'll have to spend way too much time checking up on you. So when Lizzie is feeling up to it, you'll help her with this. And I expect to see you at the store tomorrow at some point for some more practice. Yes?"

Saying no didn't seem to be an option. I'd have to call my client and tell them I'd be working off-site for a few days.

I looked at the cookies. She should have made a bigger batch.

"Did you know she was going to say that?" I asked when I came back to the kitchen after showing Cassandra out.

Lizzie was at the dishwasher, stacking plates one-handed. "I didn't know Damon was going to ask for help, so how was I supposed to know that Cassandra would say you should help me?"

"Educated guess?" I shooed her away from the dishwasher. "Let me do that."

"I have a fracture, not a head wound," Lizzie said. "I can handle putting some plates in the dishwasher."

"You're supposed to be resting. I fractured my arm when I was twenty. I was exhausted for a few weeks."

"Yeah, but you didn't have a witch speed up the healing, did you?"

"That's tiring, too." I knew that from experience.

"I have Cassandra to nag me," she said, then winced. "Sorry, bad mood. I'd rather be at work."

"Does Evie really need you right now?"

"Yeah, we do a big push as the school year wraps up and then set up for our holiday campaigns."

"Anything I can help with?"

"You have a job of your own," Lizzie said, but she smiled.

"Not one I'm much good at for the moment."

"So we need to fix that," she said. "But if you're interested in volunteering at some point, I'm sure Evie will find something you can do. We always need more hands."

"Okay." I closed up the dishwasher. "I will." It seemed the least I could do to start paying Lizzie back for all the help she'd given me. "What are you doing this afternoon?"

"More exciting sofa time, I guess." Lizzie looked less than enthused. "How about you? I could talk you through some of the stuff in that book Cassandra gave you. Easier than just reading about it?"

"Actually, I have some work-work to do," I said. "Sort of."

"Oh?"

"Damon is supposed to be sending me a data dump of everything related to the emails he's been receiving. I'm going to run some pattern analysis on them, see if anything leaps out at me. You can help if you want. You need to know what's in there anyway, I guess." And Lizzie would see things that I wouldn't even know to look for if there was something magical going on.

"Sure," she said, brightening. "I can do that from the sofa. Then no one can accuse me of not resting."

"Is anyone else likely to check up on you today? We're getting low on syncaf." And a lot of other things, particularly if we were going to be feeding a teenage boy. If Yoshi had time later, I would get him to keep digging around, see if he could find any trace of how my system could have been cloned. The methods for doing that weren't going to be strictly kosher, but I suspected he knew how even if he was a white hatter.

"I'll order groceries while you're running whatever analysis you're going to," Lizzie said, heading toward the living room. "Out of curiosity, when did Damon say those messages started?"

I frowned, trying to remember. "Back at the beginning of the month, I think."

She turned to look back at me, eyes wide. "May first?"

"I'd have to check. Why?"

"That's Beltane."

Beltane. Pagan festival. That was about all I knew about it. "Does that matter?" I tried to see if anything else popped up in my head about it. "Isn't that a ritual all about fertility and harvest?"

"Traditionally, yes, and no, we don't necessarily

pay much attention to those historic days, but some people think that the energy of such days is enhanced. It would be a good day to start a big working of some sort." She shrugged. "Or it may be just a complete coincidence. So, you run whatever it is you want to do, I'll make sure we can eat for another week, and then we'll see what there is to see."

Chapter Ten

RUNNING a basic analysis of the information Damon's team had sent me didn't take too long despite the thousands of emails. Apparently fake me had been a busy girl.

The ones that contained the threats were easy enough to separate, but there were others that appeared to be spammy gibberish, and then a subset that my system quarantined and shunted off to my vault to be transferred to an isolated computer before it would let me open them. Those would be full of viruses and malware and all the nasty things the dark side of the web could dream up. I sent a bot to scrape the text and basic identifying data off those and shunt the results into a safe file that I sent through my various levels of cleanup before the system agreed it was safe to add that file at least back to the analysis queue.

By the time our groceries arrived in the automated delivery car, my system was starting to dump reports into my inbox. I told it to send them to Lizzie as well and went to fetch the groceries.

I unpacked, stashed everything back in its place, made tea, and plated up some of Cassandra's cookies before I went back into the living room. Lizzie was curled on the sofa, frowning as she read.

"Anything interesting?" I asked. I set her tea on the coffee table and peeked at what she was reading. A breakdown of the dates and times of all the emails.

Her frown deepened. "I need to check a few things." She changed screens on the datapad, projected a keyboard, and started typing.

"Should you be using two hands?"

She didn't look up. "It's fine. This won't take long." She tapped the screen a final time and then sat back, chewing her lip.

"Spit it out," I said. "Something's bothering you."

"The first big wave was on May first," she said.

"Beltane, right."

"Then there's another spike seven days later, which happened to be the new moon."

"And that's bad?"

"Some people think the new moon is the best time to do bad magic."

Huh. I should have remembered that. Sara, my mom and a witch who had *not* been scared to dabble in the darker side of things, had paid attention to the lunar cycle. And other things I wished *I* had paid more attention to now. "Anything else?"

"There's another spike two days ago—coinciding with the next moon phase. But if I had to guess, I'd say we'd find patterns in the time the emails were sent, too. Either correlating with the moon's movements or something else that's significant."

"Is the moon thing true?"

Lizzie shrugged. "The moon affects the earth's gravity. Which changes the energy flows. So in that sense, yes."

"So you think someone is using these emails to what...do bad magic? Aimed at Damon?"

"I don't know yet," she said. "But the pattern seems to fit. If someone was trying to curse him or something." She nodded toward the printer. "Did you do an analysis of what was in the emails? Or read them?"

"I looked at a couple that contained actual threats. But not all of them do. There's a lot that are just gobbledygook, the sort of stuff you send to clog up someone's emails. And there's a bunch that the system quarantined. Delving into what's in those is trickier."

"Might be safer to leave them alone for now," Lizzie said. "And don't read any more."

My stomach sank. She really was worried if she was warning me off. "How are we supposed to figure out what's going on if we can't read them?"

She waved her hand over the screen. "We do this. Analysis. If we need to go digging into what's in the ones you quarantined, then we take precautions."

"I've already taken precautions. They're sent to a clean system, which I disconnect before I do any work on them."

"Not that sort of precaution," Lizzie said. "Though that sounds like a good start."

"Can someone send a curse through a virus?"

Her eyebrows lifted. "If a demon can use virtual reality to get to people, are you surprised? Curses are about intention, and repetition helps cement the intention."

"Crap," I said. "Damon really is going to hate this." Much like I was hating the idea that I'd be needing to see him again.

"Not much we can do about that," Lizzie said. "But if we can figure this out, we can clean it up, find who's behind it, and, hopefully, problem solved."

I didn't like that "hopefully." I wanted a "definitely" solution. One that would mean I had as little exposure to Damon as possible. The man was my own form of a virus. He got under my skin. "Okay, so what do we need to do?"

She chewed her lip. "What else have you run already? Keyword searches? That might help us narrow things down."

I grabbed my datapad, flipped through to find the right report. "I did a frequency search on some of the terms in the threats. And other things I could think of. I wasn't thinking of curses though." And that was a sentence I'd never thought I'd utter. "If you give me more keywords, I can run more."

"Let's see what's in here. It's hard to know what to look for without an idea of what the spell is trying to achieve. Maybe something in here will give me a clue."

"How does a curse work exactly?"

"The basic idea is you're trying to leach energy from your victim. Cause them bad luck, or worse."

"Does it work?"

"If someone knew what they were doing and had the power, yes," Lizzie said. "Otherwise, it's like the love potions and that sort of stuff the—" She broke off, looking up, cheeks reddening.

"The witches like my mom do?" I asked. "The ones who prey on the normals and rip them off? It's okay. I know my mom wasn't a nice person. Or a good one." Finding out she'd bound me to a demon had killed any lingering regrets I might have had about the less-than-stellar relationship I'd shared with Sara. And she'd been dead a long time. My grandparents had managed to patch up the worst hurts her lack of maternal feeling had inflicted.

I didn't know exactly how much Lizzie knew about my past. The Cestis kept tabs on any witches doing shady things. They hadn't stopped Sara at the time—more's the pity—but apparently she'd fallen off their radar. Which, knowing my mother, meant she'd done her best to hide away once she'd had me. I didn't know if she'd planned to bind my power to a demon from the outset—Cassandra had suggested it was possible, but I didn't want to think that Sara really was as evil as that would suggest—but she'd obviously come up with the plan some time between my birth and my thirteenth birthday. She wasn't one of the good guys. But I didn't know exactly how much they knew about what she'd gotten up to before I came along. I'd never asked. Either Gran or Cassandra. I wasn't sure I wanted to know. The uncomfortable truth was that Lizzie might know more about my mother's shady past than I did.

"Hey, my folks were no picnic either," Lizzie said.

My own brows lifted. "They weren't?" She'd never mentioned her family. Maybe that should have been a clue.

"That's a story for another day," Lizzie said. She tapped the printouts. "Let's focus on working out who's trying to turn your ex into a frog or whatever."

Once Lizzie started giving me words to search for, the queue of reports got longer. And she grew quieter. Finally she said, "Right. We definitely need to talk to Damon about this. You should call him."

I glanced at the time. "It's late."

"You're telling me he clocks out before 9:00 p.m? In a launch week?"

"You could call him. He asked for you."

"I'm supposed to be resting." She batted her eyelashes at me.

I scowled, leaning back on the sofa. "If you're trying some convoluted method of getting us back together, then forget it. Not going to happen."

"Just call. See if we can see him tomorrow."

"You're supposed to be resting," I parroted back at her.

"I think I can manage a meeting," she said. "I wasn't planning on getting into any combat situations."

"I'm doing this under protest," I said, reaching for my datapad, wishing I could just send an email.

But I assumed his team would still be monitoring any communications coming from me, and he'd said they didn't know about the magical implications of what happened with Archangel. So better to speak to the man himself.

As luck would have it, Damon actually answered. "Maggie?"

"Lizzie says she'll take a look," I said. "So, she wants to meet with you." I'd kept my video stream turned off. I might have to talk to the man, but I didn't have to look at him.

"Sure. Just let me check my diary." He paused. "I take it you don't mean right now?"

"No." I wasn't sure how much I should say over the phone. "But sooner would be better than later."

"Well, as luck would have it, I'm giving a guest lecture at UC Berkeley tomorrow. I'm sure they could lend me a meeting room afterward. That would save Lizzie the trip into the city."

"Guest lecture?" I said stupidly.

"They have one of the best game design and VR programs in the country,"

And I guessed his PR team would have him taking any opportunity to get his name out there doing good things. Like volunteering his time at a university. Or maybe that was just me being horribly cynical.

"Unless you'd prefer me to come by your house afterward," he said.

"No." That shot out of my mouth a little too fast. From the sofa, Lizzie snorted. I stuck out my tongue at her. "UC is fine. Just let me know where and what time."

"Lecture finishes at two. I'll get Cat to send you the details." He cut the call. Which I should have been happy about—making one round of awkward chat with him earlier had been hard enough—but there was a part of me that wanted to keep talking. I dropped my datapad and reached for a cookie, chewing with more force than may have been strictly necessary.

"Well?" Lizzie said as though she hadn't been listening to the conversation.

"Tomorrow," I said. "He's going to be in Berkley. We'll see him at the university."

"I noticed you didn't mention it was 'we,' not me," Lizzie said.

"It was you he wanted."

She smirked. "I think that depends on your definition of 'wanted.'"

"Are you sure Cassandra or Radha didn't give you some sort of weird drugs that have addled your brain? I just want to get in and get out. No, correction, I want *you* to get in and get out. I don't want to do this at all."

"That's the spirit," Lizzie said.

"Go team," I said sarcastically. My team was Team Don't Get Burned Again, not Team Yay Magic.

"I'm just saying that I'd like to keep this simple. So I'd appreciate it if you'd ease off."

She held up her hands, palms out. "Okay. You win. You and the D-man are just business. So let's figure out what we're going to tell him tomorrow."

Chapter Eleven

"So, there's a possibility that you may be cursed," Lizzie said. No beating around the bush for her.

"Excuse me?" Damon said. The day was warming up, and sunshine filled the swanky meeting room with light. One of the beams fell across his face, highlighting the laser-blue eyes and bone structure that made him a favorite of the vid-sites and gamer groupies alike. What it didn't do was hide how taken aback he looked.

I pretended I wasn't there. I'd been the one to bring mayhem into his life last time. This time Lizzie could be the bad witch.

"Cursed," Lizzie repeated. "As in someone is trying to make bad things happen to you." She looked him up and down. "Have bad things been happening to you?"

He folded his arms, posture stiff. "Define 'bad.'" The tension in his voice made my stomach tighten. Shit. I'd hoped he'd say everything had been fine; then we'd organize the checks Lizzie needed to do and get out fast. So much for that plan.

"Stuff that is not good," Lizzie said patiently. "If you need a scale, well, let's call ten what happened with Maggie's demon, and you can work down from there."

Damon shook his head. "There hasn't been another demon. I would have noticed."

Lizzie's mouth quirked. "Okay, so work your way back from there."

"What if there hasn't been anything bad?" he asked.

"Then maybe the person doing this is clueless and it's not working," Lizzie said. Then she straightened, her face, for once, deadly serious. "But something must be tickling at the back of your intuition for you to ask Maggie to call us in."

He looked as though he was regretting that decision now. "There's been nothing major," he said. "And it's hard to know what was fallout from the recall and what's just life. I was in a fender bender a few weeks ago, but Boyd and I were both unhurt. I dropped my datapad into a pond a few days ago. But that's just a minor inconvenience. It's always backed up, and I had a new one within an hour. Oh, and there was a power outage at my house last week when we had that tremor."

"You don't have batteries?" I asked. Anyone who could afford secondary power sources and storage had them these days. The damage to the grid done in the quake had shown up the flaws in relying on the power companies to get things back up and running quickly. I couldn't imagine that Damon didn't have multiple layers of backup.

"I do," he said. "But something glitched. It took a while for them to come online."

Hmmm. A system of the kind he could afford shouldn't glitch.

"How long?" Lizzie asked.

"Ten or fifteen minutes, maybe? But as far as we can tell, no one came onto the property during that time. There was no damage, and nothing was stolen."

Lizzie and I frowned in sync.

"I assume if your power glitched, all your security systems glitched, too. So no video?" she asked.

He nodded, his expression completing a trifecta of frowns. I wondered whose head had rolled over that. Damon didn't like screwups. And he wasn't enjoying this conversation.

"Were you home when it happened?" Lizzie asked

"No. At Riley. I haven't been home much at all

leading up to the launch. I've been sleeping on campus mostly."

"Right. The launch. Your new game. Archangel. I saw the trailer. It looked pretty chill."

I bumped my leg against hers under the table, hoping she'd get the message not to say anything about the character looking like me.

She glanced at me quickly, amusement lurking in her eyes. I busied myself with my datapad to avoid both her and Damon.

"How has that gone?" she asked.

"It's only been out a couple of days, but so far the reception is positive." He tilted his head at her. "You game, don't you? I could arrange for you to try it if you want. I can get a private suite at Deckers, or you can play at Riley Arts."

Lizzie lifted her arm in its sling. "Maybe once this is better. But thank you, that would be amazing." She smiled approvingly.

He nodded. "Maggie, how about you?"

I couldn't tell if he genuinely thought I might like to or if he was just being polite. "I don't game much these days," I said, trying to keep my tone neutral. "So, I'll pass, thank you."

He glanced down at my wrist, where there was only a fine silvery scar to show where my interface chip had been. His hand flexed a little, and his own chip glinted in the light. "Of course. But let me know if you change your mind."

He'd be waiting a long time. I tapped on the screen of my datapad, pretending my notes were fascinating.

"So there were no problems with the launch?" Lizzie asked, steering the conversation back to the more important topic.

A shrug. "All launches have issues."

"I didn't mean bugs in your game. Anything else?"

"No."

"And there've been no issues with any of the testers?" Lizzie said.

His jaw tightened. Strange behavior in his beta testers had been one of the first signs of the demon's influence. One that no one had picked up at the time. "Not so far. Ajax and his team have been keeping a close eye on everyone, we helped those who needed treatment—you know that, Lizzie—and we established new protocols in our selection process. Other than one guy who managed to play for ten hours straight and ended up dehydrated, everyone has been in perfect health. Even Edward Greenstone has been doing great since he was discharged last month. Ajax has been checking up on him."

Lizzie nodded at that, so I guess she knew who he was talking about.

"That all sounds good." I managed a smile. Ajax was someone else caught up in my memories of

Nat. She'd had quite a crush on him, I'd thought. But it hadn't had time to develop into anything.

Lizzie sighed. "All right, nothing major, then. But we'll do a sweep of your house and poke around Righteous again."

"We?" Damon asked.

"Maggie and me," Lizzie said.

"What happened to Lewis?" Damon asked, eyebrows lifting again.

Lewis, I assumed, must have been the guy who'd helped Lizzie last time.

"He's unavailable. Besides which, Maggie knows your business better than he does. I'm guessing she knows your house better, too. Win-win."

I kicked her again under the table. Damon just pressed his lips together, eyes on me.

I studied my datapad, acting like I had no idea he was staring at me.

"All right," he said eventually.

I glanced at him, and our eyes caught a bit too long.

"I guess that's settled, then," Lizzie said.

I tore my eyes away from Damon with an effort. "Settled. That's good," I managed.

Damon was still watching me. I could feel his gaze on my skin. Really, my body was an idiot when it came to this man. Which just meant I needed to shove my hormones back in their box and use my brain.

Silence stretched in the room. I could feel my cheeks heating and widened my eyes at Lizzie, trying to send her the telepathic message that we should leave. Pity I had no telepathic powers. I wasn't sure if any witches did. If they did, Cassandra's book hadn't mentioned it.

Lizzie, however, seemed unsympathetic to the awkwardness I was feeling. Or else she had decided to have a little fun with me. Or Damon. Or both of us. Her inner matchmaker was as unruly as my hormones. "I, er, have to make a call," she said, smiling at me. "I'm just going to step outside for a few minutes. You two can talk computer nerd stuff." She practically jogged out of the room, leaving Damon and me sitting in silence.

I decided to give him a minute, picking up my datapad and pretending to check my inbox. After all, it wasn't every day you found out that maybe someone was trying to curse you. Or that the cavalry you'd called in was going to include your ex-girlfriend.

The silence stretched. I poured myself a glass of water. The meeting room was swanky but apparently didn't come with caffeine—real or fake.

I sipped and waited, but Damon didn't say anything. I decided to just acknowledge the problem.

"If you don't want me to do this, just tell me. Lizzie can find someone else to help her."

"Did I say I didn't want you to do this?" He rubbed a hand through his hair, looking irritated.

"Not yet. I thought maybe you were working up to it."

"I hire the best." He stuck out his chin, giving me a flash of the old lord-of-the-universe Damon I'd thought I'd known. "You're the best. And Lizzie is right, you know more about Righteous than anyone else she's likely to bring in."

"I only worked for you for a short time. And I was looking at very specific code." And that was straying into territory that wasn't good to stray into. Like his damned game and why someone in it was wearing my face. "This is bigger than that." I didn't know whether I was trying to talk him or me out of doing this. Maybe both.

"You're still the best at what you do."

Damn it, he kept saying that. And if there was one thing I was damned sure about, it was that I wasn't going to lie to him. I didn't know if we could ever be more than exes, if maybe one day we might be friends, but I did know that it wouldn't happen if I kept secrets from him. He'd told me the truth when he'd needed to. It had broken my heart, but he'd told me the truth. He couldn't accept my magic. He didn't trust it. So if he was going to trust me to work on solving this for him, I needed to be honest with him.

I gulped water, steeling myself. Then put the glass down, folding my hands together so I wouldn't fidget. "Right now, I'm not so sure about that."

"What does that mean?"

"It means I mostly haven't been working since Nat died."

"I heard you'd taken on a new client."

He had? Where had he heard that? Was he keeping tabs on me? And why? "I have. But so far I haven't been able to fix their problem."

"You're telling me you're rusty?"

My hands tightened. "I'm telling you I might have lost whatever knack it was that made me good at my job."

"It's not a knack. It's skill and instinct. Stuff like that doesn't just vanish."

"Yeah, well, maybe not. Or maybe it does. Because the other thing you need to know is that right now, I can't use my magic either. And if Cassandra and Lizzie are right, then those two things are very much related."

He blinked at me. "Cassandra thinks you're good with computers because you have magic? But you didn't have magic before we met." He leaned forward. "Wait, are you saying you don't have magic now?"

I held out my hand. "Stop right there. I might not have had control of my powers before the chip did whatever it did to break the bond, but I still had magic. I've always had magic, I guess. And I still have it now, even if I can't use it. So nothing has changed. Let's be clear on that. If you decide you want me to help you with this, then all this can be is me accepting a professional engagement."

He grimaced. "Maggie—"

"No. You don't get to 'Maggie' me. You walked away. So you stay away. Maybe that's not what you meant, but it's what I mean. I'm still a witch."

His mouth flattened, but then he nodded. "All right. That's fair." He tilted his head, eyes suddenly that laser bright shade that was hard to escape. "You didn't mention this the other day."

"I wasn't sure what was going on," I said. "And I didn't think I'd be seeing you again, so it didn't seem relevant to the conversation we were having at the time. Speaking of which, how are you going to explain this to your security team? Lizzie and me, poking around, I mean?"

"Same as I did the first time. Tell them it's a confidential project that I'm overseeing myself. Mitch will know what's happening. He'll have discretion as to what he tells anyone else he needs to use."

"And they'll just accept it when you tell them that one of the people you've hired for this project is the same person they thought was sending you death threats two days ago?"

"No," he said. "I expect that Mitch is going to tell me I'm insane and that there will possibly be some shouting, and I'll have to buy him a case of Scotch to get him to calm down, but none of that particularly matters because when it gets right down to it, I own the company and he doesn't."

"Life's easy at the top," I muttered.

His mouth quirked. "So people keep telling me. I keep waiting for the easy part." He glanced toward the door. "Should we call Lizzie back in, or do you think she really had to make a phone call?"

Through the tinted windows of the meeting room, I saw Lizzie chatting away on her datapad. Whether there was actually anyone on the other end of the line was anybody's guess. "I think she's trying for some version of 'If I make them talk to each other, they'll get over the awkward part.'" Well, actually I thought it was more like if "I make them talk to each other, they'll fall back in lurve," but no way was I telling Damon that.

"Is it working?" Damon asked. His eyes were still very bright, the faintest hint of a smile flickering over his face.

"You tell me." I lifted my chin.

"I don't want things to be awkward," he said softly. "I know I made a mess of things at the end. I could have been...kinder."

"Not sure there is a kind way to dump some-one," I said. "It's fine, Damon. I'm a big girl. The past is the past." Except for the way it was cur-rently dragging me back into his present.

He blew out a breath. "Okay. Then let's be not-awkward." He pointed at my wrist. "That looks like it healed well."

I wasn't sure how bringing up my chip removal fell into the category of not-awkward, but maybe he was right. We had to be able to talk about what had happened. Particularly if what was happening now —if anything was—had any connection. "It did," I said. "Dr. Barnard does good work." I flexed my hand to demonstrate that I had full range of motion. Apart from the faint scar, the chip might never have existed.

"I'm glad." He squared his shoulders. "We've been working on that technology, added some safeguards to how the chip interacts with the ner-vous system." He held out his own wrist. "I had mine upgraded about six weeks ago. I know you said you don't game, but if you wanted to try again, then I'd be happy to pay for you to get the new model. You said it helped with your work. With the new tech, you should be fine."

It was a generous offer. Interface chips were still expensive, and having a top-of-the-line neural-cyber surgeon like Dr. Barnard didn't make them any less so. And I had to confess, the thought of having the added abilities to interact with data that a chip offered were tempting despite how badly wrong it had gone last time. "Have you tested it on any witches?"

He shifted in his chair. "Not directly. But Dr. Barnard did consult with several healers when he was working on the upgrades to the sensors and the interface. In theory, there's no reason it would interfere with your magic or have any adverse effects on someone with power."

He'd actually thought about users with magic. I hoped my surprise didn't show in my face. But maybe I shouldn't be surprised. He was, after all, a businessman. There were magic users like Lizzie who gamed or had other jobs, like mine, where an interface chip would be beneficial. The technology, like all technology, would become cheaper and more widely used with each generation, so he had to be thinking of limiting any risks. Ending up in another situation like the game recall had to be his worst nightmare.

"Who knows, it might help with your problem," Damon said.

"I'm good without for now," I said. "But if I change my mind, I'll let you know." A chip wasn't going to be my first choice in solving my magic issue, but I filed it away in my brain in case we ran out of other ideas.

I caught Lizzie's eye and beckoned. I'd had

about as much one-on-one with Damon as I could take right now.

Lizzie nodded and came back in to sit beside me "So, good chat?" When neither of us replied, she just powered on. "So let's figure out how we're going to do this. Damon, we'll start with your house. It's smaller, so my arm won't be an issue. Then we can move on to the Riley campus."

Which was huge. Checking out all the buildings was a massive task that would take days for two people. And that was before considering the computer systems, if we needed to cover those. I hoped Lizzie had a spell or something up her sleeve that would speed up the process for the buildings, at least, or we would be there for weeks. How to explain that to my actual paying client was another thing I hadn't considered.

"That makes sense," Damon agreed. "Do you need me to be at the house while you're there?"

"It would make things easier. You would know if anything looks unusual."

He tapped at his datapad. "I have a press day tomorrow. I'll be doing interviews back to back virtually all day. But I can clear a few hours the day after."

"Works for me." Lizzie reached into a pocket and pulled out a chain with a familiar-looking pendant. "Cassandra said you should wear this." She pushed it across the conference table. The sunshine glinted off the black and purple stones.

Damon stared down at the necklace as though it might bite him. "I still have the first one she gave me," he said eventually. "Do I need another?" He didn't sound as though he wanted to need even one.

"Can't hurt," Lizzie said cheerfully.

"It didn't seem to help much with the demon last time," he pointed out.

"Well, you're still here," she countered. "So wear it. You don't want to have to explain to Cassandra why you don't want to."

Chapter Twelve

When we arrived home, Yoshi's skinny figure unfolded from the front steps. Lizzie gave him a quick hug hello. I contented myself with a complicated high-five handshake thing, not sure he was ready to be hugged by a relative stranger.

The night before, we'd set him the task of coming up with a plan for analyzing the quarantined messages. Lizzie had decided it should be safe enough if he didn't read the messages themselves. I wanted to see how he got around the various traps lurking within them.

"Have you eaten?" Lizzie asked.

Yoshi nodded. "I had lunch."

It was after four now. I suspected "I had lunch" was nineteen-year-old boy code for "I could eat again." Looking at the way his bright green Hawaiian shirt and red-and-yellow plaid shorts hung loose, I suspected I was right.

"Well, I'm hungry," Lizzie announced. "So I'll make you something, too."

Yoshi picked up his battered backpack and followed us into the house. Once he was seated at the kitchen table with a bottle of orange soda, a pile of sandwiches, and a bag of corn chips, he extracted his terminal deck from his bag, then pulled out a somewhat battered-looking datapad as well.

I blinked at it. "Is that a X30 Yingen?"

He nodded.

"And it still works?" I'd spent a lot of my teens trying to keep my gran's datapad lurching along, and it had been an X50. Several gens younger than the relic in Yoshi's hand. The Yingens were one of the early gen datapads that evolved from smartphones.

He nodded again, looking pleased. "It would be more exact to say at this point, it's an X30 shell with massive interior modifications."

"Even still, that's impressive." Getting old tech to play with new wasn't easy.

A shrug. "The retro geeks love this sort of stuff. If you can find the old stuff that still looks decent and mod it, then it's a sure sale. But the beauty of this one is it's manual load only. I've killed all its connectivity. So it's a good safe sandbox to test those messages you've quarantined."

"It has enough grunt to handle them?"

"Yeah, I upped the processing specs last night. The screen is on the smaller size, but we'll be able to see what we need to see."

So far I liked his plan. I started grilling him on the rest of his approach. The quarantine system already sorted the various viruses, malware, tech-jacks, and other sundry nasty stuff into groups. I downloaded one onto a datachip for Yoshi to ex-periment on.

I wanted to see if he could defeat the virus rather than just scrape what data he could from the message before the virus ate his system. For one thing, I'd have to reimburse him for each one that got destroyed, and that could get expensive fast. I'd be better trying it on my own safe systems if he couldn't get to grips with the traps embedded in the messages. They had more grunt, and I had my suite of apps and bots and code-dumps to deal with this sort of thing. But navigating tech threats was part art, part science, and I didn't entirely trust my instincts at the moment.

After Yoshi finished explaining his proposed ap-proach, I handed over the datachip and told him to have at it. He grinned like a puppy given a treat and got to work.

"You want one of these?" Lizzie asked, pointing at her sandwich. I nodded, and she got to work.

"Let's let the kid work in peace," she said, handing me a plate. "It's a nice day to soak up some sun."

We ended up sitting on the back steps, munching in silence. But my brain kept racing, bounding between Damon and emails and demons until I felt like I would go crazy if I didn't at least say something. I put my empty plate down as Lizzie wiped her hands on her napkin, staring out into the yard. Probably mentally planning the vegetable garden she wanted.

"You asked Damon if anything weird had been happening," I said, tracing random patterns with my finger on the step. I was probably risking serious splinters, but I was feeling too edgy to sit completely still.

"Yes," Lizzie said, still gazing at the yard.

"It made me wonder. About what exactly has been going on. I know you and the Cestis have been...cleaning up. What exactly does that mean?"

That got her attention. She looked back over her shoulder as though checking on Yoshi.

"He has headphones on," I said. "He won't hear anything."

"Do you really want to know about this stuff?"

No. My gut tightened. But I'd been living with

my head in the sand for too long. Time to face the things going bump in the night again. "Yes. Or the summarized version of whatever it is you're allowed to tell me." I nodded at her sling. "Have there been many imps?"

"There are always a few around."

"More than usual, then."

She nodded. "It looked like things were calming down for a while, but there have been more again lately."

"That doesn't sound good. How can there be more if there isn't a demon controlling them?"

"It's complicated. When the demon got sent back, all its connections would have snapped. What usually happens if a connection to an imp snaps is that it goes into a frenzy. Like a rabid dog left off a leash. But some hide. Or get...knocked out I guess is the closest analogy. Or hibernate, maybe. They can go dormant until something wakes them up again."

"What can wake them up?"

"Humans doing dumb shit," Lizzie said, grimacing. "Or maybe a lesserkind. We don't know if your demon had any. No one's seen one, but that doesn't mean there weren't. We don't have much information on them."

"And imps or afrits without a demon in charge can still cause problems?" The only times I'd encountered imps, they'd been specifically hunting me. I hadn't let myself think too much about what they might have done to me had they caught me. But I knew it wouldn't have been good.

"Totally. Imps can kill a person, drain their energy. Afrits tend to just cause trouble. Though their version of causing trouble can be dangerous, too. Especially if there's a flock of them. It's like having magical roaches eating your wiring or your brake line."

"So you've been bug hunting?"

"Sort of. We've also been keeping an eye on Damon's beta testers. The ones who played the game with the old filter."

I blinked. Damon hadn't mentioned that. "Does he know that?"

"Not all the details," Lizzie said. "Like you, we thought it was best not to bother him until there was something to bother him about."

"And has there been?"

She tipped her hand back and forth. "Not yet. Most of them seem fine. There are a few who definitely had some mental health issues triggered by the filter in the game, a couple had minor demon taint, but nothing worse, far as we could tell. The last one of those was discharged from the hospital a few months ago. There were two, I think, who haven't been located."

"That doesn't sound...great."

"It depends. They may be fine and have left the

country or something. They could be—" She broke off. "I mean, there's lots of reasons for someone to disappear, but we'd feel better if they were all accounted for."

"But the demon is banished. So if it had bonded with anyone or was controlling them, that bond should be broken."

A slow nod. "Yes. In theory."

I frowned. "In theory?" Then something that had been niggling at the back of my brain popped to the front. "Wait, you said demons usually control the imps. Does that mean sometimes something else does? Can a person control an imp?"

"Normally, no. That's why we kill them when we find them. But it's possible that someone who'd been controlled by a demon might have some sort of connection. Lesserkind can control them, of course. They're not as smart or powerful as demons, but they're not simple like imps. We know they can follow commands. They know well enough to hide themselves from our magic. They can cause trouble. But they must be hard for the demons to bring through to our world because they're fairly rare."

"My demon could have had some though?"

"Your demon was well powered up, so yes. And the imp activity is still higher than we'd like this long after you fried him, so it's a possibility. But like I said, we haven't seen any signs of one." She shrugged. "And if there is a lesserkind connected to your demon, we would have expected it to come after you, try for some sort of revenge on behalf of its boss. That's the kind of thing the demons tend to use them for. They can send them through when they can't get through themselves."

I stared at her, feeling suddenly ill.

"Don't freak out," Lizzie hurried on. "There's been nothing out of the ordinary."

"Other than someone claiming to be me sending death threats to my ex," I said.

She grimaced. "Yeah, well, that. That wasn't the greatest news ever. But hey, it could just be a normal screwed-up human. One of the missing testers or someone Righteous booted. Or any random weirdo with a bone to pick with Damon. Or you." She cocked her head at me. "You don't have any other enemies you forgot to tell us about?"

"Not that I can think of. I'm a computer nerd. We don't tend to get into feuds. My mom was the one with the talent for trouble, not me."

"Yeah, I guess someone would have to be holding a grudge for a long time to come after you now for something she did. But it seems easier to start with Righteous and Damon."

Before she could say anything else, Yoshi poked his head through the door.

"I've finished with that first batch," he said. "I think I've iced the virus, and the encryption was fairly simple once I got past that. If you have an-other datachip, I'll dump the text file for you."

"That was fast," I said, impressed again. Lizzie was right. The kid had talent. If he was older, I'd think about offering him a job once I built my clien-tele back up again. See if he could learn to do what I did. Or find his own way of doing it. Before the de-mon, I'd pretty much reached the limits of what I could handle on my own—another reason losing the chip had hurt—I'd been able to work faster with it—and I'd been turning clients away. But Yoshi was young. He needed to go to school and then decide what he wanted to do with his life.

I left Lizzie in the sunshine and went to find Yoshi another datachip. He was packing up his bag as I came out. "Hey, Maggie. I have a shift at Red-line tonight. I can come back tomorrow, work on some more of these." He nodded at the datapad. "I'll leave that here if you want to work through some more on your own. And I sent the text file to your safe queue."

He left after scooping up the sole remaining half sandwich on the platter and shoving most of it into his mouth in a single bite.

"I'm going to take a look at what he found," I said to Lizzie.

She just nodded sleepily. If she wanted to stay put, that was fine with me. She needed the rest.

I'd been looking at the data and tentatively forming a plan to tackle the next lot of infected messages for about an hour when Lizzie wandered back into the living room.

She yawned and dropped down onto the sofa beside me.

"What did he find?"

I shrugged. "Mostly stuff that looks like the standard nonsense spammers use. Some of it could be Latin—and not the *lorem ipsum* variety—and there are other words that aren't English. Not anything I recognize." My high school Spanish was rusty, and the scraps of the Mandarin for Business class I'd taken one semester in college were few and far between. But none of the odd words looked like that. "I'm running them through a translation program next. Do you want to take a look?"

"Sure. Shoot it over to my account. I can do the translation while you keep processing the messages."

"You have translation-bots?" I pinged her the file.

"We deal with lots of people from lots of different places. And the other Cestis members around the world. Translation-bots come in handy. Maybe you should drop a hint to Damon. If they could make an interface chip that somehow trans-lated directly, they'd make a fortune."

I was sure he—or some other tech company—had already thought of that. There were AIs and bots that did a good enough job for your average tourist in a strange land or businesses dealing with overseas customers, suppliers, or vendors, and VR games did a basic level of captioning players who spoke other languages in English or whatever your home language was, but something that made translation seamless would be a game changer.

"Speaking of chips, Damon offered me a new one," I said.

Lizzie's head shot up from her datapad. "Did you say yes?"

"No." I shook my head. "But he said they had a new generation. And that it would be safe. He said they'd had a witch look at it. Was that you?"

"No." Her brows drew down. "No, it wasn't any of us. And whoever did it hasn't told us either."

Great. I'd just caused the Cestis more work.

"Do you think it could be safe?" I asked.

"Theoretically, maybe. Chips modify your ner-vous system. That changes your energy signature. We know that can affect spells—it broke your bond, after all. But I guess a minimal change shouldn't impact someone's magic. At least not any new magic they did." She didn't sound certain. "Do you want another chip?"

"I don't know," I said honestly. "There are things I can do with data with a chip that are much harder and slower without. That's the positive. Systems just get more complex over time. But the thought of opening myself up to another demon somehow...." I stopped, shivered. "I don't know if I'd want to go there."

"You sure you just don't want to play the game because she looks like you?" Lizzie asked. I knew she was teasing me, trying to lighten the mood.

"I'll pass on that, thanks. Wait, is that an option?" I'd assumed the character in the ads was a game character, not an avatar choice.

She grinned. "I don't know. I haven't played it yet. Do you want me to tell you when I do?"

"You're definitely going to play it?"

"Sure. I don't have a chip, and they've changed the filter. It seems safe enough to me." She tipped her head at the datapad. "I understand why you have concerns, but if you still want to game, you could." Her expression softened. "It's not disrespectful to Nat for you to have some fun, you know. She'd want you to be happy."

I opened my mouth to protest, but she held up a hand.

"I understand survivor guilt. I know this is all fresh for you still, but you've been holed up licking your wounds for most of a year. Going back to work is good, but you have to start living again, too. Go out. Drink too much." She looked me up and down. "Have an orgasm involving another person."

"If you're suggesting I do the nasty with Damon, then no."

"No. I get he broke your heart, but there are plenty of other nice guys out there. I'm not talking about Mr. For-life here, but maybe a Mr. Screaming-orgasm-or-two might be good for you. And if you really can't find someone who does it for you, then maybe that's something to think about—how you still feel about old blue eyes."

I was leaving that comment alone. Damon was a no-go. But Lizzie was painfully close to the mark. I hadn't felt a flicker of interest in any other man. Not that I'd actually left the house to try to meet any who might flicker me. Self-service had been just fine.

"How did we get from interface chips to my sex life?" I muttered.

"It's what friends do," she said. "I was happy for you to stay in your little bubble while you needed to, but now you've taken some steps, and I'm not going to let you stop walking back toward life because there are a few obstacles in the way. For one thing, I want you to have your magic back."

"So I can help out the Cestis?"

"So you can be safe. And fully who you're supposed to be," she said gently.

I sighed. "I don't think I know who that is anymore."

She shrugged. "Well, friends are here for figuring that sort of shit out, too." Her datapad beeped, and she looked down. I waited, assuming there was something more to her sentence, but Lizzie was frowning at her screen, bottom lip caught between her teeth.

After a minute or two, she snapped her fingers at me. "I need some paper. And a pen."

I didn't like the urgency in her tone, but I slid my notebook and pen toward her. I'd always copped some flak amongst my tech head friends for still using analog gear, but I found it soothing to move my hand across the paper and get stuff out of my overcrowded head at times. I'd filled far too many cheap composition books with midnight lists of worries over the last nine months.

Lizzie starting scribbling things down. I waited, tension creeping up my spine with each breath. When I couldn't take it anymore, I said, "Want to fill me in about what's so fascinating?"

There was a chance that she'd say "Cestis business," but I figured it was a pretty small one. Far more likely was that whatever her translation-bots had produced wasn't good.

"I'm not sure yet," she said, straightening in her chair. "There're snippets of phrases here that remind me of curses. And the languages themselves.

There's Polish, Russian, German, Mandarin, Hindi, a few different variants of Arabic, Scots Gaelic, Ancient Greek, Latin like you said, and something my computer says is Middle Egyptian."

"That's quite a collection."

"Yes. All from countries with, as far as our records can tell us, strong histories of having witch populations throughout the centuries."

"Doesn't every country have that?"

"Not all. We don't know why. Some countries only have smaller numbers of witches, which means for a long time, most witches wouldn't have known another witch and would have had to figure things out for themselves. And of course, in some places, certain religions took over and caused witches to be persecuted or driven out or underground. The ones with larger populations, as I said, the witches either worked alongside religion initially or learned to coexist or held enough power in their own right to establish their traditions."

"All right." I could add History of Magic 101 to my list of things to learn.

Sara hadn't really told me much, and the sorts of small towns we'd moved through in my childhood didn't tend to have the kinds of progressive educational programs—or the funding—to want to spend money on teaching their kids much about magic when most of them weren't ever going to need to know much about it. Once I'd landed in

Berkley with my grandparents, I could have taken classes if I'd chosen, but I'd only had to utter one "No" and my gran made sure I was never asked again.

"So how do we find out if any of these words add up to an actual problem?"

Lizzie grinned at me. "For that, we need the library."

Chapter Thirteen

LIZZIE DIDN'T MEAN our local library. She meant the Cestis's research library. She'd never mentioned it to me before, but I was getting used to being the one in the dark about magic. If the Cestis had pulled out broomsticks and flown, it probably wouldn't have shocked me too much at this point.

The library, as it turned out, was located beneath Cassandra's house. Which was in a much better state of repair than mine. It had clearly been rebuilt post-quake—I knew the subtle signs of a reconstructed house now—and as we descended the stairs beneath the house, I understood why.

The Cestis took their libraries seriously. Where most houses would have had a boring old basement finished to some degree, there was instead a thick steel door of the kind that conjured up mental images of bunkers and top-secret labs. The palm scan on the wall beside the door was expensive. The same brand that Riley Arts had in their buildings, unless I was mistaken.

"What exactly are you keeping down here?" I asked, only half joking as Cassandra pressed her hand against the scanner.

"The usual. Books, scrolls, information."

"Not sure your average library has scrolls these days," I said, curiosity pinging. How long had the Cestis been collecting this stuff?

"This isn't your average library, dear," Cassandra said. "We were lucky that nothing was lost or damaged in the Big One, but we learned our lesson from that, and we upgraded the facility."

The door swung open into a space that resembled the type of air lock/secure entry point I'd only encountered in state-of-the-art manufacturing facilities, Righteous, and virtual reality spaceships. White walled, with enough lighting that it was almost painful and obvious cameras mounted in all four corners.

At the other end was an identical door and a second scanner. We passed through that and emerged into a very short corridor that had a more normal-looking blue door halfway down its length, then a third solid metal door at the opposite end.

After a third scan, Cassandra pulled that one open.

"Stay there," she said to me as she and Lizzie walked through. They took position on either side of the door and pressed their hands to the inner walls. There was no flash of red light to indicate a body scan. A ward, then. Good to know. Even if someone broke through three doors, they risked being fried by something nasty if they couldn't take down the wards.

As Cassandra and Lizzie finished whatever they were doing, I hovered in the doorway, watching as rows of lights blinked into life down the length of a very long room. Cassandra's house was nice—an homage to the old bohemian-style houses—but it wasn't massive. The room was bigger than I thought should fit under its footprint. Maybe she had accommodating neighbors.

Most of the room was filled with rows of dark metal bookcases arranged like the stacks of a college library. They were an unusual style, the books pushed deeper in the shelves than normal. That made sense when I spotted the tracks cut into the edges of the front of each one. The sort of track an automatic door panel might slide down. Which would perhaps make them fireproof and quake-proof.

Along with the bookcases, there were shorter, stouter file cabinets tucked against the walls and a couple of smaller desks like you might find in a college library, each with one or two chairs. What I didn't see was any kind of monitor to indicate a comp system, though one had to exist to run the scanners.

In the remaining spare space sat a solid-looking metal and glass table with eight chairs around it. The room was cool and the air clean smelling. Filtered. And temperature controlled. Someone had spent some serious cash setting this all up.

Even though I wasn't keen on the subject matter of the books, part of me itched to step into the room. I'd always loved libraries. They'd been a haven for me in small towns where I had no friends and didn't stay long enough to make any, even if there'd been girls my age willing to overlook the fact that I was always from the wrong part of town and ignore the rumors about my mother that never seemed to take long to start swirling around.

Librarians, for the most part, had been welcoming to a quiet bookish kid. And Sara had been happy enough to have me not underfoot in the tiny RVs or apartments we'd lived in. As long as I didn't rack up any fines, she was glad to let books babysit me.

The smell of paper and ink equaled escape and safety. Ironic given I now lived so much of my life digitally.

"It's safe to come in now," Lizzie said, beckoning me forward.

Cassandra was already pulling chairs back from

the table. I joined her, unpacking printouts of the reports and my datapad.

"Have you been studying?" she asked.

"As much as I can," I said.

"Does that mean doing as little as you can and telling me you're too busy or actually studying?"

"It's been a busy few days. But I've been reading your book. Ask Lizzie." I waved a hand at the papers. "But this is more urgent."

"Protecting your power and yourself is always a priority," she retorted.

"I'm protected. I have Lizzie. And the rest of you." It was perhaps an overly optimistic view of the world, but I really didn't want a lecture.

Cassandra hmmphed but didn't press. Instead she turned to Lizzie and asked about her arm.

Lizzie's face looked much like I imagined mine did as she waved Cassandra off. "It's fine. Radha will check it again in the morning. Maggie is right, this is more important." She got a hmmmph, too.

We talked fast to explain to Cassandra what had been happening with Damon and the analysis we'd done of the messages.

As she started reading the list of words and phrases—both translated and originals—her expression, much like Lizzie's had, turned serious.

She sent Lizzie and me into the stacks several times—Lizzie to find books, me to carry them, much to Lizzie's disgust. Cassandra flipped through pages and made notes on a legal pad as she went. Her ability to know exactly what she was looking for in each of the books—not to mention where exactly each book was—was impressive. And a little intimidating. She didn't so much as glance at a catalog.

I didn't know whether there even *was* a catalog.

The thought of this much valuable information just lying around in hard copy and not backed up somehow made me twitch a little. But I wasn't here to critique their information management practices. Not today, at least.

After about an hour, Cassandra finally put her pen down.

"What's the verdict?" Lizzie asked.

"Well, I don't know much about technology, but if someone was using these words in a normal way, then I'd guess they were trying some sort of summoning." She tapped the notepad. "But how that works via email, I don't know."

"Not a curse?" Lizzie asked.

"No," Cassandra said. "It doesn't feel quite right for that."

"Lizzie said repetition helps curses. Would it help a summoning?" I asked.

"I don't really know. A summoning involves sinking your power into something specific to bring it into our reality. A curse is more general, usually. Aimed at bringing bad luck or ill will to a person but not setting an imp or any sort of demonkind on them." She tapped her pen on the pad, a series of short fast beats. "You think a curse sent over and over again might work?"

"It's possible," Lizzie said. "Lots of little bites at someone's energy field could have an impact. But if the person doesn't read the messages...I'm not sure if it would be effective. Not on its own, anyway."

I waved at the stacks and the multitude of books. "Isn't there something in here that might tell us?"

"Most of these books were written well before computers were invented," Cassandra said.

"Well, how do you share information now? There are Cestis in other countries, right? And you must have...what do you call them...operatives or something throughout the country here. Using tech-nology to curse someone can't be a completely new idea, can it?"

Granted, Sara hadn't exactly been a tech head, but even she had a datapad and used the web for shopping, planning our next moves when we had to flee, and researching her marks. Other witches must have decided to see how the digital world could help their magic. But Cassandra was still frowning, which didn't make me think she'd come across this exact problem before.

"We do share information, but each Cestis

maintains their own records and research," Cassandra said.

"Archived and backed up?" I said hopefully.

Lizzie snorted. "I asked that when I first joined. I thought they were going to rescind my nomination."

Cassandra tapped her legal pad with a finger. "We've done very well for hundreds of years without computers."

"They might make life easier for you all," I said. "If all this was digitized and archived, along with whatever collections the rest have, you'd have access to all of it. You'd be able to tag and search and find stuff fast."

"Or make it easier for this knowledge to fall into the wrong hands," Cassandra objected. "Not to mention there are spells in here that could be quite dangerous if you mixed them up if there was some sort of glitch."

I hadn't thought about that. But I wasn't sure the risk of the wrong person getting access to a digital archive outweighed the benefit of ensuring that if something happened to the physical one—if there was another quake or something and this place got damaged or caught on fire even—all the information wasn't lost for good. "Security is getting better and better. There are ways to protect the information."

"The Cestis doesn't have unlimited funds. It's not as though we can tax magic. And the government, much as they claim to appreciate our services from time to time, don't provide us with funding. Apparently the cooperation of the police and various departments is enough. We rely on investments and donations."

They'd had enough to set this place up in the first place. But I'd never stopped to really consider what running an organization that kept watch over an entire country—even though the magical population within that country was small—might take.

"Well, we're about to have a grateful tech genius on our hands," Lizzie said. "Maybe we could hit him up for some advice."

"I'm not sure the man who let demons invade one of his games is the best person for the job," Cassandra said.

I bristled on Damon's behalf. "Actually, the fact that he understands there *are* demons and what the risks are make him more qualified than most, I'd say. Or do you have a lot of rich geeks beating down your door?"

"There's you," Lizzie said. "You're the Techwitch. Well, if you get your powers back, you will be. You can't claim it's just marketing forever."

"I'm not beating down your door," I said. "And I'm not rich. I need to work. And you couldn't afford me."

"Damon can afford you," Lizzie said.

"Damon isn't hiring me," I retorted. "He came to

you." I turned my attention back to Cassandra's notes, wishing I hadn't brought up the subject. If there wasn't a fast way to search for what we needed, we'd have to do it the slow way. "So, if this is supposed to be a summoning, is there any way to find out what is being summoned?"

"It would be difficult from just this," Cassandra said, waving her hands over the notes. "Is this everything you have?"

"Everything so far. We're running more analysis." Every variation Lizzie and I had come up with.

Her mouth twisted. "It's hard if we don't have all the information. Even with it, it will be slow to do a deep dive into what this—" She tapped the notepad with her pen. "—might mean. And given that it doesn't seem to have been effective so far, I think Lizzie's instinct is right. Even if we're going to look into this, we need to check Damon's house and where he works and see if there are more summonings or hexes planted anywhere. If they're clean, we can come up with Plan B to work out what's going on."

By the time we reached Damon's house, my spine was doing a good impression of a steel bat and my jaw ached. The last time I'd been here, Damon and I had been happy. Together.

Was it shallow to hope that he was the kind of gajillionaire who got bored easily and redid his entire house and gardens every year? It would make it easier if I wasn't faced with memories of what we'd shared every few feet. Maybe I'd stick to the gardens. I'd never really gotten the chance to explore them fully. At the time, Damon and I had been more interested in, well, indoor activities.

"Relax," Lizzie whispered as the car Damon had sent for us turned into the drive and paused while the gates drew aside before rolling smoothly forward.

"I am relaxed," I said through clenched teeth.

She rolled her eyes at me. "You haven't been relaxed for a single second for the last few days except when you've been asleep."

She was right about that. Not that there'd been much time to sleep. Damon's press commitments had given us a single day of breathing room. I'd tried to cram in doing enough work to keep my client from firing me, working with Yoshi to finish the disarming of all the crap infecting the rest of the emails and running every kind of pattern analysis we could come up with over them, and working with Lizzie to start planning how to tackle the Riley campus. Not to mention candle drills with Lizzie and trying to get through more of Cassandra's book.

"Relaxation is for wimps." At this point I was

probably about 70 percent syncaf anyway. It would take me days to unwind under the best of circumstances.

Searching my ex's house and garden for magical traps wasn't the best of circumstances.

"This will be easy," Lizzie said. "Just follow my lead."

It wasn't as though I had a choice. Without my magic, I was just here to fetch and carry for Lizzie. But perhaps she was right. This would be easy. After all, if Cassandra had been seriously worried that we would run into trouble, she would have provided Lizzie with better backup than me.

The car came to a halt near the front door. As we climbed out, me hefting my backpack onto my shoulder, the front door opened. Damon stepped onto the porch.

Darn. Part of me had been hoping he'd be caught up in something at work and we'd be left alone

No such luck. Judging by his well-worn jeans and gray tee shirt, both of which were just that bit more casual than anything I'd ever seen him wear at Righteous, he was working from home.

"Ladies," he said, tipping his chin at us. I nodded back. He shoved his hands into his pockets, looking, I thought, slightly wary.

Good, I wasn't the only nervous one.

"Nice day for it," Lizzie said.

It was starting to feel almost hot after the morning fog had burned away. The sun beat down, and I was glad I'd chosen to tuck my hair up under an ancient Yosemite cap. From what I learned, imps and such tended to lean toward nocturnal. So, if there was anything magical concealed anywhere in Damon's house, hopefully it wouldn't be awake to try to eat us.

Cassandra and the other Cestis members had agreed that the snippets we'd found in the emails could be a summoning, but over the course of a long night, they hadn't reached any kind of agreement as to what might be summoned.

"I guess," Damon said. "Come in. We'll have coffee, and then you can get started."

"We can just start—" Lizzie began, but I cut her off. I maybe had already overdone the syncaf, but nothing was keeping me from Damon's never-ending supply of real coffee.

"Coffee would be great," I said far too brightly.

He lifted an eyebrow but just took us through to his kitchen. It was still a cook's dream of steel and glass and marble and blonde wood. True to his word, the tantalizing scent of fresh ground coffee filled the air. Damon did complicated things with the coffee machine, then came back with two elegant blue mugs.

I practically drooled as I reached for mine and took an ecstatic sniff.

His mouth quirked, and he passed the other mug to Lizzie.

"No sling today. Is your arm feeling better?" he asked.

"It is, thanks," she said.

"That's good," he said. He produced a plate of beautifully arranged fresh fruit, crackers, and cheese from the fridge. The handiwork, I presumed, of his housekeeper, Amy.

"Who else is in the house and grounds regularly besides you?" Lizzie asked. "Still just the gardener and your housekeeper and your driver?"

Damon nodded. "Yes. No new staff."

"You said you haven't been home much in the last two weeks," Lizzie said. "Have they still been here?"

"Amy has been in to clean. She stocked the fridge yesterday. Frank, my gardener, has had a week off. He's got a new grandkid in Arizona and went to meet him. He's back in a few more days. And Boyd has only been here to pick me up or drop me off. I gave him the day off today, so he's not here."

I'd met Boyd a few times. He was loyal and discreet. No way he wouldn't tell Damon if he'd noticed anything out of place. I couldn't imagine any of his staff would.

I could dig into their backgrounds, see if anything happened in the last nine months to turn them against Damon, but I assumed his security team would keep tabs on anyone who had easy access to him. Still, maybe it would be a good task for Yoshi. But that would have to wait.

"That makes things easier," Lizzie said.

"How exactly?" Damon said.

"Fewer people in the house equals fewer energy patterns. I know how you and Amy feel. If someone else has been using magic in here, then if they left any traces, they'll stand out. But that's a big 'if.' Any sensible witch would hide their tracks if they were working something bad." She shrugged. "Of course, if it's a curse trigger or a hex, then they could be planted by someone without magic."

I drained my coffee. "It doesn't really matter who did it if we don't get started. I'll take the garden. Lizzie, you do the house." We'd already agreed on this split. Lizzie claimed her arm felt fine, but I didn't want her doing something dumb like climbing a tree and hurting herself again. Houses at least had stepladders.

"I'll go with Maggie," Damon said, carrying my empty mug over to the sink.

Lizzie smirked at me, and I dragged a finger across my throat at her before he turned back. She just snorted as I pulled what I needed out of my backpack and headed for the back door without waiting for Damon.

Chapter Fourteen

"You know," I said, heading to the right fork of the path through Damon's garden, "you don't have to follow me round. I won't steal your prize rose-bushes or anything."

"I don't have any prize rosebushes," Damon said mildly.

I glanced back over my shoulder. "Priceless ancient relics, then?" The garden was big, as one would expect for his house. But it was cunningly landscaped with lots of trees and curves and plantings that meant you couldn't see exactly how large it was.

Lots of nooks and crannies.

Lovely if you were lord-of-the-universing and enjoying some sun and sipping a cocktail or whatever it was Damon did there, but less good if you were hunting for signs of dark magic. Still, Lizzie had managed to clear it all last time, so it must be doable. But I'd work faster without the weight of Damon's gaze burning into my back and making me annoyingly self-conscious.

"No priceless ancient statues either. Not recommended in an earthquake zone."

Was that a not-so-subtle reminder that he could have all the ancient priceless things his heart desired?

"Absolutely no reason for you to trail around after me, then."

"Maybe I just like your company," he said. "We said we'd keep things civil. So we need to practice just hanging out."

I really didn't think that was a good idea, but it seemed rude to tell him that straight up. "Lizzie could be cleaning out your house as we speak."

"No prize rosebushes or priceless antique statues there either," he said.

Not strictly true. There was plenty of expensive stuff in Damon's house. Any burglar who actually had skill enough to break in would think they'd hit the jackpot. Until the weight of his security team fell on their head.

I kept walking.

"Besides," Damon continued, "Lizzie has magic. If she runs into anything, she can defend herself. You, apparently, do not."

"Neither do you. The only way there being two of us will help is that it'll divide the attention of whatever it is for a few seconds."

"I'm pretty speedy. I lettered in track in high school." His expression was deadpan.

Damn. Now I was imagining him sweaty and buff in running shorts. *Gah.* "What sort of self-respecting nerd letters in track?" The path came to an end in front of a row of plane trees that stood behind a bank of green bushes and ferns.

"The kind who goes to schools that insist on well-rounded curriculum," Damon said, coming to stand beside me. "This is the rear boundary." He nodded at the trees. "So how do you want to do this? Some sort of grid pattern?"

"I guess that would make sense. I don't suppose you have a map of the grounds handy?"

He pulled a piece of paper out of his back pocket and waved it at me. "Here's one I prepared earlier."

Right. He'd done this before. I unfolded the paper and stared at the neatly gridded diagram of the garden. Security sensors and cameras were clearly marked. There was one a few feet away from us. I wondered if anyone on his security team was watching. Odds on, they were. Which explained why Damon had insisted on coming with me. "You came with me so you could give me an alibi or something if anything happens, didn't you?"

He tilted his head. "If I had, would you be mad about it?"

I hesitated. Part of me was pissed that his team continued to have me on the undesirables list. But Damon himself was doing his best to shield me from that. Hard to be mad about that. "No-ooo," I said slowly.

"You don't sound sure."

"No," I agreed. "But then I'm not sure about anything to do with this." I waved the grid in an arc that took in Damon, the garden, and perhaps the whole damned world.

He snorted. I took that for agreement.

I smoothed the grid out and aligned it with the fence behind the trees. "Okay, I guess we start in the far-left corner, work our way across, and then come back."

Damon shrugged agreement. "Lead on."

"If you're trying to save me from dastardly magic by being here with me, shouldn't you lead on?"

"Maybe. But of the two of us, I'm the one most likely to blunder into magic with no chance of rec-ognizing what it might be and set something off. You go first. I'll be the rearguard."

It took us nearly half an hour to work our way across the first row of the grid. In that time, I scored muddy shoes, leaves in my hair, a closer-than-I-wanted encounter with a couple of bees, and grubby hands from pulling back branches and pushing leaves off objects half-hidden in the soil. Which had all turned out to be rocks. Gloves would have been a good idea. Maybe Damon's gardener had a stash.

So far we'd found nothing I classed as suspicious.

I stretched, arching my back. Apparently my DIY-earned muscles weren't quite the same ones used to crawl around garden beds.

Damon studied the grid. He'd managed to stay cleaner than me somehow. He'd donned a nanohide jacket before we'd left the house. I hadn't thought to bring mine with me. Nanohide looked like leather but weighed hardly anything, was stronger and more flexible, shed dirt, and did temperature control. It cost a bomb but was a smart choice for trawling through a garden on a hot day. I'd left my denim jacket in the house, not wanting to get any sweatier than I had to.

It didn't matter. I was sweaty anyway, my hair damp under my cap, and my tee shirt uncomfortably clammy. "What next?" I asked. The faster we worked, the quicker we'd be done and could join Lizzie in the much cooler confines of the house.

"Maybe we should do this column back down toward the house next. Then we can have a break for coffee and whatever once we reach it."

I liked his thinking. Though if we took a break every hour, this was going to take forever.

I pulled my datapad out of my back pocket. Nothing from Lizzie. Apparently her search was going as well as ours. Which, I supposed, was actually good news.

"Coffee sounds good," I said. "Show me the grid again."

Rather than passing it to me, he moved closer so I could see. Too close for comfort. Suddenly I was hot for reasons completely unrelated to the sunshine and the physical activity.

Focus. I squinted at the grid. "What's that?" I asked, pointing to a square about halfway between where we stood and the house and set a little way away from the fence line.

"One of the garden sheds," Damon said. "I don't think Frank uses it much now. There's a bigger one on the other side, and he has a small greenhouse over there, too. More light." He pointed them out on the map.

Sheds and greenhouses. That was going to slow things down even more. So might as well get one of them out of the way. "Then let's take this column," I said and stepped into the next square of the grid.

The trees lining the fence along this side weren't as densely underplanted, so we made slightly better time. Still, by the time we got to the shed, I was beginning to dream of coffee and giving my feet a break.

Also getting far away from Damon. Who stayed close—which, granted, was hard to avoid in a six-foot by six-foot grid square. But my hormones didn't know he was only close because he had to be. They were too busy flashing back to all the memories that the smell of him and the way he moved and his voice triggered.

I tried to focus on our search and keep him out of my eye line, but I was already a nervous twitchy mess and we'd only covered 10 percent of the damned grounds. I eyed the shed, wondering if it would be totally unreasonable to lock him in it out of the way until I was done. Tempting, but I suspected the sight of me shoving their boss into a small structure and locking the door would only confirm all the worst suspicions Damon's security team had about me.

"I'm assuming that will let you in," I said, nodding at the palm scan that seemed out of place on a shed, which was a rustic style that blended in with the natural-but-deliberate aesthetic of the garden. But I guessed the idea was to not provide any hiding spots for anyone who managed to get onto the grounds.

"Unless Frank has jerry-rigged it, then yes, it'll let me in," Damon said.

Unless Frank was a gardener who'd previously

been a hacker or a top-tier burglar, I doubted he could have hacked the lock. I knew the brand. Expensive. And good.

I eyed the top of the shed. It had faux gables and a window and an old-fashioned tiled roof. The kind that had fallen out of favor since the Big One. They disintegrated too easily, but maybe that wasn't such a concern for a mere shed. The other thing about tiles was that they could be lifted...and things hidden under them. The angle of the roof suggested there could be a small crawl space.

"Inside or outside first? And do you think there's a ladder inside?" I asked.

"A ladder?"

I pointed up. "We'll need to check the roof. And by we, I mean you."

"Why me?"

"I'm not overly fond of ladders."

He snorted. "That must be hard when you're renovating a house."

"I'm fine with a ladder to paint a wall or something. Roofing I leave to the experts." If there was ever another big quake, I'd rather be squished than plunge to my death from a height. Not exactly rational, but there wasn't much I could do about that.

Damon eyed the shed. "It's about ten feet high. You'd probably survive."

I folded my arms. "Which means you'll be fine. So let's open the door and find the ladder."

He snorted at me but stretched out his hand toward the scanner. I grabbed his wrist. "Wait."

Damn. I hadn't thought about the lock itself. Could that be magicked? If my magic had been working, I might have had a chance of knowing, might have been able to see the energy field surrounding it. But now, I was flying blind.

I stepped in close and studied the lock. It looked perfectly normal. No smudges or scratches or mysterious runes. The metal surrounding it was a bit dingy, but it seemed normal for a scanner designed to be left out in the weather. The wood on either side of the lock seemed fine, too, nothing marring the paintwork. I reached out a tentative finger and touched the edge of the lock, avoiding the palm scan itself, not wanting to set off an alert because I wasn't authorized.

One breath, then two, then three. Nothing happened. *Phew.* I stepped back, waved Damon forward. "Seems safe enough. Scan away."

The door swung open obediently at the touch of his hand, releasing a waft of dust-scented air. The lights within blinked on automatically. Only high-tech garden sheds for Damon.

I followed him in, scanning the room quickly. Nothing caught my eye. Some of the tools hung in neat rows on the back wall looked dusty, as did the wooden workbench along the left-hand wall.

Damon checked the security log on his datapad. "This says no one has been inside for weeks. But there's a gap from the power outage, of course."

Meaning we couldn't rely on what the system told us.

We went over the room methodically before taking the ladder hanging on the wall back outside so Damon could climb up to the roof.

I held the ladder and tried not to wince as he clambered over the structure as blithely as a goat. Did he have to be good at everything? A comment about being able to leap tall buildings in a single bound seemed appropriate, but he didn't need an ego boost.

I half held my breath until he was safely back on the ground. He stowed the ladder and locked the door again, then bent to tie his shoelace.

"Might have been better to do that before climbing a ladder," I pointed out.

"It was fine then," he said, glancing up with a grin. "Don't be a worrywart."

That made me laugh. Damn it. I hated that he could still charm me. "A worrywart? Is that what the cool kids are calling it these days?"

"The cool kids don't worry about people having untied shoelaces."

True, because most of them wore nano-enhanced sneakers that laced themselves. I preferred old-school. It was comforting to think that my shoes couldn't stage a rebellion and send the laces up to throttle me in my sleep or something. Besides, boots were my go-to these days unless I had to get dressed up for a client. Work boots, "nice" boots, or hiking boots like the well-worn ones I wore. It was hot, but I'd been thinking about avoiding creepy crawlies getting into sandals or flip-flops.

Damon started to straighten, lost his balance, put his hand out to catch himself. I don't know whether I saw something beneath the leaves coating the ground beside him, but I lunged forward to grab him before he could make contact. Lunged and missed. His hand hit the leaf-covered dirt, and there was a weird popping sensation in my ears as though I'd suddenly gained altitude accompanied by a faint hiss of noise that I wasn't certain I'd actually heard or just imagined. Nevertheless, I lunged a second time and hauled him up and away from the spot where he'd made contact.

"What?" he said, looking confused.

I reached for his hand, turned it palm up. There was a dark smear of something that could be just dirt on his palm. But I couldn't be sure. The back of my neck prickled as I stared at it. "Does that hurt at all?"

He flexed his fingers. "I didn't fall far. It's fine."

"I'm not talking about the fall." I reached into my back pocket, pulled out my datapad. Then into the other one for the small pack of bio-wipes I'd stashed there in case one of us needed to clean our hands of something gross in a hurry. I shoved the wipes at Damon, dialing Lizzie with my other hand.

"Clean that off," I said.

Lizzie didn't pick up.

The prickling on my neck intensified. "I think we should head for the house," I said, shaking my head slowly, trying to rid myself of the sensation.

"I'm fine," Damon said. "Really." He scrubbed at his hand with the wipe and held it up. "See? All clean."

"You didn't hear anything?" I asked, fighting the urge to grab his hand and pull him back toward the house.

"I was too busy trying not to fall on my ass," he said. Then he went still. "Wait, are you saying you heard 'something'?" His air quotes were slashes in the air.

"I'm not sure," I said. "Maybe. So I think we need Lizzie." She still hadn't answered. Which didn't make me feel any better about our immediate situation. "Let's go back to the house." I tapped out a quick **HELP!** message to Lizzie and sent it.

Damon nodded. "Good plan."

He held out his left hand—the one that hadn't hit the dirt—and mine closed around it before I could remember why that was a bad idea. We started walking fast but hadn't gotten very far when the breeze shifted and I caught a flash of rot in my nose. Not good garden compost type rot, more death and decay and things my brain told me weren't good news. I knew that smell. The smell of something related to a demon.

I planted my feet, pulling against Damon's grip. "Stop."

If there was an imp or any other nasty magical creature in the garden, it could well be between us and the house. Blundering into its path would be dumb. Trouble was, I didn't know how to figure out where it was. The breeze had dropped, and I couldn't smell anything.

"What is it?" Damon asked, voice low.

"I'm not sure. An imp, maybe." He'd been with me the first time either of us had encountered an imp. "Can you smell anything or hear anything?"

I strained my ears for either the sound of Lizzie coming to our rescue or the sound of something coming to try and eat us. Imps weren't stealthy creatures. They tended to strange noises and gibbering. Then again, I'd only ever seen two. Perhaps stealthy ninja imps existed.

But if they did, I had no desire to meet one. Lacking any clue as to where the creature might be, the house still seemed like the best option.

Damon's hand was firm on mine. "What do you want to do?"

On the heels of his words came a faint chittering

sound from behind us. Back toward the shed somewhere. I caught a whiff of rot as the chittering came again.

"We should try for the house," I said, lowering my voice. "Fast."

We took off at a run, barreling along the angled path, heading to the junction where the paths met and opened onto the lawn immediately behind the house. It hadn't seemed far when we'd been walking down earlier. Now it felt like miles.

I risked a glance back, trusting Damon to lead me forward. I couldn't see anything, but the leaves in the garden beds lining the right-hand side of the path were swaying, as though something was making its way through them. I couldn't see what it was, but there was definitely something there. And I doubted it was a neighbor's cat or dog.

Not unless it had been rolling in something that had been dead for weeks. The smell caught in the back of my throat. I wanted to gag, but stopping would slow us down. Instead, I turned back to face the way I was running and tried to speed up.

I nearly stumbled when an echoing screech—now far too loud to be called chittering—rose behind us, making every hair on my neck and arms stand to attention. My body knew something bad was coming. It wanted to get away.

Apparently Damon did, too. He pulled me forward as I recovered my footing. A gun had appeared in his right hand. But I had no time to wonder where the hell that had come from. We made it another few feet, almost to the front lawn, and then the screeching came again. Louder.

Closer.

Too close, my brain whispered. *Do something*.

The first time I'd been chased by an imp, I'd fried it with magic I hadn't known I possessed. Now I knew I possessed it, but I couldn't use it. But whatever part of me it was that the magic came from was telling me that the imp—or whatever the hell it was—was too close. We wouldn't reach safety. I had to stand and fight. I let go of Damon's hand, no idea what to do as I whirled around.

The creature moving steadily down the path to-ward me was in the same family as the imps I'd dealt with before but not identical. Those had been oily black, the color of gasoline and black mold. This one looked more like it had been bleached and then rolled in some sort of grease. There was a dull gleam to the mottled white skin. And it was bigger than the other ones. Maybe half again as tall...over four feet rather than about three. It paused for a moment, studying me with eyes the color of rust, then screeched again, revealing rows of gray needlelike teeth.

"Maggie, get down," Damon said from be-hind me.

Down? What was he going to do, shoot it? I had

no idea if a gun could hurt an imp. I did know you could fry one.

I held out a hand, trying to remember what the hell summoning fire had felt like. "Burn," I hissed desperately. Nothing happened. My stomach plummeted. The creature screeched at me, and from behind me came a crack of noise. Gunshot.

A smear of black appeared on the creature's shoulder...if the place near the top of one of four arms could be called a shoulder. The bullet, if it had hit, didn't stop it though. Instead, it screamed again, face twisted, took two steps closer to me, and leaped, soaring over my head easily. I twisted, trying to follow its trajectory. It landed with a thump on the lawn a few feet from Damon, who had the gun pointed squarely at it.

The gun wasn't going to help him. It was going to reach him. Tear at him with those fangs and claws. *Kill him*.

Panic surged through me, and I lifted my hand again as my pulse beat in my ears. "Burn," I shouted so loudly my throat hurt. This time I felt a blinding surge of power in response, and the creature burst into flames.

As I stared at the burning imp, Damon fired again.

My gaze jerked up to his face, which was twisted in grim concentration as he continued shooting until the gun ran out of bullets.

"I think that's probably dead," Lizzie's voice came from behind him. She ran across the grass to stand by Damon's side, gently pushing his arm down. He stepped back but didn't let go of the gun.

We all watched the green and orange flames blaze as the imp got smaller and smaller. They were terrifying little hell beasts, but it was handy the way they burned to ash.

Fire, it seemed, had become my go-to.

"What was it?" Lizzie asked.

"Imp," I said. "I think. It was a weird color."

She frowned at the flames, head tilted. "It just appeared?"

"No," I said after looking up at Damon to see if he wanted to answer. Apparently not. He was still staring at the ashes, a muscle twitching in his jaw. "Damon touched something over there—" I pointed to where we had been. "—and then it appeared."

"That's not good," Lizzie said. "You'd better show me."

Damon looked at her, shot me one inscrutable look, then turned on his heel and stalked off. Toward the house, not back to the shed.

I took one step forward to follow him and then stopped myself. If he wanted to run from magic again, he wouldn't change his mind because a witch followed him.

"Is he okay?" Lizzie asked.

"He's not hurt, if that's what you're asking." The

memory of the imp arcing over my head, claws stretched, aiming for Damon flashed, and I had to stop and swallow.

"Are you okay?" Lizzie came to stand next to me. "Hold out your hand."

The first time I'd called fire, I'd burned my arm. This time, my hand was red and tingling, but otherwise, I felt fine. She studied my palm, fingers gentle on the back of my hand as she supported it.

When we heard the sound of a car, both of us turned to watch. Damon guided a sleek black sedan out of the garage and turned down his drive. I flinched as his front gate slid open. He really was leaving. Again. My knees wobbled, and I sucked in a breath that was close to a gasp as the realization stabbed though me.

"We should go back to the house. You need to sit down."

"D-Don't we have to watch this, make sure nothing else catches on fire?" The first word came out half choked. I didn't think it had anything to do with the stinking smoke rising from the burning imp.

"We'll sit on the steps," Lizzie said. "Come on. Breathing in this smoke won't help us."

Chapter Fifteen

"So your powers seem to be back," Lizzie said, perching beside me on Damon's front steps. We stared at the patch of scorched earth at the edge of the lawn. The imp was nothing more than ashes now. Not even a wisp of smoke.

"Apparently so," I said. Possibly a normal person would have been happier about it. My life wasn't normal anymore. Maybe I wasn't either. "Was that an imp? It didn't look like the others. It was white. Sort of." Picturing it made my stomach roll uneasily.

"They don't all look the same. But given it fried like an imp, we'll call it an imp for now. Speaking of frying, you did magic." She frowned at my hand. "Are you sure that feels okay? I can give you a jolt until we can get a better healer to check you out."

I flexed my hand. The redness on the palm was fading, but my fingers still tingled. All of me tingled, in fact, but I couldn't tell if it was adrenaline or something else running through my veins. "I think it's fine." Other than the fact that once again I was freaked out that I'd thrown fire with my bare hands.

"You should try to use your magic straight away."

"No more imps to fry," I said. I was scared to try again. Though I wasn't sure if I was scared of my powers being back or of them not. "Unless there could be another one?" Now that was a horrifying thought. "Is that likely? Could there be another one?"

"There could be more trigger spells, sure, but I've never heard of one that had enough juice to summon multiple imps. So we're probably safe for now. "

"So if that was a summoning spell, to bring the imp, is that the same kind of thing the email messages were trying to do?"

Lizzie shrugged. "Maybe. It's hard to say, other than it seems likely they're connected. But stop changing the subject. You need to try your magic again." She hitched one hip up to dig in the back pocket of her jeans. She pulled out a battered pack of matches.

"Why do you have matches?" She didn't mess around with any of the drugs that people smoked these days like Sandman or hyperhemp. At least she never had anywhere near me, and I'd never smelled it on her clothes. And she definitely wasn't rich enough to get her hands on illegal tobacco.

"I like to be prepared," she quipped. She tore a match off and passed it to me. "Light it."

There was no way she was going to let me get away with not even trying. I stared at the match, trying not to pinch it too hard between my fingers. Sure enough, it glittered faintly around the edges. *See the energy field, change the energy field.* I concentrated a moment. The match flared obediently into life. I blinked at it, not quite believing what I'd done. The flame burned down quickly. The heat began to sting my fingertips, helping connect me to the fact that it was real. I blew it out.

"Do it again," Lizzie said and passed me another.

After I'd ignited three more, she relented and put the matches away, grinning. "I guess it was psychological after all."

"How do you know?"

Lizzie nudged my shoulder with hers. "Dude. You used magic because you needed to save Damon."

Ugh. No. That was something I definitely didn't want to be true. Embarrassing. "I needed to save myself."

"I saw. Your magic didn't work until the imp went for him."

I could hear the laughter in her voice and dropped my head onto my knees with a groan. "Shut up."

"Didn't Radha say something about strong emotions getting you past the block?"

"No," I muttered.

"Yeah she did," Lizzie said. I couldn't see her stupid face, but I knew she was grinning. "So, I guess you still feel something for old billionaire boy after all, huh?"

"No I don't," I said. It was a lie. But I was sticking to it. Acknowledging I might still have feelings for the man who had left us sitting here while he drove to safety was not going to happen.

"Yes you do. And I can't help noticing that for a guy who wants nothing to do with magic, he seems to have made an effort to get back into your life."

I raised my head, fixed her with a death glare. "Because someone is trying to *curse him*."

"Or because you're not the only one with feelings."

"He has feelings about witches. He hates them."

Lizzie shook her head. "He doesn't seem to hate you. He's always been civil to me."

It was a long way from civil to allowing himself to have feelings for one. "Do you see him here right now?" I waved my hand at the grass and ashes. "One dead imp and he's out of here. His feelings about magic definitely trump whatever imaginary feelings you think he might have for me. So that kind of makes it a moot point how I feel. So please shut up before I have to kill you, too. Which I will do if you mention any of this to Damon."

She snorted. "You don't have enough control yet to kill me."

"I don't know," I countered. "I'm feeling some pretty strong emotion toward you right now. Not the good kind."

"Shut up. You lu-u-rve me."

"According to you, I love a lot of people," I said, then snapped my jaw shut.

Lizzie laughed out loud. She almost fell off the step, she laughed so hard. "Maggie Diana Lachlan, you are so screwed," she wheezed when she regained control.

"I hate you," I said.

"Wrong again."

"Again?"

Lizzie pointed down to the road, where a familiar car was heading back up the hill. "He came back."

The lurch of hope in my stomach was also humiliating. I told my brain to stop being stupid. "He kind of had to. It's his house," I pointed out.

"I'm sure he has other places he can be."

"Maybe he's back to kick us both out."

"Well, if he does, he's an idiot. We still have to clean that up"—she pointed at the pile of ash—"then you have to show me where he touched whatever it was, and we still have to see if there are any more hexes in this garden." She looked at me. "We need to tell Cassandra what just happened."

"This day just keeps getting better and better," I said.

"Well, look at this way. She'll probably stop making you try to light candles twenty-four seven."

"Yeah, but I'm fairly sure she'll replace it with something else." Having seen the library had only cemented my view that Cassandra wasn't the kind to let resources go underused. If I had my powers back, then she'd be trying to make sure I damn well knew how to use them so the Cestis had another witch at their disposal.

"You're probably right about that." Lizzie stood as Damon's car pulled to a halt. "You know, I think I'll go inside and call Cassandra now. She might want to come and see that"—she waved her hand at the ash—"for herself."

I reached for her arm. "Do *not* leave me alone with him," I hissed as Damon climbed out of the car.

"Oh no, you two need to talk." Lizzie grinned, yanked her arm free, and then waved at Damon, who still stood by the car not moving. He wore sunglasses, so I couldn't tell if he was looking at her or me. I didn't want to know. I looked away, hugging my knees again.

Lizzie patted my shoulder.

"I hate you," I muttered as she retreated up the stairs.

"No you don't," she said cheerfully. "And, pro tip, I don't think you hate him either. So stop being a wimp."

What was wrong with being a wimp? Wimps lived to wimp another day. But Lizzie was right. I didn't hate Damon. Even if I did, it didn't look like I could avoid him until we figured out what the hell was going on and the Cestis put a stop to it.

So I was just going to have to deal with him.

I sighed, flexed my still tingling hand, climbed to my feet, and began to walk toward him.

After a few seconds, he moved, too. We met in the middle of his lawn and I hesitated, not sure what to say. My hand curled again as the tingles flared stronger for a moment, as though being close to Damon made the memory of fire and magic stronger somehow.

"Are you all right?" he asked. He still wore sunglasses, hiding his eyes from me. I was tempted to reach out and take them so I could at least have some chance of guessing what he might be thinking. But that move would be too...intimate. Too close.

"I'm fine," I said, fighting not to flex my fingers again. "How are you?"

It seemed a reasonable question. He'd reacted to the imp's death by running. We'd been in tight spots before with magical creatures. His instinct then had never been to retreat.

Maybe he was as messed up by all of this as I was.

The thought made my brain stutter for a moment.

"I'm—" He paused, mouth twisting. "Sorry, that was dumb of me."

I hitched a shoulder. "If Lizzie and I had any sense, we would have joined you." Running from a magical creature possibly being controlled by a demon seemed like a sensible response to me. More sensible than trying to burn it to ash.

"I don't even know where I was going," he said. "I only got to the end of the street before I turned around."

"You don't owe me any explanations," I said.

His mouth twisted again. "It kind of feels like I do. I left you and Lizzie to deal with my mess."

"Well, Lizzie is the one who's actually qualified to deal with it," I said. "She's inside calling Cassandra. So I'm sure more help will be arriving soon." I tilted my head at him. "I'm kind of surprised there haven't been an army of Riley security people appearing from all corners. You know, with the gun-shots and all."

"I called them from the car," he said. "Told them I had a close encounter with a snake and to deal with the police if there were any reports of gunfire."

"And they believed you? I thought best practice would be for them to come investigate in case you were being...you know, coerced at gunpoint or something."

"I have code words for that kind of thing. We practice. And they can tap into any part of the house feed or my car if they need to."

"The perks of wealth," I said. Then I realized what he'd said. He practiced being kidnapped?

"Would you rather I let them arrive and we had to explain that?" He jerked his head in the direction of the ash which I assumed was still smoking slightly behind me.

"No." I wasn't volunteering to explain imps to Damon's security team. They already didn't like me. Telling them he was definitely under magical threat was a job I'd delegate to him or Lizzie.

"Speaking of that," he said, "you told me you couldn't do magic."

"Seems like I can," I said. "Maybe these things come and go." No way was I going to tell him Lizzie's theory of why I'd gotten over my block. Time to change the subject back to him. "Your se-curity guys didn't wonder why you had a gun in your garden?" He hadn't routinely carried a gun when we'd been involved.

"No. They'd prefer me to have actual guards inside the property line most of the time, so I'm sure they're happy to know that I'm following their suggestions about taking precautions. Mitch makes me practice with the gun, too."

He'd certainly seemed to know what he was doing. "Okay. Good. It's probably better if they stay out of this for now."

"I figured the Cestis would want to look around first."

He was right about that. Plus, the garden wasn't safe for anyone who didn't have magic to be poking around in yet. Not until we knew if there were more trigger spells. Someone must have set them during the power glitch. A fast worker, if there was more than one. The question was who. And why? Which made it two questions.

"I know it's been a rough time for Riley Arts," I said, "but have you been getting other threats?"

"Some," he said.

"Enough that you've started carrying a gun?"

"Maggie, we were searching my garden for magical curses. I thought bringing a gun might be sensible."

"Bullets didn't really seem to stop it," I said.

"Yeah, that was a flaw in my plan."

"I'm not sure an imp attack is something anyone

knows how to plan for," I said. "Well, maybe the Cestis."

Damon laughed. "You think I should ask Cassandra if there are magic bullets?"

"That seems awfully close to you being interested in magic," I said. "I didn't think that was your thing."

His smile died. "I guess I deserve that. But I'm a realist. If magic wants to mess with me again, then I want to be as prepared as I can be. So I'll ask Cassandra what I need to do."

My hand curled, and I winced. He was prepared to embrace magic to save himself but not when it came to accepting me. That hurt, I couldn't deny it. Which kind of pissed me off.

"Is your hand okay?" he asked. "You burned yourself the last time you did that." He tilted his head. "I mean, the last time you did that when I was with you. I guess I have no idea how many times you've done it since."

"Are you asking if I've become a demon hunter of some kind, slaying magical creatures with a single flame at every turn?"

One side of his mouth curved up. "That sounds more like something out of a game than something the Cestis might do. I can't really imagine Cassandra in black leather, wielding a knife."

"I wouldn't want to mess with her," I said, deliberately ignoring that he'd avoided answering my question. "And I'd imagine she was pretty kickass when she was younger."

"I wouldn't argue with that," he said. "So, have you? Been...Cestis-ing?"

"Cestis-ing is not a word," I said. "But no. I haven't. I'm still mostly in the dark about all of this, just like you." I didn't volunteer that Cassandra wanted me to know more. And fast.

"You didn't burn your hand though."

"Not like last time," I said. "It still feels...weird. Like I said, clueless."

"Lack of knowledge can be fixed. I would think they'd be interested in someone with your...ability."

"Doesn't mean I'm interested in them," I said. "Right now we have more pressing problems. Like who sent that imp and why they've got it in for you. So why don't we go inside, and you can start thinking who that might be?"

I turned to the patch of still faintly smoking ground, the back of my neck prickling again. Damon, despite the noise around the recall of the game and the hit Righteous had taken, seemed like a kind of obscure target for a magical attack. Kidnap, sure. He was rich as a whole barrel of sin and no doubt had insurance to cover ransom demands. But I wasn't sure who would want him physically harmed. Something was nagging at the back of my brain.

I turned back to him. "Lizzie said not all the Archangel beta testers were found."

He grimaced. "No. There were a couple we never traced. But everyone else is accounted for. We offered them all counseling and all the families support and covered any medical bills for anyone who required more serious help. But that wasn't many, thank God."

That matched what Lizzie had told me. "Counseling?" I said. "With regular counselors?"

He coughed. "Cassandra may have suggested a few names." He finally took off the sunglasses. "She probably suggested the same ones to you."

"Did she suggest some names to *you*?"

"Yes," he said matter-of-factly.

"And did you actually do it?"

"Some. Things have been pretty crazy. But enough to help in the initial...aftermath." He pressed his lips together. "I guess you probably did the same?"

"Some," I said. I didn't think I owed him more of an explanation than that. Though I was still surprised by his admission that he'd seen a magical therapist. Maybe I should have stuck with it. But no point lingering in regrets about what I had or hadn't done when I'd been trying just to survive.

"But that's sort of beside the point—" I paused as something started beeping.

Damon reached into his jacket pocket and

pulled out a datapad. Not the one he'd had at UC. This one barely filled his palm. One of the latest holo models. "This is me," he said.

I couldn't hear anything of the conversation as he listened to whoever it was on the other end.

"Yes, that's fine. Let her through." He stashed the datapad again. "Cassandra is here."

"I'll tell Lizzie she's arrived," I said, seizing my opportunity to bring our little chat to an end. "You stay and show her in." I didn't wait for him to argue with me, just pivoted and headed for the house at as fast a walk as I could manage without actually breaking into a run.

"Where's the fire?" Lizzie said as I came around the corner into Damon's kitchen, almost skidding on the highly polished floorboards about a minute later.

"Isn't it a little soon for fire jokes?" I said, then waved off her apologetic grimace. "Cassandra just arrived. I know we have to tell her I did magic, but can you hold off on the comments about Damon motivating me while he's around?"

"You two didn't kiss and make up, then?" she asked. "You were talking for quite a while out there."

"This is real life, not a rom-com. We're not going to kiss and make up. My magic doesn't improve things between us, just puts us squarely back where we were."

"So you're just going to ignore your feelings for him?"

I nodded vigorously. "I'm not an idiot, Lizzie. There's no point in pining after a guy who's never going to let himself love a witch. So you need to not say anything about this around him, okay? You can tell Cassandra another time."

"She's probably going to figure out there's a connection, you know," she said.

"I'll deal with that part when I come to it." I fixed her with a stern look. "You can mock me all you want in private, but keep it zipped around Damon."

"I'm not mocking you. I think you two should work it out. He seemed to make you happy. When I first met you, you were dealing with a lot of crap, but you still kind of glowed around him."

I had? *No. Don't think about that.* Don't think about the little bump of joy that had filled me every time I'd seen him or the way his mouth tasted or...

"Thank you for being a hopeless romantic, but in this case, you need to focus on the hopeless part and not the romance part. Damon and me, we're past tense and going to stay that way. Got it?"

She sighed. "All right. But only because I know this is stressful for you, and we all have enough to deal with. Not because I think you're right."

I'd take that for now. Hopefully once she saw that Damon remained uninterested in me, she'd give up her mad ideas once and for all. I just had to grit my teeth for however long that was.

And however long I had to keep working with the man to sort out curses and imps and assorted nonsense. Now that my magic was back, there was little chance that Cassandra would let me out of helping with this case, even if I begged. Not if this was going to tie back to my demon as my gut was suddenly insisting it did.

Which, damn it, might mean my mojo was back in more ways than one. I relied a lot on instinct in my work. I'd been missing that feeling of having a hint of heading in the right direction for months now. I may not have really noticed it until I'd taken on my client and tried to use it for something actually productive, but now that it was back, I was all too aware that it had been missing and I'd been off my game for a long time. I'd been blaming it all on grief and guilt and anger. But it seemed that maybe my magic being blocked had something to do with how weird I'd been feeling, too.

I pressed my lips together, biting back a curse.

"Everything okay?" Lizzie asked as the sound of Damon's front door clicking shut and footsteps announced that Cassandra was about to join us.

"Fine," I said and tried to look like I meant it.

Chapter Sixteen

ABOUT HALF AN HOUR LATER, I stood in the garden near the shed and tried to ignore my skin crawling as Cassandra inspected the patch of ground where Damon had fallen.

We'd watched the footage from Damon's security feeds—apparently imps photographed just fine—over cups of strong tea. After that she'd asked Lizzie a couple of questions, inspected my hands—not saying anything more than that about my magic reappearing—and shooed us all out to the garden.

"What's she looking for?" I asked Lizzie, who was watching Cassandra with a level of focus that made me think she was looking at the energy fields rather than Cassandra herself.

Which reminded me that now that I had my powers back, maybe I could see the energy fields, too. Or maybe I should just leave that to the experts.

"Trying to see what they used to set off the summoning," Lizzie said. She leaned forward, as though she wanted to see better, but didn't move closer. "Whatever it was, it was clever. They've covered their tracks nicely."

Curiosity got the better of me. I reached for my magic, hoping it would respond. Then squinted, dazzled by the blaze of swirling blue around Damon. Cassandra and Lizzie glowed, too, but they were trained and knew how to hide their auras, so Lizzie's pink and Cassandra's green were much fainter. Damon had no power, but emotion was energy, too, and he was obviously agitated, the color spiking around him.

I pulled on what I remembered from Cassandra's initial lessons and tried to block him out. I didn't completely succeed, but he receded to a dull glow, leaving me with an afterimage burned on my retinas as I blinked to clear my vision.

I couldn't see much that looked out of place in the garden among the faint hum of life that surrounded each of the plants and trees. The shed itself didn't glow, whatever it was made from magically inert.

Finally Cassandra straightened. "There's something faint here. But whoever set this was smart. The spell mostly burned itself up when Damon triggered it. There's not enough here to trace or look for any sort of signature."

"Where does that leave us?" Damon asked, blue surging brighter.

Cassandra moved away from the shed. "We have the footage of the imp—if that's what it was. That will be helpful."

"How?"

"Because there are some things that most humans wouldn't be able to summon," Lizzie said. "If it's one of those, then we're probably looking for a lesserkind."

Cassandra nodded. Neither of them looked happy at that thought.

"That's like an imp on steroids," I said to Damon.

"Not quite. More like a..." Cassandra wriggled her fingers. "A minor demon, perhaps. That's not quite right either. A lesserkind can never be as powerful as a demon, but they're descendants from the same branch of whatever hell-plane family tree demons come from." She looked at Damon. "We will ward the garden for you again," she said. "And Lizzie and I can make sure there aren't any other triggers lurking, but that's about all we can do until we get more information. You were going to get your team to look at your employees. Did they find anything yet?"

Damon shook his head. "Not yet. Not that I've

heard. We have a lot of employees. Unless you can narrow it down?" he asked Cassandra.

"If it's a lesserkind summoning, then the most obvious connection will be to look for anyone with a link to your static filter," Cassandra said.

"And if it's not?" Damon said.

"Then your security team has more work to do." She tipped her chin up, one hand tugging down the sleeve of her mustard-colored linen shirt. "I assume you'll be telling them about this?"

"I'll tell Mitch when I get back to the office," he said. "He isn't going to like it. He wasn't happy the last time you were all involved."

"He doesn't have to like it," Cassandra said sharply. "He just has to not interfere. And I told you the last time that your team would do well to recruit someone with some magical expertise."

"We've been busy with other things," Damon said. "And security experts with magic seem to be a little scarce on the ground. At least in the private sector."

Cassandra regarded him for a moment. Then turned her gaze to me.

"Oh no," I said, shaking my head firmly. "Personal security is not something I know anything about. Nor do I know anything about—" I stopped and flapped a hand back at the shed. "—this kind of thing. I have my own business to run. You must have contacts from the Cestis. If you want him to have a witch on his team, you can do some magical headhunting for him."

"We're getting off track," Lizzie broke in. "We have more important problems to fix than finding Damon extra staff. We need to clear the garden, and then we need to research." She turned to Damon. "Can you send a copy of the security footage to all of us?"

"Of course." He pulled out the small datapad. "Give me a minute."

We watched as he waved up a holoscreen, typed a message, pulled down the file we wanted, and sent it. It only took a minute.

Lizzie's eyes lit up at the sight of the datapad. "I want one of those," she said.

"I'm pretty sure neither of us can afford them," I said. "I'm not even entirely sure that one is available to the public."

"It's not," Damon said. "We're doing a collaboration on something with Legacy, and they sent me a prototype."

My eyebrows lifted. Legacy was the most successful survivor of the post-Big One tech upheaval. With half of California in disarray and other parts of the world hit hard by similar natural disasters and climate events, there'd been alliances and takeovers and restructures throughout in a number of global industries. Legacy was made up of parts of several OG tech companies that had wanted to spin off data devices into a new direction and needed more funds than any of them could muster alone.

They'd been successful—more than successful. They now dominated the datapad market in the same way that Righteous dominated VR. Were they working on VR for datapads? There were simple systems available already—more augmented reality and meta-holo—but nothing approaching a true VR system. Maybe now that interface chips were becoming commercially viable, that would change. In which case a project between Righteous and Legacy made sense.

"Damn," Lizzie said. "It's pretty."

Damon grinned at her as he shoved the datapad back in his jacket.

"Pretty won't help us find imps," Cassandra said. "Let's get this garden checked out, and then Damon can have the rest of his day back while we research some more."

"Maybe I could help with the research," he said. "I mean, I do have a whole tech empire at my disposal. I know my way around data."

I hid a smile. "How are you with a card catalog?"

He looked blank.

"The Cestis research library is analog," I added.

For a moment his expression turned genuinely horrified. "It is? Why?"

"Lack of funding," I said before Lizzie or Cassandra could interrupt me. "At least that's what they told me."

His brows drew down. "I thought the Cestis was a global organization? How do you run a global organization without tech?"

"We have tech," Lizzie said. "We just, er, don't use it for everything." She glanced at Cassandra, expression more than a little exasperated.

Cassandra hmmphed. "Many of the materials in our library are very old and exceedingly fragile. They could be destroyed by over handling. Impossible to scan them safely."

"Oh, there are ways around that," Damon said.

Cassandra gave him one of her disapproving glares. "I hardly think the kinds of artifacts we hold fall within your area of expertise."

He waved her off. "We did some VR installations for the Met a few years ago. One of them explained their conservation processes, which includes digitizing collections. Making digital reproductions of all kinds of original objects. Including documents. The whole project was fascinating."

Cassandra stared at him like he'd grown a second head. Lizzie coughed.

"What?" he said. "I'm one of their big donors. They tell me stuff. And we needed to know what they were doing to build the displays. We might have even suggested some improvements to their processes. They've made copies of things now that they thought they would never be able to."

"The Cestis take donations, too," I said. "Save lives, not art. Or something. Or, you being you, do both because you have the cash."

At least I hoped he did. His finances could have taken a hit along with Righteous. But he didn't seem to have made any adjustments to his lifestyle that I had seen. So I figured he was doing okay.

"Why don't you show me your library, and I'll see what we can do?" Damon said.

Cassandra shook her head. "The library is off-limits to anyone without magic. Anyone not approved by us."

He turned one of his killer smiles on her. "You approve of me," he said. "I can't help with the magic part, but you can trust my discretion." His smile widened. "After all, I trust yours. And even if it's not digital, four sets of eyes are better than three. Unless it takes magic to read whatever you want us to read?"

"Nothing I'd give to either of you is going to require magic, no." She sounded almost offended, as though the thought that she might give idiots like us more than we could handle was ridiculous.

Did that mean that some books in the library did require magic? Note to self. Do not randomly touch anything in there. Avoid ending up as a smoking blob of ash on the floor.

"So I can come?" Damon asked, still working his smile.

"Only if you agree to do as I say," Cassandra said. She didn't look entirely happy about it, but maybe she'd decided it might be worthwhile having him involved.

"Of course." He dipped his head in something close to a bow.

Cassandra snorted. "Your charm is wasted on me, young man. So, let's get to work." She nodded at me. "Maggie can help me clean up after the imp. That will give Damon a chance to check in with his office, and Lizzie can call the others and see if anyone else is free to help." She fixed me with a stern look. "I suppose you've forgotten the ritual we used on the imps last time?"

"I remember it required a couple of buckets." I was about to ask Damon where the laundry room was when something else occurred to me. "Do we need to save some of the ash for anything? Last time we just...disappeared it."

"This isn't magical CSI," Lizzie said. She blew her bangs out of her eyes and shook her head at me. "We don't have a secret lab hidden away."

"Well, you have a secret library," I said. "It's not an entirely unreasonable idea. I thought maybe the ash could help identify it."

"The footage from the security cameras should be enough," Cassandra said. "I don't think anyone's ever written a book about the composition of imp ash. I doubt any one witch ever comes across enough imps in a lifetime to do so." She peered at me again. "You're running well above average for someone who's not in the business."

The Cestis business, I assumed. I held up my hands. "Not by choice. I'd be happy to never see another one of those things again in my life."

Cassandra looked as though she didn't think that was likely to be my fate. "We'll deal with the cleanup first, and then we can start working on how to stop any more appearing."

Damon, it turned out, had a well-stocked laundry room—especially considering that only one person lived in his house—and we found several metal buckets to fill with hot water. Cassandra produced a small metal case that looked like a cross between a very old-fashioned doctor's bag and the type of high-tech security cases I'd seen clients use to transport very important information. It took a palm scan and Cassandra's voice to open it, the lid concertinaing up and out, revealing three foam-lined trays of things in tiny vials and jars. They had labels, but the tiny print was symbols and short combos of letters rather than full words.

Some sort of code, I guessed. Cassandra

plucked four of them out without even glancing at the labels and carried them, and the bag of salt she'd also taken from the car, over to the ring of scorched earth where we'd left the buckets.

"Right," she said, pushing back her sleeves and passing me a pair of gloves. "Time to take care of this. Give Damon's gardener a fighting chance to regrow some grass here. And while we do that, you can tell me how you managed to fry another imp when yesterday you couldn't even light a candle."

"That would be easier to do if I knew," I said, snapping on the gloves. I bent over the nearest bucket and poured in a few handfuls of salt. That much I remembered from the last time we'd done this ritual. Salt was used for wards and for banishing. Anything that involved blocking magic, sending power away, or obliterating it altogether.

"From the video it looked like you succeeded when the imp went after Damon," Cassandra said.

"Not you, too," I muttered.

She ignored that, passed me one of the vials, and instructed me to add three drops to each bucket. The scent from the oil within was bitter and green. I knew I should ask what it was, but I wasn't ready for a magic lesson just then. Then again, it might distract Cassandra from talking about Damon.

"What is it?" I asked.

"Feverfew," she said.

That left me none the wiser. Herb lore hadn't been part of my hasty preparation to fight the demon, and the name didn't ring any bells from the bits and pieces Sara had taught me. I tucked the name in the back of my mind and carefully dripped the oil, then recapped the vial.

"Good," she said approvingly as I passed her the oil back and opened the next one she handed me, asking what that was, too. After we'd mixed everything together, the aroma rising from the steam reminded me of a garden beginning to grow after winter. Green and strong. No sweetness or perfume to it. Powerful but vaguely unsettling. It didn't quite mask the still acidic rotten smell that wafted from the ashes every time the breeze flirted our way entirely, but it was an improvement.

Cassandra leaned down, holding her hands over the buckets and muttering under her breath. I half saw, half felt the subtle wave of power she released. The mixture in the buckets bubbled, and the steam briefly flashed a ghostly green.

As she straightened she said, "Don't worry, I won't try to make a match between you and Damon. I'm not Lizzie. I don't think men really change their spots, and I think that one did you the courtesy of telling you the truth before either of you got too far in."

I bit back the "It would have been nice to know

a bit earlier" that rose in my throat, limiting myself to nodding.

"So no, I think you'd be far wiser to give the man a wide berth. But from what we saw with the imp, it's clear you may have some untangling of feelings to complete first. Not to mention trying to figure out what's trying to kill him." She nodded down at the steaming scorch mark.

"You think it would have killed him?" I hadn't had time to stop and think about what was happening. Now, the memory of the creature's teeth and claws and the thought of them tearing into Damon made my knees feel wobbly. The green scent rising around me caught in my throat, and I swallowed hard, hoping I wasn't going to disgrace myself by barfing into the buckets we'd just so carefully prepared.

"It looked as though it had violence on its mind on the video. Imps usually do," Cassandra said as she picked up one of the buckets and pointed at the other one.

I lifted it with fingers suddenly sweaty and clumsy.

Cassandra walked to the opposite side of the scorch mark to me, then frowned, studying my face. "You've gone pale again. Are you feeling all right?"

"I don't even know how to answer that," I said

honestly. "Can we just finish this, and then I might be able to start figuring it out?"

"You probably need sugar," Cassandra said. Feeding me sugar and tea was her answer to many things, I was starting to realize. I guess if magic was going to mean regularly dealing with things that freaked me the hell out, it was at least some small consolation that I got cookies. Though right then, I wasn't sure I could stomach them. Or the tea, for that matter.

"Imp goo first, then snacks," I said, trying to sound calmer than I felt. Damon was fine. I was fine. The imp was a smoldering pile of ash. I had won. I should focus on that.

Cassandra lifted her bucket and walked around the blackened patch of grass, pouring the water gently onto the ash. The smell got worse before it got better. But by the time she'd made two circuits and her bucket was empty, it was beginning to clear.

"Now you," she said. "Cover any parts I missed."

It was surprisingly quick. The water soaked into the ash and seemed to melt it away, though the ground was still burned and blackened.

"There," Cassandra said. "That's done."

"Does it really make a difference?" I asked. I'd helped clean up after an imp death once before. I'd been too distracted by the fact that I was actually dealing with a magical creature trying to get to me for the second time in a few days to wonder what the cleanup did other than clear the mess.

"Well, now the grass will grow back," she said, handing me her bucket. "And nothing else will be drawn to that spot." She turned to look back past the house.

"Drawn?"

"Magic can attract magic. The aftermath of a spell leaves a signature of a sort. If nothing else, someone could exploit it to get within the grounds to try another kind of attack. Now they won't be able to. At least not after we finish checking that—" Her hand took in the garden with a sweeping gesture. "—and adding more wards."

Damn. I'd forgotten we hadn't finished. There could still be any number of booby traps, magical or otherwise, hiding in the greenery.

"I'll take the buckets inside. Then we can get started," I said.

Cassandra smiled. "That's the spirit."

I bent to grab the second bucket. As I straightened, I heard the front gate opening.

"Did you call someone?" I asked Cassandra, turning to watch the gate. I doubted Damon had. Not when he'd told his security team not to come.

She shook her head, frowning as the gate completed its inward swing and an expensive-looking dark gray sedan glided through.

It slowed as it drove past Cassandra and me, the gravel on the drive crunching under its wheels, but didn't stop. The tinted windows hid whoever was driving from view. And there was nothing on the car to give any hint. No corporate logos or stickers.

As the car halted by the house, Damon walked onto the porch, a frown darkening his face. Lizzie followed a step or two behind him.

Two men climbed out of the car. The older one, who had sandy gray hair that might have been red once, was tall, broad-shouldered, and wearing the kind of well-tailored charcoal suit I associated with expensive men's magazines. His eyes were hidden behind gold-rimmed sunglasses. I didn't know him, but the other guy—younger, blonder, taller, and wearing an equally slick suit—was Ajax Fields.

My stomach tightened. Ajax worked for Damon. Last time I'd seen him, he'd been in charge of one of the beta testing teams. The one Nat had joined just before everything went wrong. I'd thought he'd had a bit of a crush on her. Or stronger feelings. The last time I'd actually seen him had been her funeral. I hadn't had much ability to focus on anyone but Nat's parents, but the pain on Ajax's face as he'd watched Nat's coffin being carried out of the chapel had stuck in my mind.

"Ajax," I said, not really meaning for it to be loud enough for him to hear me, but he glanced in my direction. He didn't look happy to see me. I tried to smile, but his expression didn't change, and he snapped his gaze back fast enough that it was a clear dismissal before walking around the car to join the other guy.

The knot in my gut worsened.

"What are you doing here?" Damon said, descending the front steps. Lizzie stayed where she was.

The older guy folded his arms. "You didn't actually think we weren't going to turn up after you used a gun here, did you?"

"I told you it was a snake."

Sandy brows lifted above the rims of the sunglasses. "And that was a lie, wasn't it? That's the other reason we came. I wanted to see if you fell and hit your head somehow to explain why you're lying to us or whether you forgot that we can review your security footage." His gaze swiveled in my direction. "And to see why the woman who seemed to be sending you death threats is at your house when you had to discharge your weapon."

So this was Mitch, Damon's head of security. I met his stare, refusing to be the one to look away. His mouth flattened. It seemed, like Ajax, he wasn't currently a member of Team Maggie. Well, the feeling was mutual. Especially if he was still going to see me as a threat. If he'd reviewed the footage, he knew damned well that I had saved Damon's life. What more could he want as proof of my lack of nefarious intentions?

I had no good answer. Nor did I understand what Ajax was doing with him.

I could understand why Damon's security had turned up despite orders not to, but I still wasn't sure what a tester was doing tagging along.

"We've covered that," Damon said flatly. "Maggie is not the problem here. She saved my ass today."

"So she 'shot' the 'snake,' did she?" Mitch said, making air quotes as he spoke.

"If you've watched the tapes, you know what happened," Damon said.

"Nothing good," Mitch said. "And now I see we have your other magical friends here again." He made a sweeping sort of gesture that took in Lizzie at the top of the stairs before moving around to Cassandra.

Cassandra made a hissing sort of noise under her breath, and I had to fight the urge to smile. I was sure Mitch was good at his job—his misconceptions about me aside, Damon didn't hire idiots —but I was pretty sure Cassandra could wipe the floor with him if she wanted to.

"They're here at my invitation," Damon said. "And you're going to work together for a while. So be nice. You don't want to tempt them to turn you into a frog." He beckoned at Cassandra and me. "If you two are done, why don't we all go inside and talk?" He turned and walked back into the house. Lizzie followed, and Mitch and Ajax started up the stairs in his wake.

"Master of the freaking universe," I muttered, tempted to stay right where I was out of sheer contrariness.

Cassandra chuckled. "You're the one who dated him." She nodded toward the house. "If we weren't done here, he could just wait until we were, but seeing as we are, no point putting this off, I guess. Mr. Angelico is an impatient man."

I assumed she meant Mitch. "You've met him before?"

"Briefly, when we helped Damon previously. I got the impression he wasn't thrilled about us, but he didn't interfere. Of course, we didn't find anything that time."

Meaning she thought he'd want to be hands-on this time? I guess the Cestis had to work with all kinds of law enforcement at times. Including personal security. Cassandra would know how to navigate the situation. I would keep my mouth shut and watch.

Chapter Seventeen

WATCHING myself fry the imp on a holoscreen didn't make the experience any less weird. Nor was it less creepy sitting in Damon's kitchen. I hadn't known his kitchen had a holoscreen, but it shouldn't have surprised me that he had technology at his fingertips no matter where he was in his house. Of course, most of the meals I'd eaten here, we hadn't really been focused on business. Sure, we were dealing with magical mayhem like we were again, but we'd also been in the kind of haze of first-lust, great-sex, new-couple that made the world go away a lot of the time. Maybe that was how I'd made it through dealing with the demon.

But this time I would be doing it cold turkey. I made myself watch the footage as Mitch demanded to see it from several angles. When he finally indicated he'd had enough with a wave of his hand, Damon left the last image—the flickering flames on the grass—frozen in place.

"So what happens now?" Mitch asked, directing the question at Cassandra rather than Damon. He'd removed his sunglasses, revealing bright blue eyes that didn't miss a thing.

"We'll check the garden to make sure that won't happen again. Then we'll need to search the Riley campus as well."

Mitch pointed at the screen. "You want to explain to me exactly what that was?"

"A summoning spell," Cassandra said. "Most likely set to be triggered by Damon."

"Set by who?"

"You're his security, you tell me," she replied. Clearly she wasn't going to let him imply that any of this was her fault. She and Mitch stared each other down, the atmosphere in the room, tense to begin with, turning even cooler.

"Anybody could have come onto the property during the power outage. A trigger spell doesn't necessarily take a long time to set up," Lizzie said to Damon.

"We checked after the outage," Ajax said. "We didn't find anything."

"You wouldn't have known what you were looking at," Cassandra said. "Unless you've added someone with magic to your team?"

I shot her a glance. She knew they didn't. Was she trying to annoy Mitch?

Mitch's mouth flattened. "No."

"Well, then, I guess you did the best you could." Her tone was sweet, but her eyes were steely. "So now you need to let the experts handle this particular problem."

Mitch opened his mouth, but Damon said, "Mitch, can I talk to you in the other room a minute?" He pushed back his chair and walked out of the kitchen.

After one last glare at Cassandra, Mitch followed, leaving Lizzie, Cassandra, Ajax, and me sitting in awkward silence around the table.

"So you're in security now?" I said eventually to Ajax.

He nodded ,and for a moment I thought that was all the response I was getting. Then he shifted in his seat and seemed to focus.

"I switched departments nearly six months ago," he said.

Not exactly the warmest of responses, but it was better than nothing.

I smiled tentatively at him. "It must be quite a change."

He shrugged. "I started working with the security teams when we were following up on all the beta testers after—" He hesitated, "—you know."

I nodded. I did know. And I didn't think he

wanted to talk about the demon any more than I did. And it made sense that Mitch had chosen Ajax to bring with him when dealing with a magical issue if he was one of the few people in the know about what had really happened.

"I found I enjoyed it. The testing work is fun for a while, but I guess this felt more...real, in a way."

"Damon said the testers were all okay now," I said. "That's good to hear."

"There's still a couple we're helping with some follow-up care, but yes, everyone is doing well."

I wanted to ask how he was doing but got the feeling that might be pushing things too far. For now I would be happy that he and I could have a conversation, at least. That would have made Nat happy.

Lizzie leaned forward as though she wanted to ask a question, but the kitchen door opened, and Damon and Mitch rejoined us at the table. Mitch still didn't look happy, but Damon looked slightly more relaxed. I hoped that meant he'd gotten his way in whatever their discussion had been.

"Well?" Cassandra asked.

"Mitch and Ajax will be going back to Righteous," Damon said. "You three can finish your sweep of the garden, and we'll all meet tomorrow to work out the plan for covering the campus." He looked at Cassandra. "I assume if there are more of those things, then they're most likely aimed at me? Not likely to be triggered by someone random?"

Cassandra nodded. "Given that nothing has happened before today, that seems a fairly safe assumption. We can't be certain, of course, until we've done some more investigations, but if you haven't had any imps trying to take a piece out of your staff until now, one more night isn't going to hurt."

Damon turned to Mitch. "See? She agrees with me."

"Plenty of people agree with you," Mitch retorted. "Doesn't mean they're right all the time."

I hid a smile. If he wasn't so anti-me, I'd probably like Mitch.

"I take people's safety just as seriously as you do, Mr. Angelico," Cassandra said. "You look after a company. Granted, it's a very large company, and I'm sure you're good at your job. But I'm responsible for a whole damned country. I'm good at mine, too. If I thought your people were at any real risk, I'd be telling you to shut the place down for a few days. But given what Riley Arts has had to deal with so far this year, I didn't think you'd appreciate me recommending you do that when I don't think it's justified." She nodded at Damon. "We'll keep an eye on your boss here. He'll be as safe as I can keep him. You have my word on that."

A muscle twitched in Mitch's jaw, but he nodded. "All right."

"I could stay," Ajax offered, voice eager. "Help out here."

Mitch shook his head. "You and I have some planning to do. Damon, you know how to reach us if you need to."

"I haven't forgotten how to use the panic mode, no," Damon said. "Everything is fine."

That was a big fat lie. Everything wasn't fine, and I could tell Mitch thought so, too. But apparently he'd decided there was no point to arguing, so he just jerked his chin at Ajax, muttered, "I'll see you all tomorrow," in the direction of the rest of us, and stalked out before any of us could reply.

Ajax managed a hasty "Bye" before he jogged after his boss.

"Panic mode?" I asked Damon after Ajax left.

He nodded. "Added feature of my latest chip. If I make a certain gesture, it transmits an alarm signal and my location."

"You're GPS tagged like a fancy car," I said, not sure if it was funny or vaguely creepy.

"Not all the time," he said. "Only if I engage it."

"What happens if something happens to you and you're out of range of anything to transmit to?" Lizzie asked.

"Well, then, I'm out of luck," Damon said easily.

"What did you do before the chip?" Lizzie asked, sounding fascinated.

"Panic code on my datapad," he said, shrugging. "And I have a small panic button sewn somewhere into most of my clothes." His mouth quirked. "The less glamorous side of making lots of money. No one has ever actually tried anything physical up until now, but we have enough threats and weirdness on the regular that it's better to be safe than sorry." He brushed his hands together as though the subject was one he wasn't entirely comfortable with. "Speaking of better safe than sorry, let's get this garden done. Then you can show me this library of yours."

Watching Damon's face as he stood in the library and Cassandra explained the card catalog to him was the most entertainment I'd had all day. After a few fruitless hours going over his property with the magical equivalent of a fine-tooth comb, watching his brain almost short out trying to process that, yes, there really were a lot of very old and valuable books here, and no, no one had digitized them or even produced a digital catalog was amusing. Given I'd spent the entire time at his house wondering if another imp was going to appear out of nowhere every time I touched something, I'd take my entertainment when I could.

To Damon's credit, he didn't immediately ask any of the questions I knew he must have been burning to ask. Instead he just shoved his hands in his pockets and said, "Okay, where do we start?"

Cassandra looked almost approving. "You and Maggie got the best look at that imp. We have records of imp sightings. You two can look through those, see if you can find one that matches."

"How many kinds are there?" Damon asked.

"At last count there were somewhere around ten thousand."

His brows flew up. Mine, too. "So many?"

"There are probably more," Lizzie said. "Or maybe there's only one kind and they look different depending on how they're brought through."

"Shapeshifters?" Damon said. His mouth twisted as though he wasn't pleased by the idea.

"Perhaps. Of a sort," Cassandra said.

Did that mean there were other kinds of shapeshifters? I wasn't game to ask. One day I needed to know exactly what was real and not real in the stories that humans told about magic and the supernatural, but for now demons were enough to deal with. I wasn't sure I wouldn't just have a total meltdown if I found out werewolves, vampires, and the like really existed.

"So if we can find this thing in your books, what does that tell you?" Damon asked.

"Maybe how it was summoned. Something about its habits. It depends on how often we've come across one like it before and how good the notes are."

"And how often do you come across them?"

"Well, imps aren't exactly common, but they're not rare either."

Damon looked like he had more questions, but Cassandra turned to Lizzie and rattled off a bunch of letters and numbers. Lizzie nodded and headed into the stacks. Perhaps the Cestis had their own version of the Dewey Decimal system.

I took a seat at the table, glad to be off my feet. Cassandra had made me drink tea at Damon's, and they'd found me crackers to nibble on, but that had been all I could stomach after the adrenaline rush of the attack. I'd rinsed the worst of the sweat and grime off in his bathroom before we left for Cassandra's house.

That had been hours ago, and now I felt like I'd been hit by a whole convoy of trucks. And in need of caffeine. But there was still work to be done. I just had to suck it up and keep going.

Damon took the chair next to mine, removing his jacket and hanging it over the chair. He'd swapped his tee for a dark blue Henley. He rolled his shoulders and tilted his head to stretch his neck in a way that made me think he was just as tired as me.

"Sorry about all of this," I said.

He stopped stretching, face puzzled. "It's not your fault. In fact, if it weren't for you, that thing in my garden could have killed me today. You have nothing to apologize for."

"It feels like I do. They tried to get to you through me. Or me through you. Either way, it still feels like if we hadn't crossed paths, this wouldn't have happened."

"Maybe. But we can't change the past. And dwelling on 'if onlys' has always felt like a waste of time to me. I mean, how far back do you go? If only I'd never stayed here after the quake? If only your mom hadn't died and you'd never moved here? If only she had been the kind of person who didn't sell her daughter's powers to a demon?"

I'd spent quite a bit of time "if only-ing" that one myself since I'd found out that was what she'd done. And some more regretting what happened between Damon and me. Maybe I needed to learn from him and lock all that away somewhere.

Though he was the last person I wanted to ask to teach me how.

Fortunately Lizzie arrived to dump an armful of books between us before our conversation could continue. "Demonkind mugshots, volumes 1 to 5," she said cheerfully. "That should keep you busy for a while."

She was right about that. The books were thick. Cassandra had said there were at least ten thousand different kinds of imps. So I could only assume there were more volumes to come.

"Mugshots?" Damon said hopefully. "Photographs?"

Lizzie shook her head. "Nope, drawings for the most part. I was paraphrasing."

"Will you be helping?" I asked, hoping she'd correctly translate this as "I'd rather not sit here doing this with Damon." Which was a long shot given her view on our relationship.

"Cassandra and I are going to be neck-deep in summoning and trigger spells. See if we can work out how the spell in the garden shed might have worked."

"Cassandra said that would be easier if we knew what kind of imp it was," I said. "If you help, we might find that out faster."

"Maybe, but no harm working the problem from both directions." She pointed at the books. "Enjoy. Yell if you find your creepy pale friend." She headed back to join Cassandra.

I narrowed my eyes at her retreating back as I reached for the nearest book. Volume 1, according to the neatly lettered spine. Prosaic brown leather, faintly worn, and the edges of the pages had yellowed slightly. Obviously old. I didn't want to damage it. Lizzie hadn't told us to wear gloves or anything though, so maybe it wasn't too fragile.

Using my fingertips, I cautiously flipped it open, supporting the front cover as I lowered it down to the table. The title page had a border of swirls and flourishes in black ink that was turning red-brown with age. The title read simply *Demonkind I*. No further explanations offered. I guess whoever wrote it assumed that if you were allowed to read the book, you probably didn't need them.

I turned the page gently. No table of contents or index. Just a half-page drawing of an imp. Whoever drew it had been skilled. Even sketched in careful strokes and shadowed with tiny lines, the creature was creepy. Tall with bony features beneath a dark skin—the illustration was black-and-white, so I couldn't tell if it was supposed to be black or dark gray or some other shade. Arms that bent at too many angles ended in hands more like clawed spikes. Beside it were a few lines of neat text, but the words were in what I thought was Latin. Somehow the need to learn Latin had never come up in my education.

But then again, if I could read the descriptions and stopped to do just that for each picture these books contained, it would only slow down the search. What mattered was that this creature did not look much like the one I'd killed in Damon's garden. I flipped the page, then another, then another.

Beside me, I was dimly aware that Damon had started a search of his own. Good. Less talking was good.

I flipped another page.

By the time I reached the end of the book, my eyes were already sore. And my brain was full of images that I wasn't happy about. Imps and what-ever else these things were came in a dizzying vari-ation of bodies that ranged from gross to truly frightening.

Nothing quite as primordially terrifying as the demon was, but that had been more than just its appearance. Something about its presence had by-passed all sensible thought to hit the part of the human nervous system that still remembered being a small helpless thing that other things with teeth and claws would kill without blinking.

These were just pictures. They couldn't hurt me. They might make my nightmares less pleasant, of course, but I'd lived with nightmares so long that they were normal in a weird way.

Damon closed the book he'd been looking through and sat back in his chair.

"My kingdom for a tagging system," he muttered. "There has got to be an easier way."

He was right. There should be. Even without stopping to read anything, it had taken us over thirty minutes to get through the first volumes.

"Well, you could build a time travel machine and go back and fund the Cestis better so they had microfiche, at least. Of course, you'd have to figure out how to convince them that digitizing all this was safe, as well." I didn't doubt that if he set his mind to it, he could talk Cassandra round. After all, his kingdom could buy a lot of tagging systems. And his charm could probably pay for even more. But that didn't help us here and now.

"If I could build a time travel machine, we wouldn't be sitting here in the first place," Damon said. But then he sighed and reached for the next book.

Asking exactly what he would do with a time travel machine seemed like a bad idea, so I did the same.

The second volume was just as gross as the first. But still not helpful. There were a couple of lighter imps, so I noted the page numbers. Before I could worry about whether Damon and I might have to go through the fifth volume together, Lizzie reemerged with another armful of books.

"Any luck?" she asked.

"Not really," I replied. Damon shook his head, too. "How about you?"

"Cassandra has a few ideas. But I'm mostly of book-fetching duty at this point, so I can't tell you exactly what they are. Happy reading." She turned and headed away again.

The book on top of the pile was volume six. There didn't seem any particular need to go in order, so I took it. The text of the first page actually looked printed rather than inked onto the page. I got about halfway through before a pale imp caught my eye.

"Does this look about right?" I said to Damon, pushing the book in his direction.

He pulled out his datapad. "I have the footage. We can check."

Of course he had the footage. I wouldn't have been surprised if he was able to project a whole 3D image of the thing from his garden and map it somehow against the picture to do a full image match.

But we didn't need anything that sophisticated. Whoever had drawn the creature in the book had been accurate. It wasn't exactly identical once we lined the screenshot against the drawing, but if they'd been together in a freaky demon monster lineup, I would have labeled them as the same species or whatever the right term was.

"We have a winner," I said and picked up the

book. Lizzie and Cassandra were sitting at one of the desks in the stacks, heads bent over another book. They looked up as I approached.

"Find something?" Lizzie asked.

I put the book down on the table and tapped the page. "This one."

Cassandra pulled the book closer, studying the picture.

"What does it say?" I asked.

"Still an imp," Lizzie said absently. "Not common."

"Is 'still an imp' good or bad?"

Cassandra looked up from the picture. "Well, it means it was sent. Or someone set it up to be summoned. Which is consistent with what the traces from the spell in the shed tell us. It says here..." She leaned closer and squinted. "Contagious. I think. It's not quite clear."

"Contagious?" Lizzie said. "That's weird."

"Is anything about these things not weird?" Damon muttered.

Lizzie pointed at the picture. "Well, imps mostly just try to eat your face off if they're attacking you. At least the ones we usually see. Not sure there's much point in them infecting you with something when they can kill you pretty easily. I mean, look at the claws and teeth on it."

I didn't look. I didn't need the reminder.

"Are they saying this one does more than that?"

Cassandra hitched a shoulder. "Hard to say. There's nothing else here. It could be contagious, or it could work with sickness somehow. Or it could be the language means something closer to venomous. Or poisonous. This note is from a few centuries ago." She tapped a notation at the top of the page.

"Well, it didn't touch either of us, so I guess it doesn't matter," I said. "And we cleansed the ashes."

Cassandra nodded at that. "Yes. And we can do some more to reinforce that cleansing if we need to."

"Does it help you figure out who summoned it, knowing what kind it is?" I asked.

"There's nothing here about that either, to say how common this kind is. Or what it takes to summon one." She peered at the image. "The remnants I felt in the garden made me think human magic. Which is possible given it's an imp."

"Humans can summon imps?"

"Sometimes. And they can definitely set a trigger spell to help make a target for something else doing a summoning. This one is large though. And the contagion thing is unusual. If it's some sort of stronger imp, then it's more likely to be a lesserkind controlling it. Or a demon using a witch who is far gone into its control."

I didn't like the sound of that. "Why far gone?"

"The sort of power it would take to bring a stronger manifestation over would burn out most humans," Cassandra said. "It's not like a binding. It takes a lot more power. For a witch to funnel that much power from a demon, they would have to cede total control to it. At which point it's safe enough to say that they're really no longer a person. More a person-shaped home for the demon to walk around in."

The thought of that made me want to gag. "Why would anyone do that?"

"I doubt many people set out to end up that way," Cassandra said. "People are foolish. They think they'll be able to control what they give to the demon, to resist it. Most of them cannot. Which is why only fools dabble in such things to begin with." She looked at me. I met her gaze. Yes, my mother had been a fool who had bound her only daughter's powers to a demon. But I had no desire to follow in her footsteps.

She'd paid dearly for her choices in the end. And I'd had the love and care of my grandparents to help me heal the worst of the scars from my childhood with her from the time I'd turned thirteen. True, the last of her legacy had only come to light when I'd accidentally broken the bond with the demon, and I hadn't yet truly dealt with that final betrayal.

Then again, perhaps she had cared for me a

little. Whatever she'd done to bind me to the demon, she'd also kept it from influencing me in any other way other than siphoning my magic. I hadn't turned into the kind of mindless demon meat suit Cassandra was describing—and no, no thinking about what a close call it might have been or I'd risk losing my lunch right here in the library—and the Cestis had declared me free from demon taint twice now.

My mother had been powerful. Possibly as strong as Cassandra or Lizzie. Why she'd chosen the life of a grifter and to be the kind of witch who preyed on the hopeful or the hopeless, selling them love potions or luck spells and taking their money for years, was something I would never understand. Maybe it was the only way she could play out whatever her plan for me had been or get whatever the demon paid for me. But she hadn't lived long enough to reap whatever reward she thought she was earning.

"So we're looking for a person?" Damon asked.

"I think a person most likely set the spell in your garden," Cassandra corrected. "But it's unlikely they're working on their own."

He pressed his fingers to the bridge of his nose, grimacing.

"Which brings us back to working out who wants to get to you," I said. "And Righteous."

Lizzie nodded agreement.

Damon shook his head. "Just when I thought things were getting back to normal."

I flinched. Just when he'd fought to bring his company back from the disaster my demon caused the first time. He could tell me he didn't blame me all he wanted, but it was hard to see how he could feel anything else.

Cassandra looked sympathetic. "We will start there. You have a good team working for you. If Mr. Angelico will cooperate, then hopefully we can narrow down a list of people to talk to. In the mean-time, we're also talking to our networks. See if anyone has noticed any unusual activity."

How unusual would something have to be to stand out from whatever the Cestis had already been dealing with?

As if she could sense what I was thinking, Lizzie rubbed her arm, flexing her fingers.

Cassandra pursed her lips. "But I think all of this can wait until the morning. Lizzie and Maggie need to rest. I need to speak to the other members of the Cestis. Damon, I would recommend you go to a hotel for the night. I would prefer to check your home one more time before you stay there alone. Choose one you haven't stayed in before."

"We have suites at the Riley campus," he said. "I don't usually stay there. They're more secure than a hotel would be."

"Perhaps. But it seems likely that someone who

is targeting you will be watching the place you work," Cassandra said.

Damon nodded. "I understand that. And I'll think about it."

Cassandra nodded. "It is, of course, your decision. Just be careful. Lizzie will let you out. We can reconvene at your office in the morning."

Chapter Eighteen

"CHRIST, I COULD EAT A HORSE," Damon said as we emerged blinking into the golden light of early evening.

"Me, too," I said. Then regretted it. I didn't want him to think I was angling for an invitation.

"That place is..." Damon turned back to look at Cassandra's house.

"Weird? Archaic? Fascinating and terrifying?" I offered.

"I don't know about fascinating," he said, "but yes to the others."

He didn't fool me. The man didn't like magic, but he'd been interested in what we'd been doing. Beyond the horrified curiosity of a techno geek trying to assimilate that a global network could operate without his favorite toys and gadgets. I knew what his face looked like when something caught his attention. Because once upon a time, it was the expression I'd seen when he'd looked at me.

But there I went thinking foolish thoughts again.

"It's definitely lacking in snacks," I joked.

"Yes. I guess they save their money for the books," Damon said. "I wonder where they buy them."

"Some sort of magical dark web?" I said. "Or maybe not the web if Cassandra's aversion to tech is the norm. Maybe those weird little spooky book-stores you see in fantasy films are based on real places."

"I don't know how weird and spooky they'd be," he said. "Those books were old. They can't be cheap. Maybe the magical booksellers are making bank, and that's why Cassandra doesn't have money to digitize the whole thing."

"Maybe she thinks this is safer," I said lightly. "We can't all be billionaire uber-geeks who think tech holds all the answers."

His mouth twitched, but I couldn't tell if the expression he was hiding was a smile or a wince because he'd put his sunglasses back on.

"You could let the billionaire uber-geek buy you dinner," he said.

What the heck? I opened my mouth to answer and then closed it again as confusion rushed through me. Swiftly followed by a spike of "Yes!"

that almost made me step toward him, pulled in his direction by emotions too dumb to know when to quit.

"I'm not sure that would be smart," I said after an awkward pause as I tried to think of a better answer.

"Just dinner," he said. "You have to let me say thank you. You did save my life today."

The first time he'd taken me to dinner, there'd been stupidly good steak and wickedly expensive scotch, and the night had ended in scorching-hot sex. Three things that sounded hard to regret, but I did regret them. Well, not so much the steak and the scotch because I wasn't dumb enough to pass those up when offered, but the sex had been...a beginning all too soon ended. A regret to add to the tally of regrets that had dogged the last year.

That tally wasn't going to get any higher if there was any way to avoid it.

"That still doesn't make it a good idea. You, me. Together."

"I'm not talking candles and low lighting," he said. "One of the UC professors told me about a great taco truck near the marina where they built that new park."

He knew I liked tacos. Or maybe he'd forgotten and had just picked them at random. My stomach hadn't. It rumbled at the thought, and he grinned.

"That's one yes. What does the rest of you say?"

Tacos weren't sexy, I told myself. And they were fast. I could eat and leave. Get out with my stomach full and my emotions no more ruffled than they already had been today. Simple, right?

"I think Cassandra wouldn't want us hanging around in the open."

"She wants me to be unpredictable. I don't think anyone is expecting me to go for dinner at a taco truck in Berkeley. I've never been there before. Ji-Lin said they were really good."

Right now the tacos didn't even have to be good. I just needed them to be hot and edible.

"Well?" Damon asked, as though he could sense my resolve crumbling.

"One hour. I have...things to do." Now that I had my magic back, I wanted to take another stab at my client's problem. See if the solution suddenly leaped out at me.

But I didn't actually have to do that right away. So, as excuses went, it was weak. But it seemed so was my willpower when it came to Damon. It didn't matter what truth I knew or how much logic I tried to apply to the situation. Not when my heart still wanted to leap when he smiled at me and the scent of him in the warm afternoon air made my mouth water for more than fast food.

So I would indulge myself. To a point. Let myself

have an hour to pretend we could perhaps be friends. Friends who ate tacos in the summer twilight and had magic-free lives and no complicated past.

Normal friends.

Since magic had come back into my life, I wasn't sure I even knew what normal was anymore. Didn't I deserve a taste? Even if it was a lie?

"Things?" Damon said.

"Work. I'm sure you do, too."

He nodded. "Yes. But food first. One hour. It's a deal."

Forty-five minutes later, I had a belly full of near perfect fish tacos, a half-drunk so-called Tijuana Iced Tea that I was beginning to suspect featured more tequila than one might expect from a cocktail poured by a business operating on taco truck margins, a sunny spot on the grass near the waterfront, and an increasing reluctance to stick to my own time limit.

Clinging to the illusion of normal was seductive even when I knew exactly what I was doing. I needed to summon some willpower soon and haul my butt out of there.

Trouble was, the sight of Damon lounging on the grass, jacket off, olive skin near golden where he'd pushed up his sleeves, and a lazy smile on his face as he slurped the last of his own drink was apparently my form of personal kryptonite.

He wasn't sitting particularly close to me, and he'd been careful not to touch me as we'd walked from his car to the truck and waited in line to order. He'd kept the conversation light, sticking to safe topics that didn't involve magic or anything that had happened earlier. Weather. Movies. Taco preferences. Apparently he wanted the illusion of normality, too.

Simple everyday small talk. I should have been immune to small talk. But he made even that charming.

I blamed the tequila. I'd started drinking the tea before I'd eaten my tacos, and it had clearly hit me too hard. That was the only reasonable explanation for why I wanted to scoot across the grass and lay my hand over his heart just to feel it beating.

If I hadn't found my powers, then he could be dead right now.

That knowledge stole my breath for a moment.

My fingers flexed, then curled as I fought the need to reassure myself that he was real. And alive. Because he was both. But he still wasn't mine, and I needed to...accept that.

Or just get the hell out before I made a fool of myself all over again.

The chill of acknowledging what we could have

lost this morning melted my relaxed mood away. We could temporarily ignore the fact as hard as we liked, but we had a problem on our hands. And eating tacos and letting myself play "if only" in the lingering sunshine wasn't going to solve it. I crumpled the remains of my takeout containers into a ball and stood. "I really need to get home. And you need to figure out where you're going to stay tonight."

I didn't wait for his answer, just started walking across the grass toward the park boundaries and the lot where he'd parked the car.

"Maggie, wait," he called.

I stopped, turned. Damon was on his feet, but he hadn't moved from our picnic spot. I couldn't quite read the expression on his face. Or maybe I could.

No.

I was wrong. There was no reason for him to be looking like that at me. He'd walked away from looking like that at me. Still, I felt my stupid heart speed up a little. "What?"

His mouth twisted. "Nothing."

See. I was right. He wasn't looking at me like that. Stupid girl. "Okay, fine. Then let's move. It's going to get dark soon." I turned away, trying to tell myself there was nothing to feel disappointed about.

"Wait."

I stopped again. Turned back even though I knew it was truly a terrible idea. I'd thought I could do it—spend time with him and not want what I couldn't have. Turned out I couldn't. Because I did want it. And with every little bone he threw me, every smile, every time he made me laugh, or even, really, every time he breathed in my direction, I wanted more. Wished I could turn back time and become the nice uncomplicated nonmagical woman he wanted.

My fingers curled into my palms as we stared at each other. Seriously, this had to be over with fast or I was going to be in a world of hurt. Solve the puzzle, get the hell out of Dodge and away from the man who could shred my heart just by stepping into a room.

"What?" I repeated. "Is something wrong?"

"Not exactly."

I blew out a breath, trying not to let him see my frustration. Because he might just guess what was behind it. The only thing worse than carrying an embarrassing, can't-kill-it-no-matter-what torch for the man would be for him to realize it. "Then let's move."

"It's just—"

"Just what?" I asked when he paused again.

"Hell." He closed the gap between us with two long strides. "Just this." And his mouth came down on mine.

My brain shut down. I couldn't move. Couldn't think. For a moment, some part of me clung to the last dregs of sanity and came up with "This is a really bad idea." The thought flashed through my mind as the taste of him registered on my tongue, and then there was no more thinking as I wrapped my arms around his neck and kissed him back.

This.

This was what I'd been missing.

In this kiss was the gap in my life that needed to be filled. The lack I hadn't let myself try to fill. The touch and taste of Damon's mouth and the warmth of him against my body and the sheer screaming pleasure of sparking lust and delight.

I'm not sure how long we stayed there kissing like crazed teenagers. A minute. Maybe more.

A delicious span of time that just was. Where there were no demons or curses or trouble. No magic beyond what flared between us due to good old-fashioned chemistry.

But all good things have to come to an end, and somehow we disentangled and sprang apart, watching each other warily like two cats who weren't sure whether to attack or flee the scene.

Damon rubbed a hand over his head. "I'm sorry," he said. "That was...."

"Stupid?" I said, my voice uneven because I was still trying to catch my breath.

"Yeah," he agreed. "Won't happen again." The

words sounded sincere, but there was a certain alley cat glint in his eye that told me he wasn't. That maybe he wanted to play a little.

The thought was like a slap of cold water. I stepped back.

"No," I agreed. "It won't."

It was his turn to look surprised. "You didn't like it?"

"Doesn't matter whether I did or not. I'm not in the mood for—" I waved my hand back and forth between us. "—whatever you had in mind."

"I didn't have anything 'in mind,'" he said, sounding indignant.

"And that's the problem," I retorted. I shoved my hands into the pockets of my jeans. "You and I...we were careless last time. We tumbled into bed and played it casual, and well, maybe it started casual, but it didn't finish that way. Not for me."

"You don't do casual?" he said.

I lifted my chin. "I do casual if I want. If I want no strings, well, there are a hundred guys in a hundred bars in the city who would do just fine. I have boobs and long legs, and I know how to use them if I need to scratch an itch." The fact that I hadn't scratched that itch since he'd left me was beside the point. "But I'm not scratching an itch with you. I was careless last time. And it was fast, and yes, maybe there were extenuating circumstances driving us together. But I won't be careless again. And I won't let you be careless with me."

"I—" His jaw snapped shut as his eyes searched my face. Then he straightened his shoulders. "I didn't mean to hurt you. I didn't know how it was going to end."

"I know you didn't," I said softly. It hurt to say it but it was true. Just as it was true that he had hurt me, whether he meant to or not. "Neither of us did. Which is why we should be smarter this time. We can be colleagues. Friends, maybe. But that's all I can give you."

"I guess I'll see you tomorrow," I said as the car stopped. Damon had insisted on driving me home, even though I told him I'd call a ride-share. The short drive had been quiet. Apparently he was all out of small talk. We'd brooded as separately as two people in a car could. Me staring determinedly out the window, and Damon, from what I could see of his profile reflected in the tinted windows, focused doggedly on the road ahead.

I reached for the door handle, eager for the awkwardness to be over. I needed some space. Away from him. Needed to give myself the chance to remember why I had to ignore the echoes of his kiss that still had my body humming softly. I'd told him the truth. I wasn't going to be careless. Wasn't going to let him hurt me again.

But apparently that determination didn't quite translate to me being able to not want him.

"Maggie—" he said, and I held up a hand before he could finish.

"Don't. I'm tired. It's been a day. I just want to go inside, shower, and then fall face-first onto my bed to sleep for about one hundred hours."

"But that would make you late tomorrow morning," he said, one side of his mouth lifting slightly.

The part of me that wasn't immune to his charms felt that little quirk of his lips like they were pressed against my skin.

"As close to one hundred hours as I can manage, then," I said and pushed the door open. "I'll see you tomorrow."

I climbed out and shut the door fast, the thud of it close to a slam. The sound of safety. Proof of a solid barrier between me and him.

But as I walked a few steps up the drive, the sense of safety vanished, replaced by crawling unease.

I stopped dead, staring up at the house. No movement. No lights. Lizzie must still be at Cassandra's. The outer lights came on, dispelling the twilight shadows that lingered around the foot of the stairs and the front door where the porch roof shaded it. Being able to see that there was clearly nothing there did nothing to chase away the sensation.

Surely I was just jumping at shadows? My datapad would have pinged me and Lizzie if someone had broken in. My computer mojo may have been lacking lately, but our system was rock solid. And it had layers and backups. Unlike Damon, we hadn't had any unexplained power outages recently that would let someone bypass it.

Check the wards. The thought popped into my head in a voice so like Lizzie's that for a moment I wondered if she'd walked up behind me without me noticing. I made myself focus, calling on my magic. It felt sluggish, as though I was pulling it from somewhere sticky. Fair enough. I was exhausted. It made sense my magic would be, too.

But there was a shimmer over the house, as though I was looking at it through a faulty UV filter. I couldn't see any gaps or holes or any variations in the faint rainbow haze. I could see that I was standing outside it. Did that mean only the house was warded?

I looked behind me. There was a matching shimmer along the boundary line where my front lawn met the sidewalk. But it seemed fainter, flickering rather than shimmering.

"Maggie? Is everything okay?" Damon pushed his door open.

I held up my hand again, hoping like hell he'd be

smart and stay where he was. I looked back at the wards on the house. I wasn't imagining things. The wards along the boundary line looked different. The crawling sensation had crept up my spine and flowed down my arms, making my hands tingle, a sensation somewhere between an itch and pain that made me want to flex them in readiness.

Readiness to do what exactly?

Protect myself from whatever the hell it was that was freaking my spidey senses out?

"Maggie?" Damon said again.

I turned slowly, still caught between the urge to flee and the fear that I was simply overreacting. After all, I was clueless about what the wards on my lawn were supposed to look like. But even as I stared at it, my bracelet suddenly went hot, and the ward glitched like a video pixelating before it vanished.

Chapter Nineteen

Fᴜᴄᴋ.

I jerked backward, but before I could do more, an imp appeared on the grass in front of me. If the one from Damon's garden had an older, meaner brother, this was it. Half again as tall and broader, not so spindly. But it shared the sickly white, grease-bruised skin and the mouthful of teeth.

And the aggression. It lunged at me, arms reaching.

I dodged, moving faster than I knew I was capable of. But apparently not fast enough. Its hand clamped around my arm, and rot and death choked me as its breath hit my face. I jerked back instinctively and, by some miracle, pulled my arm free. The imp stumbled back, caught off balance as my jacket came loose and my weight was no longer there. I pinwheeled my arms to stay on my feet, then started backing up as rapidly as I could without taking my eyes off the creature.

The imp hissed and flung the jacket away, then bounded forward, but it didn't reach me. Instead it was flung sideways by Damon tackling it to the ground.

The imp shrieked and swiped at him with a long-clawed hand. Damon yelped but didn't let go.

I froze, not sure what to do. I couldn't fry the damn thing when Damon was in the way. I needed a weapon to at least distract it. A gun would have been handy, but I didn't have one. What I did have was a rebar off-cut sticking out of the pile of construction junk in the front yard, the sensor lights from the house spotlighting it perfectly, about ten feet from where I stood.

I bolted, grabbed the bar, and ran back. The imp was starting to get the upper hand and had rolled on top of Damon, teeth glinting in the light. One thing nine months of renovating had done was improve my upper body strength. I smashed the bar down on its head. There was a sickening thud and crunch, and the imp collapsed.

Damon scrambled free and I grabbed his arm, pulling him to his feet. The imp hadn't moved. Was it going to wake up? But even as I lifted my hand, hoping like hell that I could summon the power to fry it again and could come up with a good excuse for a fire on my front lawn if any of the neighbors decided to report me, the imp vanished.

I stepped back, startled, relief sparking through me. But before I relaxed, common sense kicked in. Where there was one imp, there could be another. The ward around the house was still up, but after seeing the wards at the boundaries fail, I didn't have a lot of faith in them. At least not without Lizzie or someone else who knew what the hell they were doing there to reinforce them.

"We need to get out of here," I snatched my jacket from the grass, then grabbed his hand again and started for the car.

He didn't reply, but he didn't resist, and by the time we reached the car, his focus had snapped back. He flung open his door and slid behind the wheel. I staggered around to the passenger side and climbed in too. I'd barely pulled the door shut when Damon gunned the engine to life and we took off down the street.

I was twisted in the seat, staring out the rear windshield, making sure another imp hadn't appeared, but the lawn remained empty until Damon turned the corner and headed down the hill.

Then I started to shiver as the adrenaline crash hit me.

I closed my eyes and tried to remember how to breathe. How the hell had another imp found us? Or broken the wards? If I wasn't safe at home, then...

It didn't bear thinking about, and I forced my mind to go blank, to just not think. But Damon hitting the horn to warn another car out of the way as he drove like a bat out of hell shook me back to reality.

I was freaked out. But he'd tackled that damn thing. My eyes flew open. Fuck. Was he hurt? It didn't take long to spot the tear in his jacket; the nanohide had peeled away in a jagged gash. And there was blood on the blue shirt below it.

"It got you?" I said. "Shit."

Damon didn't take his eyes off the road. Just as well. According to the car's jet-engine suite of dashboard gauges, he was driving faster than it should have been possible to drive through Berkeley. "I'm fine."

"You're bleeding."

"It's not gushing. It's a scratch. I can hardly feel it."

I put that down more to adrenaline than reality. Sometimes it took your body time to catch up with an injury.

"Maybe you should let me drive."

That earned me a sideways glance. "Your hands are shaking."

"Shaking is better than bleeding." My hands tightened on the jacket in my lap as he overtook the car in front of us, coming a little too close for comfort.

"What's better is us getting to Riley."

"We're going to Riley?" I hadn't paid much attention to where he was headed other than registering we were going in the general direction of the bridge. "We should go back to Cassandra's. Or maybe a hotel like she said."

"You think we should go somewhere with lots of people? What happens if one of those things follows us?"

"Righteous has lots of people, too," I pointed out.

"Not where we're going. And not by this time of night. Everyone was busting their asses for months before the launch. They're under strict instructions to go home at a reasonable time for a few weeks at least, if they're not taking actual vacation."

Most of the people I'd met who worked at Riley adored their jobs to an unhealthy degree. And I'd worked plenty of late nights with them. I doubted all of them would obey an order. If Damon did a headcount, he might be surprised how many were ignoring his rules.

"No people at Cassandra's."

"She has neighbors. And we don't know if they're still there. Cassandra was going to talk to Ian and Radha. Riley is the best option. You can call Cassandra or Lizzie once we arrive."

I could keep arguing, but short of somehow wrestling control of the car from him, I didn't think

I'd be able to change his mind. Lizzie or Cassandra might know how to put a convenient whammy on him and make him do what I wanted, but I didn't. I'd done it once, accidentally when we were fighting the demon, and it hadn't ended well. And his ex-wife had manipulated him with magic. If he and I were to have any kind of friendship going forward, I could never use magic on him again without his permission.

I wriggled into my jacket, settled back into my seat and let him drive, still shivering despite the extra layer. I couldn't call Lizzie or Cassandra with my teeth chattering, so I focused on trying to calm down.

I wasn't sure whether he had some sort of "one of the richest guys in town" free pass with the SF police department, but no one stopped us as he sped through the city streets. We entered the Riley Arts campus by an entrance I wasn't familiar with, one on the opposite side of the swathe of city real estate that the company controlled to the main gate that I was used to. There was a guard and a gate that meant business, but the gate swung open as soon as Damon nosed his car toward it, and the guard didn't try to stop us.

We drove along one of the interior campus roads for a minute or so before pulling up in front of a small building I'd never seen. Which didn't mean anything in particular. I'd spent most of my time at

Riley in the main building where Damon's office was or the development lab suite where the Archangel team had been working, which was several floors underground.

The building was only two floors, and other than a dim light coming through the frosted glass of the front door, there were no lights in any of the windows.

Damon said, "Madge, it's me," and a panel beside the door slid open. He pressed his palm to it, and the door swung inward with a soft click. We stepped inside.

"Unidentified person in building, Mr. Riley," a soft female voice said.

I smiled, recognizing the voice of the computer system that ran the security for the development buildings. Apparently she did more than that. I started to say, "It's Maggie," but realized there was no reason for me to assume I was still in the system. Madge hadn't spoken to me when I'd been in Damon's office earlier in the week.

"Lachlan, Maggie Diana," Damon said. "Reinstate security clearance and palm/body/retina scan records."

"Please confirm," the voice, said and another panel on the wall closest to the door began to flash.

"Stay still," Damon said and walked to the panel. He pressed his palm against it, and the blink-buzz-flash red light of a body scan washed through the room. I wasn't sure if it was verifying him or me. The door swung shut with a decisive click. I stayed still. I didn't know anything about what security countermeasures Riley might employ, but I had no doubt some of them might be unpleasant.

"Your respiration rate is high, Damon," Madge said as he stepped away from the panel. "Do you require assistance?"

"I'm fine, Madge," he said, but he was holding his left arm close to his body.

"Very well," Madge said. "Please ask Maggie Diana Lachlan to place her hand on the scanner."

Damon beckoned me over, and I followed the instructions. There was another scan-buzz-flash.

"Verified. Welcome back, Maggie," Madge said. "Damon, Mitch has asked for notification when you return to campus."

"Negative," Damon said. "I'll contact him later. For now, no one knows I'm here. No one else is to enter this building. Full Bond mode."

I lifted an eyebrow at him. *Bond mode? Like 007?* My grandad had loved Bond movies. I was familiar with all the movies in the franchise, including the last few holo extravaganzas that he had insisted were nowhere near as fun as the old ones.

"Password?" Madge said.

"Vesper Lynd likes it shaken," Damon said.

I clapped a hand over my mouth so I wouldn't laugh.

"What's the point of having fancy voiceprint systems if you can't have some fun with it?" he muttered when a giggle escaped me.

"Some people never grow up," I said, grinning. "At least you didn't call Madge Moneypenny."

"Obvious is less fun."

"Bond mode. The building is secure," Madge said.

"Good," Damon said. "We'll be in Suite 1."

Madge didn't reply to that. Damon strode away. I followed. There was a single elevator door—matte black metal—across the foyer. It slid open when he touched the button.

Not unexpectedly, the elevator headed down. Like many companies, Riley favored underground secure locations these days. Underground rooms might get shaken around in a quake, but they didn't collapse. At least, that was the theory.

"Is this one of the employee accommodation buildings?" I asked. I knew Riley kept rooms and suites for employees on sensitive projects, executives visiting from other places, and the odd consultant they wanted to keep under wraps. Damon had wanted me to live on campus when I'd worked for him, but I'd refused. But I wasn't sure this building was simple living quarters; the security seemed over the top for that.

"No," he said. He didn't offer an explanation.

I followed him out of the elevator and through a

series of security checks and scans to arrive at another matte black door that Damon pushed open with his good hand. He had to push hard. The door was several inches thick, the kind of thing it would take a small bulldozer to get through. He was right. With all these layers of security, unless the imps were somehow locking onto Damon or me, then I doubted one would get anywhere near us.

"Okay, where exactly are we?" I asked. The room was small with blank white walls. A standard-issue Riley workstation big enough for two people stood against one wall, and there were two game chairs side by side in the middle of the room. Opposite the door we'd entered was another black door.

"It's a clean suite for testing," Damon said. "The system in here is completely isolated. It has its own server and internal network. It's not connected to the internet or any of our other networks. We use it for testing early versions or, lately, for testing any variations to our virtual reality generation code. In case of—" He waved his injured arm, then winced.

In case another demon decided to see if it could piggyback virtual reality to get to humans. I kind of wanted to wince, too. But better to focus on the more prosaic reason that Damon had.

"Does this place come with a first aid kit? You're hurt."

"Through here," he said. He led me through a

small basic kitchen, then farther down a short corridor toward a utilitarian bedroom containing a double bed neatly made up with a navy quilt and pillows. Next to the bedroom was a gleaming white bathroom with a shower, a basin over a cabinet, and a toilet. A white plastic and metal chair stood beside the cabinet, topped with a neat pile of fluffy white towels.

I put the towels on the floor and pointed at the chair. "Sit".

Damon didn't argue. He was cradling his left arm against his body and, I suspected, working hard not to let on just how much it hurt.

I opened the cabinets beneath the basin. Sure enough, a portable first aid kit was tucked on one of the shelves. I pulled it free and flipped it open.

Gauze, bandages, scissors, dressings, Band-Aids, antiseptic sprays and creams, tweezers, various painkillers, disposable gloves, safety pins. That should get me started. There was a bottle of saline solution and a plastic version of the kind of metal pan doctors used to hold supplies. There were other packets of other medications that I ignored for the moment. Get him cleaned up, and then we could call Cassandra and whoever else we needed.

"Let's take off your jacket."

Damon started to remove it but winced as the torn sleeve began to move down. I stepped closer and helped him ease it off. His breath hissed a little as I pulled it away.

"Maybe we should just skip to the part where we call Cassandra? Radha or someone should look at this," I said.

He shook his head. "It has to be cleaned up at some point. Just do it."

I took him at his word. Part of his sleeve was torn, too, and blood stained the navy. But there was less of it than I had feared, so maybe the wound wasn't too bad. I cut his sleeve away rather than trying to save it, schooling myself not to wince. Blood had never been my favorite thing. I'd gotten first-aid certified after the Big One, and I did refreshers, but thankfully I'd never had to use my skills on anything more difficult than patching myself or Lizzie up after a cut or scrape at home.

Three thin cuts scored down the flesh of Damon's inner arm, but they didn't look deep and were only oozing blood in patches, some parts already crusted over. Not the kind of thing that needed stitches. There'd been some butterfly strips in the kit; I could use those after I cleaned him up to make sure the cuts stayed closed until someone better qualified could look at them.

Damon glanced down at his arm and then turned his face to look straight ahead. I rinsed the wounds with saline, then gently cleaned them with the antiseptic. He stayed silent.

"You were right, it's not too bad," I offered. Which earned me only a grunt of agreement. I placed a couple of butterfly strips over the widest parts of the cuts, sprayed again with a different antiseptic that said it had a numbing action on the label, and taped a dressing over it. "How does that feel?"

"Better," he said.

"Wait here. I'll get you some water and you can take a couple painkillers."

"It's not that bad."

"You're probably still in shock. Wait until that wears off and you might just feel differently. Better to get on top of pain early."

When I got back with the water, Damon was still in the chair, his right hand rubbing his left shoulder.

"Is that sore?" I asked, heart going to my throat. I'd been so focused on his arm that I hadn't stopped to think he might have other injuries.

"A little," he admitted. I interpreted that particular bit of man speak as "Yes, it hurts."

"Scoot forward. Let me look."

He rolled his eyes but did as I asked. The back of his shirt was clean, no bloodstains at least. But that didn't mean no bruises or scrapes beneath it. He'd hit the ground hard.

"You're going to need to take that shirt off so I can see properly."

"Is anything bleeding?"

"Not that I can see."

"Then it's probably fine."

"Don't be a baby. Let me check, and then we'll be done."

"You just want to see me with my shirt off," he muttered.

"I can think of easier ways to get you to take your shirt off," I retorted, then blushed as he lifted an eyebrow at me.

"Oh, and what might those be?"

"Just take it off."

He reached his injured arm across to his right to pull the sleeve down and winced again.

"On second thought, let me take that off for you," I said. I stepped between his legs and started easing his right arm out of the Henley. That would give me access to his back without me having to try to wrangle the whole thing over his bad arm.

Damon went very still. Our heads hovered close together even though I was taking care not to touch the man anywhere I didn't have to. But being so close filled my head with the scent of him again, and it became very hard not to remember just how good his mouth had felt on mine. Which was a testament to just how stupid I was when it came to him. I was supposed to be checking him over, not checking him out.

I freed his arm as fast as I could, but leaning over to pull the shirt around to one side meant his head pressed against the side of my abdomen, and I swallowed hard at the sensation.

Imp attack, remember?

Right.

I studied his back. The skin was reddened in places, and there were, as I had suspected, grazes in a few spots. But there were no cuts, and nothing looked swollen in a way that might suggest he'd torn a muscle or cracked a rib or something. In fact, if you ignored the scraped skin, his back looked just as I remembered. A long reach of olive skin smoothed over muscles that told me he'd still managed to stay in shape while steering Riley back to success.

But I wasn't here to ogle the man. And I definitely wasn't going to stay leaning over him to clean those grazes up. That would just be asking for trouble. I eased myself away from him, bending to rummage in the first aid kit for more gauze and antiseptic

"You have some grazes. If you stand up, I'll clean them, and then we'll be done."

Fabric rustled as he followed my instructions. Which meant when I straightened, I was faced with a wall of pecs and abs.

"Turn around," I said a little too fast.

He stared down at me for a second, blue eyes darkened with an emotion I didn't care to name, before he turned.

I dabbed at the scrapes gently, working as fast as I could so he could put his shirt back on. "You're going to have some bruises tomorrow." Maybe not too bad if Lizzie or Cassandra needed to work some healing on him.

"Probably," he admitted. "But that's why they invented Tylenol."

Well, he could take plenty of that. I swiped the last of the grazes and stepped back, dropping the gauze into the small waste basket beside the cabinet. "You can put your shirt back on."

"You sure about that?"

I wasn't taking that bait. "Yes I'm sure. I can't see anything else that needs my attention." I busied myself with packing up the first aid kit so I wouldn't have to look at him, pretending I hadn't heard the note of invitation in his voice. Because, quite frankly, there was quite a bit of him that drew my attention. But no way in hell was I telling him that.

I gave him what I thought would be enough time to dress before I turned back. He was looking down at the sleeve I'd cut away.

"Sorry."

"Not a problem. I have plenty of shirts." He reached for his jacket.

"Actually, if you're going to put that back on, it might be better if I put a bandage over the dressing. Less chance of the jacket dragging on it."

"You're the boss," he said.

"Just remember that." I smiled at him as I unrolled one of the bandages and started wrapping his arm.

"Probably not the smartest thing you ever did," I said. "But thank you for doing it."

"You'd do the same for me. Well, in your own way. Please don't ever physically tackle one of those things on my behalf. Or on anyone's behalf."

I looked up. His face was serious, brows drawn down.

"I have no intention of doing that," I said.

"That's not the same thing as a promise not to."

"I try to make it a habit not to make promises I might not be able to keep," I said, trying for light-hearted but falling short as I realized it was true. I was back in this world now, and short of me pulling the kind of disappearing act my mother had, Cassandra wasn't going to leave me alone to stew in self-pity again. I had power. I owed it to everyone my demon had put at risk to at least learn to use it. And to help others who might face the same kind of problems one day.

If I ever learned what the heck I was doing.

A chill ran through me, and I almost lost my grip on the bandage.

"Maggie," he said softly. "You know, I didn't mean to be careless with you."

I flinched. I could tell he meant what he said. And worse, the way the words stung, made it even clearer that, despite what I'd said to him back by the taco truck, my feelings for the man, complicated and stupid and probably futile as they were, hadn't really gone away. And maybe as complicated and stupid and probably futile as they were, I should at least tell him.

I took in a breath. "You know in the movies how someone always has something big to tell someone important, but then, at the last minute, something happens to interrupt?" I pressed the tape down and he grunted.

"Yes."

"And then later, the someone important says something like 'Wait, you had something to tell me,' and the person says, 'It doesn't matter,' and because they didn't tell, lots of shit happens and one of them nearly always dies tragically?" I wrapped the bandage one last time and reached for the surgical tape to hold it in place.

"Yes," he said again, gaze not shifting.

"Let's not do that." I took another breath.

"Is there something you want to tell me?"

"I miss you," I said simply. "And I'm happy you didn't die today." Even as I said the words, the fear I'd felt came rushing back. Whether I'd reached the point in the day where I just couldn't deal any more or whether it was delayed shock, I didn't know, but suddenly the panic overwhelmed me, my throat closing and my heart going into overdrive.

I bent over, trying to breathe.

"Maggie?" Damon said, sounding alarmed.

I held up a hand, unable to speak.

"Shit," he muttered. "Listen to me. Listen to my voice. You're okay. It's okay. Just breathe." He kept murmuring to me, one hand rubbing my back. "Just breathe. It's okay."

It seemed to work, a little. I took another slow breath, the fear receding. But as it did, grief or something like it rushed in, and I started to sob.

Chapter Twenty

WHEN MY CRYING eased off to a level where I could think again, I was in Damon's lap, his arms around me. He was sitting back in one of the game chairs. I didn't remember him carrying me out of the bathroom, but apparently he had at some point while I was freaking out. He was still murmuring soft soothing reminders to breathe and that I was okay.

"Yes. I'm o-kay." The words hitched. I clamped my teeth shut.

"Have you ever had a panic attack before?" he asked, voice gentle.

"I had a couple after Nat," I admitted. "But not for months now."

"Okay." His tone didn't change, just stayed steady and calm. Which made me think he'd dealt with someone having an attack before. "Are you starting to feel better?"

"Sort of?"

His arms tightened. Guilt twinged as I remembered that one of them was currently held together with a bandage and Band-Aids. "Sorry."

"Nothing to be sorry about. But I think you need something to help you calm down. I can't offer you whiskey, and I know we don't stock anything strong in those first aid kits." He hesitated a moment. "I have another suggestion though."

"Which is?" I had Kleenex in my purse, which was abandoned somewhere on the floor back in the bathroom. I wiped my eyes with my fingers.

"The VR modules we use all have some basic relaxation modes."

I stiffened.

He murmured again and rubbed my back until I relaxed.

"I know you don't like VR," he said. "I understand why, and if I could do this the normal way, I would. But right now, that's not an option, and you need a breather. I need to know you're okay before we can figure out what we do next."

I stared at him, stomach twisting. There was nothing but concern in his eyes. I knew I could trust him, but...

"Virtual reality is not exactly what I associate with calm."

"I know. I understand. But you asked me to trust you, so I'm asking you to trust me. This system is safe. It's fully contained in this room. If we load something to it, it's brought in on a drive and side loaded. And it's checked every way we can before we do that." His voice was low and soothing, the voice of someone trying to coax a child into doing something that scared them. "There's no way anyone or anything has gotten into this system."

My breath hitched again as I released it slowly. He was right, of course. I needed something that would help me lose the lingering edge of panic. Besides, I needed to get over this fear. If I couldn't work with VR, my career would be dead in a few more years at most. As chips became more common and VR became more than just gaming, more and more systems would start to interface with humans that way. I'd already heard rumors about experimental systems that did. I hadn't seen one yet, other than at Righteous, but if I couldn't get over my fear, I'd be making myself obsolete.

"I don't want to play a game." My voice wobbled slightly.

"Not a game. Just relaxation."

If he'd really wanted to help me relax, he could at least have offered me a screaming orgasm or two.

I clamped down on that thought. Bad idea. *Very* bad idea.

I just wasn't sure it was as bad as letting my brain be hooked into a computer again.

I could almost hear my mother's laughter in my head. She'd never been big on giving in to fear. "Get tough or get trampled" had been one of the charming buds of wisdom she'd embedded in my head from the time I was old enough to toddle. Fear got short shrift. She'd gone after whatever—or whoever—she'd wanted. Granted, half the time what she wanted resulted in us having to leave town in a hurry, not to mention her bonding me to a demon, but maybe she'd been right in the basic philosophy. Being scared didn't matter. Doing something you needed to do whether or not you were scared did. Even Gran would have agreed with that one.

I tried to unclench my jaw. "Define relaxing."

"It would be easier for *you* to define relaxing. Let's start with something simple. Beach or mountains?"

Mountains meant woods. Trees. The first time I'd encountered my demon was in a wooded area in one of Damon's games. The second time was in real woods. If I was already pushing buttons by agreeing to use VR, it might be easier to take one fear at a time.

"Beach," I said firmly.

"California, Hawaii, Mexico, Caribbean, Pacific?"

I shrugged. "When I travel, it's usually for work. There's not much beach time involved. You choose."

"Okay." His arms tightened. "I'm going to put you on the other chair now."

I wriggled in his lap. "Your arm is hurt. You shouldn't be lifting me."

"Let me decide what my arm can handle." Before I could protest any further, he stood. My arms wrapped around his neck instinctively, and his grip tightened. I heard him suck in a quick breath, but then he moved and smoothly transferred me into the game chair, peeling my hands away.

"There." He stepped back. "Get yourself settled."

I looked down, scooting back in the chair, hoping the heat in my cheeks wasn't showing. The sensation of buttery soft leather under my hands and body was familiar enough to be soothing. I laid my head back and focused on keeping my breathing steady.

"Okay. I'm going to put the headset on you now." Damon's fingers were gentle. I closed my eyes, trying not to think about what I was about to do. He touched my right hand. "Lift your hand so I can open the control panel."

I obeyed. Something clicked, and then Damon pressed my hand down until it rested gently on a big button. "That's your kill switch," he said, "Right there under your palm. If you get scared or want out, just hit it, same as any other system. Go switch is just above it."

"Got it." I resisted the urge to wipe my palm on my jeans.

"I'll meet you in the lobby," he said. I listened as he settled into the other chair.

My hand hovered over the button as I fought down the squirming fear in my stomach once more. I didn't feel brave, but I wasn't going to let the fear win. I closed my eyes and hit the go switch.

I stood in a fairly standard VR lobby. White walls and floor and ceiling that varied slightly in shade to give the illusion of standing in an actual room. Damon was waiting for me. I hadn't seen his avatar since the very first night we met. Back then I'd thought it had to be idealized, but now I knew there wasn't really much difference between the man and the virtual version. Though here in game space, he didn't look tired or stressed. Which only made him more attractive. His avatar wore khaki shorts and a white tee shirt.

I looked down at mine, wearing my default black jeans and black tank. "Am I overdressed?"

His avatar grinned. "Well, if you wanted to dial up a bikini, I wouldn't argue, but without a chip, you're not going to feel the heat."

I glanced at his wrist, but the avatar didn't have a chip. "Are you using your chip?"

"Nope, just a headset, same as you."

That should have made me feel better, but it only pinged my guilt again. This was a moment of escape for him, too, but without his chip, he wouldn't get the full immersive experience, just sight and sound.

I didn't know what showed on my face, but he said, "It's okay, Maggie. I'm perfectly happy with a headset."

He stretched out one hand and made a downward gesture. A menu appeared in the air before him, and he typed something in. Keeping our destination a surprise rather than using voice commands. "Ready?"

I nodded.

The lobby faded out, and suddenly I stood on pure white sand rather than tile. The beach curved away on either side of me, the sand gleaming in the sunlight. The water was a shocking shade of tropical blue, almost unreal, stretching out into the distance before it deepened to a darker shade. The waves rolled in gently, curling into froths of white. Apart from a few seagulls riding the air currents above us, we were alone, only the sound of wind and waves breaking the silence.

"Where are we?"

"Whitehaven Beach, Australia. You like?"

"I do." As fake relaxation spots went, it was gorgeous. The sound of lapping water eased the tension in my spine.

"Good." Damon sat on the sand, leaning back on his hands. He closed his eyes and tipped his face up to the sun. Another benefit of a virtual beach. No need for sunscreen.

He just sat quietly, clearly not intending to talk unless I wanted to. I lowered myself beside him, staring at the water, focusing on the sea. Without a chip, I knew I wasn't really sitting on sand, but it was soothing just the same.

My breathing slowed down to the rhythms of the waves curling onto the sand and receding back again in sparkling coils of froth and sunlit water. The lingering edges of fear melted away. Ironic that the thing I was most afraid of had relaxed me faster than anything back in reality could.

Back there, since Nat died, I'd been too busy trying to keep myself busy to stop and be brave enough to just let myself breathe.

Maybe it was time to stop running. Running hadn't stopped the past catching up with my mother. And so far, it hadn't stopped it catching up with me either.

"That thing at the house," I said, still staring out at the waves. "It was coming for me, not you." Somehow it was easier to talk about the imp in here.

"Hard to tell. It could have been trying to go

through you to get to me. Or take you out to get to me."

I swiveled to face him. "I'm the more likely target. You don't have magic."

He shrugged and tossed a shell toward the water, where it landed with a gentle splash. "I have billions of dollars."

"Not sure demons are into extortion."

"Who says it's a demon? Cassandra said humans can summon imps. So it could be someone getting creative with an old-fashioned snatch-and-grab plot."

I opened my mouth to argue with him, then closed it. Fighting about it wasn't helpful when we had no idea what the truth was. If the imp was after me, then Damon would be safer if he got away from me, but if it was after him, then he was more vulnerable without a witch by his side. There was no way to know. Not unless Cassandra had figured out more about how these things were being summoned.

That was a problem for later. Now that I'd calmed down again, I wanted Damon to get checked out by someone who had more medical experience than me.

"We should log out and call Cassandra, get someone to look at your arm." I climbed to my feet. Even if this was a basic relaxation module, it was still detailed enough that my avatar's jeans were coated with sand, and I brushed at them without thinking.

He held out his good hand. "Help me up."

"If you need my help to stand, then I'm going to hit the kill switch and call Cassandra right now."

"Humor me," he said.

I reached out and took his hand. Without the benefit of a chip, I couldn't actually feel him, but there was something still weirdly intimate about holding his hand. I tugged at it and he stood, all the long lean length of him suddenly too close. I knew he was still safely several feet away from me, lying on the game chair next to mine, but my heart sped up anyway. I started to let go of his hand, but he tightened his grip.

"You know, we didn't finish the conversation we were having back there."

Now he brought that up? "I know. But I'm not sure there was much more to say." I'd told him as much as I was willing to tell him. As much as it was smart to tell him. I had to cling to a shred of common sense to protect my heart.

"I didn't get to answer you. Maybe I have something to tell you as well."

"You do?" I gazed up at him. His avatar was not quite him, but the eyes were the exact brilliant shade of blue they were in real life. The kind of clear skies and sunlit seas blue I just might get lost in. But I had to remember that really, sunlit seas could be home to the kinds of mythical creatures that tempted humans to madness in the name of love. That blue had certainly made me throw caution to the wind a time or three in the past. I didn't want to be dazzled again.

"I do," he said, expression intent.

"Something that doesn't fall under the definition of careless?" I asked, hoping to prevent him from saying the kind of thing my heart wanted to hear from him. The kind of thing I couldn't trust.

"It falls under the definition of honest. Does that count?"

"Honesty isn't always the best policy." I sounded breathless. Embarrassing.

"You said you didn't think we should leave things unsaid."

"Maybe I was wrong."

"No, you were right. I listened to you. And now you should listen to me."

"All right." I tugged my hand away. "But if you're going to say it, tell me in the real world. I want to hear it from you, not a bunch of electrons."

The quirk of the mouth the avatar gave me was so precisely Damon that I had to admire whoever it was who had put this particular bunch of electrons together. It was a damned good job. Knowing Damon, he may have even built it himself.

"Okay. Real world it is. See you there."

He blinked out of existence, leaving me alone

on the beach. Me and my big mouth. I could have stayed here sitting in peace, ignoring the world just a little longer. But I'd made my choice now. And part of me really wanted to know what he had to say.

I flexed my fingers in real life to hit the kill switch. The beach evaporated, and suddenly all I could see was the darkness behind my own eyelids. I opened them slowly and sat up, tugging the headset free.

Beside me, Damon was untangling himself as well. He was faster at it than me. When he finished, he swung his legs around to the right side of his chair and stood, offering me a hand up, the gesture the mirror of mine in the simulation.

If it had been hard to hold his hand in the simulation, it was near excruciating in real life. His fingers were warm and strong around mine, his thumb moving just the smallest fraction back and forth against my palm. Or maybe I was imagining that part.

Imaginary or not, the tiny caress was equal parts reassuring and just plain hot. What kind of idiot got hot and bothered from just holding the hand of a man who'd broken her heart? But I couldn't make myself let go. Instead, I stood there, rooted to the floor as firmly as though my feet were welded to the carpet somehow, my heart so loud in my ears that he had to be able to hear it.

"What did you want to tell me?" I was impressed that I managed to get the words out.

"I've missed you, too," he said.

And then toppled sideways.

I lunged for him, but he was bigger and heavier than me, and all I really managed to do was make sure he landed a bit more gently on the floor before I barely managed to avoid landing on him.

I dropped to my knees, feeling frantically for a pulse. It was there but seemed too fast.

What the hell was going on?

And where was the damned panic button when I needed one? The fancy one inbuilt in Damon's chip was no use to me when only he could set it off. But surely it would have some sort of backup for a situation just like this, something that reported back if his vitals went weird?

Then my brain kicked back into gear. "Madge," I yelled. "We need some help in here."

"Damon gave the 'do not disturb' order," Madge said. "Is there an emergency situation?"

"Maggie, your boss is currently passed out on the floor. Call Mitch. Or someone."

There was a buzz/flash tingle. Another body scan.

"Confirmed. Assistance will be on the way, Maggie. Please remain where you are."

Like I was going anywhere.

I rolled Damon onto his side and made sure his

breathing seemed okay, trying not to freak out all over again. Madge would send help.

But maybe she couldn't actually provide the kind of help he might actually need. I had to call Cassandra.

My datapad was back with my purse in the bathroom. I practically levitated as I sprinted to grab it.

I told the pad to call Cassandra while I was still running back to Damon.

"Maggie?" Cassandra said, sounding slightly sleepy. "Is something wrong?"

"I'm at Righteous. Damon just collapsed. There was another imp at my house. It scratched him. It didn't look bad, and I cleaned it up and he seemed fine—"

"Another imp? Like the first?" She didn't sound sleepy now.

"Yes. Sort of. Bigger."

"When was this?"

I looked at the datapad. It was getting close to midnight. "Nine, nine thirty, maybe?" I said. I hadn't been paying strict attention to the time when Damon drove me home.

"And you're only just calling now?"

I heard a rustle as though she was climbing out of bed.

"We were kind of busy getting out of there," I said. "And then—Look, I'll explain it all when you get here. But get here. Bring Radha or whoever you think can best help him. I'll make sure his security team don't freak out too much until you can get here." I ended the call. "Madge, do you have security clearance on file for Cassandra Tallant? And Lizzie Reagan?" Hopefully my own clearance was high enough that she would answer the question for me.

"Yes," Madge said. "They both have existing high access clearance."

"Good. One or both of them will be arriving on campus soon. Please make sure they're admitted and brought to wherever Damon is at that time."

"Acknowledged," Madge said. There was another buzz and flash. "Damon's vitals are unchanged. Is he still unconscious?"

"Yes."

"Security team ETA is approximately three minutes."

Great. I had three minutes to come up with a plan to make sure Mitch didn't get stubborn about all of this and airlift Damon to the nearest hospital.

All I could do was bluff my way through it.

I checked Damon's pulse again and prodded him a few times. "Wake up, damn it."

He remained stubbornly unconscious.

"Not helpful," I muttered at him.

Lacking smelling salts or any desire to try to wake him with magic when I was clueless about how to do that safely, I just had to sit there, trying to work out what could have caused his collapse. There was no sign of blood on the bandage over his arm, so I didn't think it could be blood loss. Unless he had internal bleeding? But I'd seen no evidence of a blow hard enough to cause that sort of damage. The imp had been big, but not bigger than Damon, and they'd been rolling on grass.

My gut told me his collapse was magical, not medical. Not that that was necessarily the better option.

"The security team is at the outer doors," Madge said. "Mr. Fields and Mr. Angelico are incoming. Should I admit them?"

I didn't have much choice on that. I couldn't help Damon on my own. And I was pretty sure Mitch would find a way to get into the building by hook or by crook if the alternative was leaving his apparently injured boss alone in here with me. So I had to let them in. And then make sure they didn't toss me out.

Chapter Twenty-One

"How long has he been like this?" Mitch demanded as he marched through the door.

"Not long," I snapped back. "I called for help as soon as it happened."

The look he shot me suggested he didn't believe me.

"I know you don't like me, but give me credit. If I meant him harm, I wouldn't have called for help, would I?"

Mitch grunted, busy doing the same sorts of things I had, checking Damon's pulse and shaking him gently to see if he would wake up. "What happened to his arm?"

"There was another...incident."

That earned me a look of fury. "And you didn't tell us? Ajax, how long on the doc?"

"She said about ten minutes," Ajax said. "Should we move him to the clinic?"

"Until we know what's going on, it's safer to leave him here," I said. "His breathing is fine, and his pulse is stable. Cassandra is on her way, too. She'll bring a healer with her."

"You didn't have authority to call her," Mitch growled.

"Damon trusts Cassandra. And if this has anything to do with the things that have been going on, then you need magical help, not just medical."

"I think you'd better start telling me what happened," Mitch said, straightening.

"We tangled with another imp. At my house. It went for me, Damon intervened. That's when it clawed his arm."

Mitch glanced back down at Damon.

"It's not a bad wound. More like scratches," I added.

"Scratches don't usually result in people passed out on the floor. Keep talking."

"We got away. We came here. I cleaned up Damon's arm, and then we...well, we both needed to calm down a bit, so we sat in the VR here for a while. Not long."

"He collapsed after the VR?" Ajax asked, looking alarmed.

"Yes. But I don't think it was that. There wasn't anything like the times weird things happened to me in a game. No weird noises or anything." Still, the thought was sending a chill down my spine. "Damon said this system was isolated. All we did was sit on a beach."

"Whitehaven?" Mitch asked absently. "He likes that one."

I nodded. "But I'm fine. If there was something in the system, it would affect both of us. Which is why you need Cassandra and whoever she brings. I know Dr. Chen is great, but she won't be able to help if it's not just physical.

"Magic," Mitch grimaced. "More trouble than it's worth."

I agreed but wasn't going to tell him that. "Right now it might be just what Damon needs."

"Can't you heal him?" Ajax asked. He was staring down at Damon, eyes wide.

"No." I shook my head. "When it comes to all of this, I'm a relative newbie. I'm not trained in healing magic, so anything I tried could do more harm than good."

"All right," Mitch said. "Madge, Ajax is going to wait in the lobby to let Doc Chen in when she arrives. Or Ms. Tallant and her associates if they get here first." He stood, then looked up at one of the cameras in the room.

"Yes, Mitch," Madge said as Ajax disappeared out the door. "Do you require any further assistance?"

"No, thank you." He turned back to me. "I didn't get a notification that you two were here. I take it that was Damon?"

"He didn't want to put anyone else in the path of the imps," I said. "He figured this place was more secure than a hotel even though it might be more predictable that he would come here. You were his next call after we'd had a chance to talk to Cassandra."

"Always was a stubborn pain in my ass," Mitch said, shaking his head. "Doesn't always take my advice."

"He's in charge. He has to trust his own instincts." I said. "Besides, if he'd listened to you, I wouldn't have been with him in his garden today. He could be dead."

"Or you could be doing a very long play where that's a way to win back his confidence," he said.

"Why do I need to win back his confidence? I haven't spoken to him for months. I don't need his money. I get paid very well for what I do. I'm not a crazed Righteous groupie. If I was, I wouldn't have gone away quietly when he broke up with me. I know it's your job to protect him, and I respect that, but this is all going to be a lot easier if you decide that he's right about me and that someone else is behind this. If only to make sure you're looking in the right places."

"Do you have any idea where those right places might be?" Mitch said.

"Whoever it is knew about him and me to target me in the way they did. And they're tech savvy. And they know about magic, judging by their preferred methods of attack. Any witches on staff here?" Somewhere as big as Riley had to have at least a few staff with some level of power unless they were actively trying to recruit people without magic. And people could still lie. True, only a small percentage of the population had power, but Righteous had something like fifteen thousand employees. There had to be some with power. Or who knew people who did.

"You really think it's someone who works here?"

I threw up my hands. "Do we really need to have this conversation again?"

His mouth twisted. "We vet people well."

"You vet them well when they start. But people can change." Or be changed. But no. Damon told me they'd hunted down all the beta testers and helped them. I stared down at him. The last time I'd seen someone collapse, it had been Nat, bleeding out. My breath caught suddenly.

Mitch looked at me sharply. "Are you sure you're okay?"

"It's—"

"Dr. Chen has arrived," Madge announced, cutting me off. I made myself back away from Damon. The doctor would need room to check him out.

Ellen Chen looked much the same as the last time I'd seen her. Her dark hair was cut into a sharp short bob now, but her expression was calm and professional as always. She spared me a quick glance, curiosity clear in her brown eyes before she bent to Damon.

"What happened?" she asked as she took his wrist in one hand, putting a medical bag down beside him.

Mitch started in with a rapid-fire description of events before I could get started. Ellen nodded and made "keep going" noises as she examined Damon. She wrapped a pressure cuff around his arm. She reeled off a series of figures, and Madge said, "Noted, Dr. Chen. Consistent with normal vitals."

Damon didn't move through any of it. I concentrated on the rise and fall of his chest, willing myself not to freak out again. Dr. Chen needed to focus on him, not deal with me having a panic attack.

Apparently satisfied with the results she was getting, the doctor turned her attention to Damon's arm. "What did you put on this?" she asked me as she started to unwind the bandage.

"Just what was in the first aid kit in the bathroom. Saline and antiseptics."

"Painkillers?"

"Just Tylenol."

"Okay." She studied the wound. "No obvious signs of infection, and his temp is normal. Other than the fact that he's nonresponsive, I can't find anything out of the ordinary. I'll take some blood, but this is all I can do without moving him to a hospital and consulting with a healer." She looked at me. "I understand there has been a magical...incident?"

"Yes. And there's a healer on the way. Several, in fact."

That had her dark brows lifting. "Who?"

"Cassandra Tallant." If Ellen knew anything much about magic, she may know Cassandra. Or Radha.

"All right. I'd still be happier if we at least moved him to the medical suite, but we'll wait and see what the healers say."

She peered up at me. "You look pale, too. Are you all right? Last time I saw you, you had the wobbles after using a VR system."

"I'm fine. It wasn't the system. It wasn't like Archangel."

"I can check—"

"Cassandra Tallant has entered the campus," Madge interrupted. "She will be directed here. She has two companions. Reagan, Lizzie has clearance. Morgan, Radha does not."

"Grant her temporary clearance," Mitch said. "Tonight only, unless I say otherwise."

"Registered. They will be here shortly."

"Go wait at the door again," Mitch said to Ajax, who was hovering in the background.

Ajax frowned but turned and left.

I sat on the game couch closest to the door, figuring if I was there, I was taking up less floor space. The room wasn't huge, and it was going to start feeling crowded with seven people in it.

Cassandra entered the room first, her gaze raking over all of us before she focused on Damon. Radha was close on her heels. The two of them exchanged a look and then went to join Ellen. Lizzie came in with Ajax. She looked at the crowd around Damon and came to stand by me instead.

"You've been having quite the day," she said quietly.

"Tell me about it," I said.

Lizzie tucked her arm through mine. She was shorter than me, but it was comforting to lean into her. "He'll be okay. Radha will be all over it. And if she doesn't know what to do, she'll call in one of the other healers."

Radha was already kneeling by Damon, both hands resting lightly on his arm, bracketing the ends of the wound. Her eyes closed, her forehead wrinkling slightly in concentration. Ellen was typing something into her datapad.

Ajax moved over to where Lizzie and I stood. "Should I call for an ambulance?"

Lizzie shook her head. "Not yet. If Radha can handle this, then no point moving him. And easier for you guys to keep the security tight." She smiled up at him, then tugged on my arm. "How about you and I go out in the hall? You can tell me a bit more about what happened at the house?.

"I don't want—"

She tugged harder. "He's fine, Maggie. They'll call us if they need us or if he wakes up. Let's give them a bit more space to work. You can tell me what happened."

Meaning she really wanted to talk about the imp. Preferably out of Ajax and Mitch's earshot. Not that it was really out of their earshot when Madge was listening in. I doubted my clearance was high enough to tell her not to snoop, so we'd just have to live with it.

Lizzie took me back to the break room/kitchen and told me to sit. She grilled me about the imp while she busied herself making tea from the well-stocked cabinets. She loaded one mug with sugar and handed it to me.

"You're too pale." She sat opposite me, another mug cradled in her hands. "Did you have a panic attack?"

I grimaced. Lizzie was the only other person who knew I had them. She'd even seen me once. "What makes you ask that?"

"You have that look. Wild around the eyes, sort of. And your aura is jittery."

"Two imp attacks in half a day. I'm allowed to be jittery."

She nodded. "Sure, but you're also allowed to admit if you had a panic attack. There's nothing wrong with having them."

I sipped tea. Then sighed. "I thought I was done with them."

"Well, if anything was likely to trigger them again, it would be this." She made a vague gesture. "Back at Righteous, dealing with magic, dealing with Damon." Her head tilted. "Why did you come here?"

"Damon was driving. He chose here. He said a hotel had too many people."

"You could have come back to Cassandra's."

"I told him that. He wanted to come here. He was pretty freaked out. I guess this is where he feels safe." Something suddenly occurred to me. "I think the wards on the yard went down. Shouldn't you have felt that somehow?" I didn't know entirely how the wards worked, but I would have expected them to have some sort of magical intruder alert like the housecomp would send me if someone broke in.

Lizzie's mouth flattened. "It should have. It didn't. Which is a concern. So tell me exactly what happened. The imp didn't attack Damon, it went for you first?"

I nodded. "Yes. I was closer to where it appeared, but it made no effort to get around me and get to Damon. It attacked me straightaway. Of course, it could have been under orders to take me out to get to Damon after what happened at his house."

She nodded. "That's a possibility. And it just vanished after you hit it?"

"Yep. Disappeared the same way it appeared. Do they usually do that?" Before tonight, every encounter I'd had with an imp had ended with dead imps.

Lizzie tapped her fingers on the mug. "They can move around that way. It takes a lot of energy from what we can figure out. Harder for the smaller ones, but as they get bigger—or smarter, at least—they have more skills of their own to help whoever is moving them around. At least, we think so. Some of them might just do it on their own."

"We don't know for sure?"

"Not many witches get a chance for cozy chats with imps or lesserkind. There have been a few witches, of course, who we've taken away from demons over the centuries. But generally at that point they're not very coherent. And they get executed if found guilty of consorting with a demon voluntarily. If they survive the demon stone. I've read a lot of the books in the archive. Big on descriptions and some sort of classification but a bit lacking in any real insight." She pushed her mug around the table for a moment. "Fortunately, we're mostly dealing with humans doing bad magic on their own rather than toying with demons."

"Until I came along."

"We live in interesting times," Lizzie said blandly. "None of this is your fault."

"Will they use demon stone on Damon?" I asked.

"Radha might be able to read him," she said. "It's unlikely an imp could have forged a connection from just a wound. They'll check him out."

"This one looked like the one at his house. Taller but pretty close. The book in the archive said contagion. Could that be it?"

It was Lizzie's turn to grimace. "That will fall under the category of 'we'll have to wait and see.' Cassandra and I went looking for more about imps and infection, but so far we haven't found anything that gives us much to go on. There have been cases of imps spreading sickness in the past. So Dr. Chen can pump him full of antibiotics and antivirals and we'll see what happens. Was there anything weird about the wound?"

"No, it was clean. And Doc Chen said his temp was normal."

"Well, that's good." Lizzie frowned. "Damon's

not wrong about the archive. This would be a lot easier if we could do a search digitally."

"Maybe he'll convince Cassandra," I said.

She smirked. "Sounds like you think he's sticking around. What was he doing taking you home?"

"He was giving me a lift. Nothing more." I gulped tea, trying not to think about the kiss. Or his almost confession. Time enough to worry about that once the man was awake. "Stop matchmaking. We have bigger problems than my love life."

"Maybe. Your love life is a pretty big mess," Lizzie said, but then she relented. "All right, a subject for another time. Shall we go back to panic attacks?"

I groaned. "Can we not? I feel okay now. Damon made me sit on a beach in VR for a while. It worked."

Her mouth fell open. "VR calmed you down?"

"Is that a bad sign?" I asked.

She blinked, then shook her head, bangs bouncing. "I'd say it's progress. You used to enjoy gaming. I know it reminds you of Nat, but she loved VR. She wouldn't want you to never play again, would she?"

She'd made this point to me before. Then, I hadn't really wanted to listen to her. But now, well, maybe she wasn't completely wrong. Nat would definitely want me to game. In fact, if there was such a thing as ghosts, she was probably haunting me right now just to be back in Righteous. But I'd never been the gamehead she was and nowhere near as good as she'd been. But my geek heart found what Righteous did fascinating, and the technology they were creating—and the potential it had beyond games—even more fascinating. I was reluctant to cut myself off from being part of that world forever. So I had to get over my fears.

That was beginning to be a theme. I'd been hiding away. Apparently rejoining the real world was going to be more of a rip-the-Band-Aid-off process rather than baby steps if this week was anything to go by.

"We didn't game, we just sat on a beach."

"Was he wearing speedos?" Lizzie waggled her eyebrows suggestively.

"Everyone kept their clothes on," I said, but my mouth twitched.

"Pity. But you doing some VR sunbathing is a step in the right direction, at least."

"Perhaps. But that step is a long way from being all the way in. And who knows if I could even have a chip again." Damon might be full of confidence about his new technology, but that didn't mean it would work.

Lizzie cocked her head. "Would you get one if it was safe?"

"The tech is heading that way," I said. "I'll be obsolete if I can't make the leap."

"Speaking of tech," she said, "Yoshi called me earlier to check in."

"Crap." I'd completely forgotten about him. "I suck. I should have called him."

"Will you have more work for him?"

"The kid has skills," I said. "And good instincts. And I'd like to help him out. So I'll think of something. Of course, what he needs is to go to school. I mean, I assume he's not?"

Lizzie shook her head. "He got through high school. Aced everything. But college...we probably could have wrangled him a scholarship. The charity has connections, but he balked. Never have quite gotten it out of him why."

"Did you meet him through the charity?"

"Yes," she said.

I didn't press. Yoshi could tell me his story one day himself if we continued working together. But Lizzie worked with kids from some pretty messed-up backgrounds. Kids who'd ended up on the street. "Does he have family?"

"A sister. She's with a foster family now, finishing high school. Next year is her last year. They're good people. They would have taken him in, too, but once he finished school, he said he wanted to do things for himself. I think he doesn't trust anyone else, deep down."

I knew how that felt. I'd had trust issues of my own, thanks to my mother. But I was thirteen when she died, and I'd started living with my grandparents. Their love had gone a long way to rebuild my faith in humanity. It didn't sound like Yoshi had anything like that. Not really. So I wouldn't let him down.

"I'll call him. Get him to come in once all this is sorted out. I don't want him mixed up in this." I paused. "He doesn't have any magic, does he?"

Lizzie shrugged. "Not that he's ever told me. He has an interesting energy field, but that could mean any number of things. Would it matter to you if he did?'

"Of course not."

"What about Damon?"

"Damon doesn't get to choose who I work with. And if—and this is a big if—we have any sort of friendship after we get to the bottom of what's going on, he's going to have to put on his big-boy pants and get over his thing with magic, isn't he? I mean, if I can do VR, he can do witches. Or he can just go away again."

That thought had my fingers tightening around my mug.

Lizzie looked like she wanted to say something, but Cassandra appeared in the doorway.

"He's awake," she said. "We need to figure out what happens next."

Chapter Twenty-Two

WHAT HAPPENED NEXT involved Mitch insisting that Damon should go to the hospital. Dr. Chen looked as though she'd be in favor of that particular option, too, but Radha and Cassandra stood firm.

"Hospitals are hard to secure," Cassandra said, echoing my earlier arguments.

"And he's not actually sick," Radha added. She turned to Ellen. "Did you find anything that gives you immediate concern?"

"He fainted and wouldn't wake up," Ellen said. "I'd be happier if he had an MRI."

"His brain seems fine," Radha said. "His energy fields are normal, other than being a little low, which is consistent with him being tired. I can't sense any infection. Or anything else."

What exactly did that mean? No demon taint? I

glanced at Cassandra, but she shook her head slightly. Apparently we weren't going to be discussing the magical nitty-gritty in front of the civilians.

"Do I get a say?" Damon asked. He was lying on the game couch he'd used earlier, looking somewhat exasperated.

"No," said Mitch.

"Overruled," Damon said. "If a hospital isn't needed right now, then I think staying here, or in one of the other suites, is a better option. I don't want to be poked and prodded any more tonight. We can do whatever tests you want tomorrow, Ellen, but right now, I think everyone should just go to bed. We can keep a suite here more secure than the hospital."

"We can't necessarily keep one of those things out," Mitch said.

"I can take care of that," Cassandra said. "There are things we can do. Short of there being another trigger spell, he'll be safe."

I hoped that was true. The imp had appeared at my house despite the wards. But maybe that was just a fluke. "I'll stay with Damon," I said without thinking. Then felt myself start to blush as Lizzie snorted. "I mean, it makes sense. We still don't know if those things want him or me. Splitting us up just splits the resources in trying to keep them out."

Cassandra nodded. In the harsh light of the

game room, she looked tired, too, not even the bright red sweater she wore distracting from the shadows under her eyes. Normally she exuded energy that meant I never thought of her as old, but tonight, I was aware that she carried more years than the rest of us. "I can't argue with that logic." She turned to Mitch. "And you have ample evidence that Maggie knows what to do if we hit the worst-case scenario and something gets through."

Damon's gaze was fixed on mine. "If Maggie is going to stay, then we should move to another suite. They're more comfortable, and we need somewhere with two bedrooms."

The weight of his eyes on me made my blush deepen. I had the feeling one bedroom would be just fine with him. But it seemed safer to blame that on him having hit his head.

Eventually he turned his gaze to Mitch. "How about the suites near building twelve? They're the most secure."

Mitch nodded. "I'd agree they're our best bet." He turned to Ajax. "You go over there, do a sweep, check everything out. Call me when you're all set."

"I'll go with him," Lizzie said. "I can do our sort of sweep. Radha, maybe you should check Maggie out, too. Just in case." She raised her eyebrows at me as though daring me to object. If I did, I was sure she'd just rat me out to Cassandra about the panic attack. I stayed silent.

Cassandra nodded. "That's a good idea. I want to talk to Maggie, too."

Oh joy. I closed my eyes a moment, suddenly exhausted. The thought of a lecture from Cassandra was a step too far.

"I'll go back to the clinic and grab some things, take them over to the suite, just in case they're needed later," Dr. Chen said. I opened my eyes again. "Maggie, I'll send you some details about things to watch for with Damon and the medications I'll leave for him." She fixed Damon with a stern gaze. "I'd give you a sleeping tablet if I was happier that you had no head injury. But I can't do that. So I'll just tell you that you need to rest. Both of you, by the look of you. Get some sleep, and we'll talk again in the morning."

She and Ajax and Lizzie left the room together.

"Maggie, why don't you take a seat on the other game chair?" Radha said. "Let me take a look at you."

I did as she asked, somewhat amused that she knew what a game chair was. I had a hard time picturing her running around a virtual world killing monsters. She was always so elegant and contained. But what did I know? Maybe that was how she blew off steam so she could be elegant and contained.

Radha took my pulse, then bent to look in my eyes. She made a displeased sort of humming sound, then rested her hands on either side of my head. "Close your eyes."

I obeyed, concentrated on breathing. There was a tingling sensation, as though I'd brushed up against something full of static, that rapidly dissolved into something more soothing, like a mild warm breeze traveling over my skin.

It melted away slowly. I opened my eyes again.

"Fatigue, mostly," Radha said, talking to Cassandra. "She used a lot of power, and she's out of practice." She looked at me. "Sleep would be best for you, too." She raised an eyebrow. "But it's getting late already, and tomorrow will be busy. So I can give you an energy boost for now. Don't use it as an excuse to sit up all night."

I didn't think there'd be much chance of that. The prospect of crawling into bed was pretty enticing. But then Radha laid her hands on me again. This time the sensation that swept through me was more like a jolt of adrenaline. The good kind, if there was such a thing. My fatigue vanished as though I'd just had twelve hours' sleep. Now *that* was a trick that could come in handy. I wondered if I could learn to do it for myself.

I smiled, and Radha said, "I mean it. You still need to rest even though you might not feel like it. Otherwise you'll just crash even harder. Probably at an inconvenient time. You hear me, Maggie?"

"Yes," I said meekly, but almost immediately I found myself on my feet, the urge to move strong.

"I'll have what she's having," Damon said, sounding exhausted.

"You'll get sleep," Cassandra said. "Mitch, how much longer do you think it will take for Ajax to do his sweep? How far is this other building?"

"About five minutes away," Mitch said. "It'll take him maybe thirty minutes to do a thorough sweep. How long will Lizzie need?"

"About the same," Cassandra said. "Which means there's time for tea." She rummaged in her huge purse and pulled out a small metal canister. "Maggie, come help me. I think I saw a kitchen back there."

I nodded. I'd had tea with Lizzie, but clearly Cassandra wanted to talk to me alone.

I showed her the kitchen and watched as she sniffed at the lack of a teapot.

Undeterred, she pulled a couple of tea infuser balls out of her bag—making me wonder exactly what else she was carting around in it—and set the kettle to boil.

"Was there something you wanted to ask me?" I said.

"No, I'm sure Lizzie will fill me in about what happened."

O-kay, then. I wasn't sure why she'd dragged

me out here. "Do you think we'll find who's doing this?"

"Two attacks in one day," Cassandra said. "I don't think we'll have to try very hard. I'm not sure exactly what's set all of this off all of a sudden, but whoever is behind it all seems to be in a hurry. So if you find Radha's boost means you're not sleepy, I suggest you read that book I gave you. Start with the parts on shielding."

She turned back to the kettle as it began to beep. I got the message. Homework. And the pop quiz in the morning could be life or death.

"What are you reading?" Damon's voice was soft and slightly scratchy.

I jumped and shielded the light coming from my datapad. "Just something Cassandra gave me." I put the book down. "Do you feel all right? Do you need anything?"

"What time is it?"

The room was mostly dark, but I could still make out the outline of his body as he shifted under the sheets, propping himself up on his good arm.

"Late," I said. It had been after two when I'd last checked the time. After we'd been moved to the suite and Cassandra and Lizzie set up wards to reinforce

Riley's security systems, Cassandra sent Damon off to bed with a touch of something I had to assume was the opposite of what Radha had given me by the way he'd started yawning as soon as she'd finished.

He'd already fallen asleep by the time I'd shooed everyone out and gone to check on him. I, silly as it was, hadn't wanted to leave him alone. So I'd settled myself into the armchair in the corner of the bedroom he'd chosen and started reading about magic again.

It was tempting to try some of the spells, but I didn't want Damon to wake up because I accidentally set off the wards or something worse. I read about shields as Cassandra suggested, which made my brain hurt a little as I tried to follow the theory. Then I'd skipped around, looking for stuff that sounded interesting. Like how to give someone the sort of nudges Cassandra had given Damon. Or the opposite. How spells could be connected or pulled apart. Of course, the knowledge was, at this point, purely theoretical, but I couldn't deny it held my interest. Or at least distracted me from Damon's sleeping form and the sneaking temptation to lie down beside him.

"How late?" Damon asked.

"Three, maybe? Go back to sleep."

He ignored me. "What are you doing up?"

He didn't ask me what I was doing in his room,

which was a relief. I wasn't entirely sure I could explain my decision.

"Just checking on you. I didn't mean to wake you. So go back to sleep."

"I've *been* sleeping," he pointed out.

"I'm pretty sure Radha was aiming for you to get at least eight hours rather than two or three."

"Well, she should have given me the good drugs, then."

He sounded grumpy. Was his arm hurting? "Doc Chen left painkillers. I can get them for you."

"No. Nothing hurts. I'm just awake. It's not that unusual these days."

"You haven't been sleeping well?" When we were together, he'd slept like a log—well, apart from the hours he'd spent giving me world-class orgasms. And with him beside me, even my insomnia had eased off. The thought of him not sleeping well made me weirdly sad.

"I sleep okay. There's just been a lot to do. Not enough hours in the day."

I couldn't see his face clearly, so I didn't know if that was the truth. I mean, I knew the man threw himself tirelessly into his work. You didn't build what he had without that. But even masters of the universe needed sleep. "Well, there's still hours left in this day."

"I'll sleep if you sleep," he said.

I hesitated. I wanted him to sleep but was reluctant to leave him alone. Sure, I could go into another room for a while until he went to sleep again, then resume my now not-so-secret vigil, but even that made me feel uneasy. Which was probably just me being paranoid, but there it was.

Sometimes it was better to go with instinct.

"I'll sleep later," I said. "You sleep now."

"I'll sleep if you come lie beside me, at least," he said. "That chair can't be comfortable."

I froze, forgetting how to breathe for a moment. He wanted me to *what*?

My brain stuttered back into gear. "I don't think that's a very good idea."

"If you come lie down here, I can tell you what I was going to say."

It took me a moment to make the connection. He meant what he'd been going to tell me before he'd so inconveniently collapsed. My skin prickled to life with a combination of nerves and heat. I wanted to know what he had to say. I also wanted to run before he could.

"How about you tell me first, then we'll see?" I countered.

He chuckled softly. "No. I want to be able to see your face when I tell you. You're just a gray blob over there."

"I'll turn the lights on," I said.

"Well, then I'll be wide awake."

I rolled my eyes even though he couldn't see me. "Are you five?"

"No," he said. "But this day has been, as Benji or Eli would say, jagged up, and quite frankly painful, and yet through it all, the one good thing has been that you've been here with me. I know how you feel about...us. I respect it. But even if we can only be friends, can't you be my friend right now and come here and hold my hand against the dark?"

His voice was both rough and wistful, and it appealed to a part of my brain that had nothing to do with reason, tugging straight on my heart, easing the part of it that had ached since we'd been apart. "If I lie down on that bed with you, that's all that's going to happen," I said.

"Maggie, I'm not sure I have the energy to do anything more exciting than that, even if you wanted me to."

I wasn't sure I trusted that. But I wanted to believe him. I'd spent a lot of sleepless, lonely nights with an empty bed. No warm solid male body to reach out and wrap his arms around me and pull me close. And maybe this wasn't that, but in the darkness and the strangeness of it all, I knew I was going to give in. Just for a few hours, maybe I could lie beside him and pretend everything was okay again.

"All right," I said softly. I put the datapad down, laying it on top of the book, and slipped off my boots. The rest of my clothes I left on. That seemed like another layer of reminders that I had to be smart when it came to Damon.

I walked around the bed and eased myself down onto the mattress.

"Lie down," he said softly.

Damn the man. He could probably tempt an angel into breaking into hell for him.

I swung my leg up and around and inched closer to him, almost holding my breath, as though I was expecting the mattress to catch fire or something. I stopped when our bodies were maybe twenty inches apart. Close enough to be safe. To keep my grip on sanity.

Damon had kicked off the blankets at some point when he was sleeping, leaving him covered only with a sheet. I hadn't wanted to risk waking him, so I hadn't picked the covers back up. Now I was regretting that choice, all too aware that nothing but a thin layer of cotton separated me from his bare chest and, well, what I hoped were the usual boxer briefs he slept in.

"Happy now?" I asked softly.

"Happier," he said.

My eyes had adjusted to the darkness, and I could make out the lines and angles of his face and the whites of his eyes as he watched me. At least the color was darkened to a shade of gray. No blue to lure me in. But then, gray had its own dangers. Too many layers and shades of it between us. Too many memories and missteps and fractures.

I should remember that and stay safely where I was. But I couldn't resist asking, "What was it you were going to say?"

He took a long breath. "Where did I get to?"

"You said you missed me." The answer came fast and certain, and I flinched a little, knowing the fact that I remembered it so clearly meant it had hit closer to home than I wanted it to.

"Ah." The sound was half a sigh, accompanied by a rustle and slide of cotton over skin as he moved slightly in the dark. The air smelled like him, and I could sense the heat of his body, so close. Still so far. Out of limits.

"I did miss you," he said softly. "I do miss you. And I'm sorry. For what I did. Leaving you that way. That was a dick move."

"You told me the truth."

"Maybe," he said. "Or maybe I was just running."

"Ah," I said, echoing him. "I know a little about that." Running for my life. Running from pain. Running from things had never really gotten me anywhere that I wanted to be.

And suddenly I knew I wanted to run *to* something for once. Even if it was for a night, for an hour or two if that was all we had. Even if it left me with more regrets in the morning. Damon and I had never had a true ending, a resolution that meant I could put him behind me. Maybe it was stupid to think that, there in the dark, I could find a way to have that. Or if I even wanted to.

But I did want him. And lying there, so close I could, I fancied, almost hear the thump of his heart. That same reassuring beat I'd hear if I just moved closer. If I laid my head on his chest and asked him to put his arms around me.

But I wanted more than comfort and closeness. I wanted something to chase everything away. To let me just *be*. To let me feel good. And if I knew one thing about Damon Riley, it was that he was the one who could do that for me.

"It was stupid," he said. "Selfish. You deserved better."

"So you owe me one?" I said. I inched closer on the mattress and felt him tense.

"I guess so," he said, tone very careful. Like a man who didn't want to scare a wild creature away.

"Then maybe it's time to pay up," I said and kissed him.

He stayed still for a moment before he kissed me back. Not as fierce as I'd been expecting. Gentle. As though he was kissing something precious. As though *I* was something precious. Something that might melt away and vanish if he did the wrong thing.

Maybe I would.

But right then I wanted to melt in other ways. I pressed myself closer, easing my arms around his neck.

"Maggie, are you sure about this?"

It was a reasonable question, given the speeches I'd thrown at him only hours ago. A question I couldn't answer "Yes" to. I wasn't sure. Not about whether this was a good idea. But I was sure I was going to do it anyway.

"I want this," I said. "I want you. If that's on the table?"

He laughed then, the sound spilling around me. "God, yes," he said, and then he kissed me again. This time he wasn't so gentle. This time his lips were hungry, coaxing mine open until our tongues touched and the taste of him flooded my mouth.

At the same time, his hands went to the bottom of my tee, lifting it up. I lifted my arms so he could slip it off me, then reached for the buttons at my waistband, all the while kissing him wildly.

Damn it, I had missed this. All those nights I'd fought against remembering, this was what I'd been fighting off. The memory of his touch and the way he knew exactly how to set me alight. My jeans joined my shirt, and I gasped as his mouth moved lower, licking kisses of fire against my skin, against neck and collarbone and chest until it settled over one of my nipples under the lace of my bra. Even without skin-on-skin contact, it was enough to send me arcing off the bed.

The noise I made was needy, and he went to work driving me crazy. He hadn't forgotten the things I liked. The things he'd learned in the short time we'd had together. Where I needed hard and soft. Where he could push me to the edge of pain, perhaps, to feed the fire between us. I tangled my hands into his hair, tugging him closer, urging him on.

He pushed the sheet away, pulling me onto his lap. I straddled him, moaning louder when the heavy length of him pressed against me.

I fell into the sensation, glorying in his mouth on mine as I rocked into him. His breath was as loud as mine in the darkness as we played with touch and taste.

This. All of this. This was what I wanted.

I slid my hand down between us and into his briefs, closing my fingers around him.

"Christ, Maggie," he breathed when he finally tore his mouth away from me. Even one-handed, he managed to flick the catch of my bra open, the straps falling down my arms. I shrugged it off, arching my back just to see his expression turn avid again.

His hands tugged me closer again, a groan escaping him as I stroked his cock. The sound vibrated through my lips and down every nerve ending in my body. I shifted slightly, pulling his briefs farther down. One of his hands steadied me while the other pulled the crotch of my panties out of the way.

I wasn't even sure what I was saying or what he was either as I slid down over him, shaking now from the need to be with him. Both of us froze a moment, the only movement our chests heaving. He pushed my hair back from my face.

"Maggie." This time it was reverence, not lust, coloring my name.

I'd thought we'd be wild and frantic, but suddenly, everything slowed. The kiss he pulled me down to was hungry but gentle, and it spun through my veins like smoked honey. The taste of him under my tongue was as addictive as the slow roll of his hips driving up into me, a sensation as electric as any touch of magic. I didn't need to look to know his aura would be blue fire. There was enough fire melting through me, narrowing the world to Damon, Damon, Damon.

To pleasure, the slow kind of wild that would melt me to nothing.

And for him, I'd burn. However he wanted me. I

felt the build of it with every touch and kiss and thrust. A dance of the two of us twined around each other, skin slick and heart struck and touch drunk until it was too much, and I came with his arms around me and his mouth on mine, pleasure spiking through me and dissolving me into nothing.

Chapter Twenty-Three

I woke with Damon's hands closing around my throat. Adrenaline spiked through me, taking me from fast asleep to red alert. His hands were tight but not choking, and his face twisted as though he was struggling with himself.

"Damon. Stop." I rasped the words as an order, trying not to let fear take over.

Not even a flicker of response.

Survival instinct kicked in. It didn't matter why he was seemingly about to choke me, what mattered was getting him off me.

He was bigger than me. Stronger. Just shoving him wasn't going to work. Instead, I needed to make him let go. I'd taken self-defense classes in my teens, and my teacher had been full of good ideas of how to cause pain fast. I remembered them but didn't know if I could pull any of them off.

Something from Cassandra's book flashed into my head, and my brain latched onto it. I leaned into the instinct, reaching for the same part of my brain that could set an imp on fire, and let myself look at him with my magic. His aura was weird and jittery, the energy field pulsing blue static against the dark.

I reached for it and yanked, trying to disrupt it.

To my shock, it worked. Damon collapsed like I'd whacked him over the head. Luckily he fell slightly sideways, and I managed to push him all the way off me, fueled by panic. I scrambled free of the bed and stood, panting, near the doorway.

Now what? I didn't know how long he might stay unconscious. I couldn't risk him waking up and attacking me again. There was a lock on the bedroom door, but it was electronic. And sure, Madge might follow my instructions and lock it for me once I was out of the room, but I had exactly zero faith that she would keep it locked if Damon ordered her to let him out. She seemed smart, but she was still just a computer system. I needed to restrain him.

Where was a bag of cable ties when I needed them?

But the kitchen yielded both a knife and scissors, and with them, I managed to slash the top sheet into strips. Fortunately, Damon didn't wake up as I tied his wrists.

Then I stopped. The man was butt naked, and I didn't want anyone asking why. I mean, I knew he generally slept in boxer briefs or nothing, but I didn't think he'd want his staff to know that. Wrangling his underwear on was harder than you'd think, but I managed and then tied his ankles with more sheet strips before knotting yet another strip to join wrists and ankles, hoping that might at least slow him down if he woke and came for me again. I dressed myself, my hands awkward and shaky as I fumbled with zips and buttons, trying not to take my eyes off Damon.

Then I picked up my datapad to call Cassandra. As I waited for her to answer, Madge's voice came from above me.

"Maggie, is Damon well? His respiration is slow."

"He's fine," I said. "He's sleeping. Just what the doctors ordered."

Hopefully she couldn't tell I was lying. But I wanted to talk to Cassandra before I called for Mitch's help.

Cassandra sounded half asleep when she finally answered the call.

"Damon attacked me," I said, keeping my voice down, not wanting to risk waking him.

"What?" Now she sounded awake. "Are you hurt?"

"He tried to strangle me. Or actually, he started

to try to strangle me, and then he sort of stopped."
I paused as my voice spiraled upward. *Deal with the situation now, freak out later.*

"Stopped?" She sounded confused.

"His hands were round my throat, but he didn't squeeze." The memory of it made my stomach clench and I tugged my jacket closer around me. "His face was weird. And he didn't respond when I yelled at him."

"But you must have managed to stop him somehow," she said. "If you're calling me."

"I knocked him out with magic. I was reading that book you gave me before I fell asleep."

"Well done," she said. There was a pause. "We'll talk about that later. Where's Damon now?"

"He's still out. I tied him up on the bed. With the sheets." *Don't ask what we were doing near a bed. Don't ask what we were doing near a bed.* "I haven't called Mitch yet. Because this kind of seems like our sort of problem. Not to mention I'm confused. Radha said he was fine."

"And Radha is rarely wrong, but she's not infallible. No healer is," Cassandra said. "Call Mitch. I think it's time we got Damon into a hospital and brought in some other healers. I'll call Ian."

Ian. Was she talking about demon stone? Fuck. That wasn't good.

"Which hospital? We can meet you there. Not much point in you coming all the way here first."

"St. Isidore. I'll call ahead and let Meredith know we're coming."

Meredith Dempsey was the witch who treated me after the first imp attack. Good. Someone I knew, at least. "Should I try to wake him up?"

"You have been studying up," Cassandra said, sounding almost amused.

"You told me to! I think I understand the parts about knocking someone out and waking them up."

"The first one, at least," she agreed. "But it might be best to let him sleep for now."

"Okay." I had to admit it was a relief. And not just because I wasn't sure I'd be able to perform the spell if I tried. "I'll let you know when we're on our way."

"Be careful," Cassandra said. "Don't untie Damon if he does wake up, even if he seems fine. And don't touch him any more than you have to. Particularly if he wakes up."

"You think this could be contagious?" I asked.

"I think we need to be careful. Now, call Mitch."

My conversation with Mitch didn't take long, but while I waited for his team to arrive, time dragged. Damon didn't wake as I dressed and splashed water on my face in the bathroom before pulling my hair back. My neck was reddened where he'd gripped me but not sore. The suite was well stocked. I found deodorant, toothpaste, and un-opened toothbrushes, so I used them, hoping there was no lingering smell of sex on me. There wasn't much I could do about the marks on my neck, so I ignored them and went back to the bedroom. I shoved my datapad and Cassandra's book into my purse, then added Damon's tiny datapad as well.

After that I just paced until I heard the door to the suite click open. Relief filled me as Ajax came in, pulling the sort of stretcher on wheels I associ-ated with paramedics and ambulances. With him, rather than Mitch, was a shorter dark-haired man I'd never met.

"Maggie, this is Ted. He's on my team," Ajax said.

"Where's Mitch?" Mitch, to his credit, had been instantly professional when I'd raised the alarm.

"He'll meet us at the hospital. He has some calls to make, get things squared away in case Damon has to be admitted."

That made sense. Big companies had protocols for this kind of thing. Someone had to act as CEO if Damon was unwell. Especially while they were still in a launch phase.

I nodded and stepped back so they could get the stretcher past me. Ted had what I was coming to think of as the "Righteous security team" look about him. Dressed in a button-down blue shirt and dark jeans that were neater than what I remembered the programmers wearing. Gold wire-rimmed glasses, brown hair short and neat. He tipped his chin at me but didn't speak.

"Is Damon in the main bedroom?" Ajax asked.

"The one at the end of the hall."

He nodded at Ted, who started pushing the stretcher in that direction. "Mitch said he's unconscious again? And you had to restrain him?"

"I cut up one of the sheets."

Ajax smiled reassuringly. "That was smart thinking. We can swap those for something a bit more reliable though." He moved closer to me. "Did he hurt you?" He gestured at my neck.

Damn, where was a little magical concealer when I needed it?

I waved him off, not wanting to go into any detail. "I'm fine."

"Okay," Ajax said. "I'm sure they'll take a look at the hospital. I'll go help Ted, and we'll be on our way." He gave me that smile again. "Everything will be all right, Maggie."

I hoped he was right. But it felt awfully like things were spiraling out of control.

I followed them out of the suite and into the elevator, standing awkwardly in the corner. Damon was covered by a blanket and strapped into place. A pulse monitor beeped softly and steadily.

We reached the ground floor and exited the elevator and the building. A truck that I would have said was an ambulance had it not been painted black was pulled up by the front doors. The first light of sunrise was just starting to creep over the horizon. Which meant I must have only slept for an hour, maybe two after Damon and I fell asleep.

What had happened in that time to make him attack me? Had the imp managed to infect him with something? Or establish a link? But how had Radha missed it if that was true?

My thoughts whirled. I tried to push them away. Fretting wasn't going to help right now.

Riley employees were enthusiastic, but it must have been too early for anyone to be out and about on campus, as I didn't see anybody else while Ted and Ajax slid the stretcher into the back of the truck.

"Ted will ride with Damon," Ajax said. "You're in front with me." He closed the rear doors. I climbed into the passenger seat and pulled on my seat belt, clutching my purse on my lap too hard, feeling my pulse start to quicken.

I would not have another panic attack now.

I reminded myself to breathe, and Ajax started the truck. He stayed silent as he drove, and I stared out the window. St. Isidore was maybe twenty minutes away. Maybe less this time of day when the traffic wasn't yet hitting the early commuter peak. Though traffic was never as bad as it had been before the Big One. Fewer businesses in the center of town and more remote working.

"Maggie, I need you to look at something for me," Ajax said. His tone had lost the reassuring note it held before. Now it was just cool and flat.

I turned to face him, frowning.

He tapped a screen on the dash I hadn't noticed. "I'm going to show you something, okay? And I need you to stay calm."

Calm? The hairs on the nape of my neck lifted.

The screen came to life. It showed the rear cabin. Where Ted was strapped into a seat next to Damon's stretcher. It took me a second to register that he was holding a gun pointed at Damon's head and that he was watching a datapad resting on his lap.

"What the—"

"I asked you to stay calm," Ajax said sharply. "Look at me."

I looked. He had a gun, too. Fuck.

"Now, I know you can probably do something to me and make me crash," Ajax said. "But if Ted feels this truck jerk or sway or go off course, he'll shoot Damon. He's watching us on that datapad. And if he sees something happen to me, he'll shoot him. But if you do as I say, then Damon will be just fine."

That was almost certainly a lie. But if there was a shred of hope that it was true, I needed to cooperate. At least until there was a chance to do otherwise.

I swallowed, my mouth dry with fear. "What do you want me to do?"

"Take your datapad out of your purse and turn it off, please."

The ice in my stomach solidified. He wanted my datapad off so I couldn't be tracked. I opened my purse carefully and took out my datapad. Damon's smaller one glinted at me from the bottom of the bag. Ajax didn't know I had it. I prayed it was set to silent and withdrew my own, making a show of swiping to turn it off.

"Good," Ajax said. "Now I'm going to turn down this alley. Your window will lower. Toss the datapad into one of the dumpsters. Don't try anything stupid."

I nodded and turned toward the window. No one outside would be able to see me through the UV tinting. And, knowing Damon, his security team's vehicles would be fitted with bulletproof glass and armored doors. Nothing I could break through myself.

Ajax slowed the car, and my window slid down. I tossed the datapad into the dumpster that stood in front of a nondescript brick building wall. Before I heard it land, the window slid closed again and the truck sped up.

They'd planned this well, it seemed. Ajax didn't

seem panicked or worried as he drove with one hand and kept the gun in his lap pointed in my direction with the other.

"Are you going to tell me what the hell this is about?" I asked. It was worth a shot.

"You'll find out soon enough," Ajax said. "Until then, just stay quiet and don't try anything dumb."

Chapter Twenty-Four

I GRITTED MY TEETH. *Okay. Think, Maggie.* My datapad was shut off and in a dumpster. Sure, Lizzie could track me to wherever we'd been when I'd switched it off via our housecomp, but after that, my trail would be gone.

Damon's datapad was still on, and Ajax didn't know I had it, so that was good. I just needed to make sure he didn't search my bag. Or find some way to hide the datapad somewhere within the truck.

Of course, the truck could have shielding, designed to block someone outside trying to track a high-value individual. Though, if it did, why would Ajax make me ditch my pad? We were still within the limits of downtown, heading toward the piers. Away from the hospital. If the truck itself had any

Riley-installed tracking devices, I had to assume that had been disabled or messed with to send a false signal. Ajax was too calm to be worried about immediate pursuit. So the plan must have been for us to arrive at our destination—wherever the hell that might be—before any alarm bells started to ring. Either that or we'd change vehicles at some point and vanish from sight that way.

Because once an alert went out on Damon, I had no doubt that Mitch would move heaven and earth to track down his boss. San Francisco was as wired as any city these days with traffic cams and security feeds galore. It would be difficult to avoid detection for very long.

But not impossible, I realized when Ajax made a series of turns that made it clear we were heading to Dockside, where the surveillance system was minimal at best. Dockside was, however, one of the few places in the city that would be busy so early in the morning, as the various clubs and gambling rooms and other establishments finally kicked out their last patrons of the night. But I didn't think I wanted to rely on the chance of boozed-up or drugged-up clubbers remembering a very boring black truck passing by.

Ajax threaded a path through the back blocks of Dockside, down streets where there were no lights other than his headlights to show our way, and past half-ruined buildings that not even the criminal side of the city seemed inclined to re-claim. When we emerged, it was into a back en-trance of some sort of transport depot, where huge semitrailers were parked in front of a ware-house that had no signage to indicate who might own it.

I tried to commit a few of the license plates to memory but lost my train of thought when Ajax drove down the side of the warehouse and up a ramp into the open cargo trailer of a waiting semi. A series of clicks echoed through the truck, then a jolt as something locked into place below us. Some sort of restraint to hold us steady?

I swore under my breath. So that was how we were going to vanish. There was little chance the cameras had traced us through Dockside, and now there would be nothing to see at all as the truck took us to our destination.

"Clever," I said.

Ajax shot me a glance but didn't respond. He tapped the screen and said, "Ted, five minutes be-fore we move."

"On it." Ted unstrapped himself.

"What's he—" I stopped as Ajax pressed his gun against my temple.

"Now, Maggie, you're just going to sit there and not try anything stupid."

I'd never had anyone pull a gun on me before. It was freaking terrifying. Every part of me froze while

my pulse screamed into overdrive, terror beating
through me.

"Good. Just like that," Ajax said.

His eyes flicked to the screen. Ted had peeled
part of the blanket covering Damon back and had
his left wrist in his hand. And a scalpel in the other.

That jerked me out of my stupor. "What the hell
is he doing?" I demanded. I didn't move, still
frozen by the steady pressure of the gun at my
temple.

"Relax. He's just going to clip his chip."

"Clip his chip? What does that mean?" Damn it,
there went my other backup plan. Damon's chip
and its panic button. Clearly they meant to disable
it. But that sounded crazy to me. Interface chips
were woven into the nervous system, installed by
very delicate surgery, and I had firsthand experience of how unpleasant it could be if one went
haywire.

"Ted knows what he's doing," Ajax said.

Unless Ted was a world-class cyber-surgeon, I
doubted that.

"You could cripple him. Or worse," I said. "Not
smart."

The gun pressed harder. "No commentary from
you. I'm smart enough to get this far. Just stay still
and behave, and everything will be just fine."

The more he said the word "fine," the less I believed him. And the more I wanted to try to take him

out. But I couldn't. Not while Ted had a gun and Damon was helpless.

The traitorous bastard had me right where he wanted me.

I stared at the screen. Whatever Ted was doing, he did it fast. He finished, sprayed Damon's arm down with an antiseptic, covered his wrist with a surgical shield, and then fastened the blanket back over him. Damon didn't stir. Whatever I'd done to him, I'd done a good job. Maybe too good. Or had Ted drugged him, too?

My jaw clenched as I sat and focused on how I was going to make Ajax regret his choices rather than how terrified I felt.

The semi's engine roared to life, making the floor of the trailer vibrate, and then we began to move. Ajax had killed the engine and the head-lights, so the only light came from the gray glow of the screen showing us what was happening be-hind us.

Ted aimed his gun back at Damon. The pressure from Ajax's gun at my temple vanished. I flicked a glance sideways. Yep, the gun was still pointed at me, but he was holding it back against his body now, still looking unnaturally calm for a man in the process of kidnapping one of the wealthiest men in the country.

I wished I could share his chill.

Or had any idea what happened to him to make

him do this. When I first met him, he'd seemed the perfect model of the happy-to-be-here Righteous employee, full of enthusiasm for his job. And now he was a full-fledged criminal.

It had to have something to do with the demon or at least whoever was sending the imps.

But still, why Ajax? Because he'd moved to security? Had he been contaminated somehow by one of the beta testers? Had he moved to security already under the influence of whoever it was?

Ugh. There were too many possibilities, and I didn't have enough information. Never my favorite situation.

Which meant I had no choice but to sit and wait until we arrived at our destination, where hopefully there'd be some more light shed on what they wanted.

And hopefully I could figure out how the hell to get us out of this when it was.

I kept track of the time showing on the dashboard. Ten minutes. Then twenty. Then thirty. Forty. Fifty. Maybe closer to an hour since we'd first left Righteous. Enough time for us to get quite some distance from the center of the city, if not out of it altogether at this time of day. But also long past the time that we should have arrived at St. Isidore.

Hopefully that meant people were now looking for us.

The thought was a small comfort. But in the face of Ajax's continued lack of concern, it was hard to believe this was going to end well for me or Damon.

All I could do was hope like hell that Mitch could zero in on Damon's datapad. I took care not to draw any attention to my purse. Cassandra's book was in there, too, and I didn't necessarily want Ajax and who—or what—he may be working with getting hold of that either. Though maybe that was a silly thing to worry about when clearly at least one of the people he was working with knew enough magic to summon imps.

I had no idea what direction we were headed. Whatever the restraints were that were locking the truck in place in the semi's trailer, it kept us very stable, leaving me with only a faint sense of movement from the vibration transmitted through the floor. There were a few turns that were sharper where I had a fleeting impression that we were going left or right, but as for overall direction, no. I didn't even have a reliable sense of speed. We weren't coming to a halt very often, which made me think that maybe we were outside the city now.

The semi came to another halt, and then, to my surprise, the engine noise stopped.

Ajax, who'd spent the trip in silence, raised his

gun once more. "All right, we're here. Don't try any-thing stupid. Ted is going to unload Damon, and then you and I will get out and walk down the ramp. You will remain in front of me. You will keep your hands in the air. If Ted sees you do anything else, then your boyfriend will be a permanent ex."

"He's not my boyfriend," I said automatically.

"Fuck buddy, then," Ajax said, eyes narrowing. "Either way, I'm guessing you don't want him dead." He prodded me with the gun. "Or maybe you do. Killing people seems to be part of your MO."

What? "Is this about Nat? I—"

The gun prodded harder. "Don't talk about her," he hissed in one of the first real displays of emotion I'd seen from him.

Was this about her? Some crazed revenge plot? Had he been in love with her? They'd only known each other a short time. But people could fall fast. I knew that myself.

That unfortunate fact was the reason they were able to use Damon against me now. I was sure it was me they wanted rather than him. If they needed him, they wouldn't keep threatening to shoot him. Which meant they only really needed him to keep me in line.

Light bloomed around us, which I assumed meant the semi's doors were now open.

Well, whatever the hell was happening, I was about to find out what came next.

I swallowed hard, fighting back the knot of terror in my stomach and the catch in my breath as I listened to the sounds of Ted taking the stretcher out of the truck. I wanted to turn and look but wasn't going to risk aggravating Ajax until I had to.

"Out," he ordered with another jab of the gun.

The light made me squint as I walked down the ramp from the back of the semi. I didn't dare lower my hands to shield my eyes, so I just blinked furiously, hoping I wouldn't trip and fall.

By the time my vision started to clear, I realized that actually the light wasn't that bright—just one lone floodlight shining from above the door of a large two-story house, making the early morning light brighter than the gray and gloomy sky warranted, but not by much. There were no other houses close by, the sweep of drive where we stood edged by gardens that dissolved into groves of trees. They didn't look like orchards, so maybe this was private property?

The thud of the semi's trailer doors closing drew my attention back toward the house itself.

Expensive from the size of it. The sort of Mediterranean stucco-and-arch mansion that wasn't that unusual for California. There was a shimmer of wards crawling over the walls, a darker oil slick sheen than I was used to. Exactly the sort of color I was starting to associate with demon magic.

But at this point, that wasn't a surprise. If this was about me, it was about magic. If it was about Damon, we'd be sitting tied in a room somewhere while a ransom demand was sent. Of course, I had no way of knowing that one hadn't been, but I was the one free and Damon was leverage. Our positions would be reversed if they were after his money.

The air was cold after the warmth of the truck, one of those unusually sullen and cool summer days that the bay air currents can blow across the city. I shivered. One of the things in Cassandra's book had been how to draw warmth from the air, but I couldn't afford to waste the energy. I had a feeling I was going to need all the magic I could muster to get us both out of here.

Ted started pushing the stretcher toward the house.

"Follow them," Ajax said from behind me, and I walked forward, happy to be moving away from the truck and Damon's datapad safely stowed in my bag still in its cabin. Until the semi's engine rumbled to life. I twisted my head and saw it headed back down the drive.

Fuck.

"Walk," Ajax said, scowling and gesturing with the gun. I faced the house. If Mitch was tracking

Damon's datapad, they'd at least have this location as somewhere it had stopped for a few minutes. They'd check it out. They had to, didn't they?

God, I hoped so.

The front door swung open as Ted approached, and he pushed the stretcher through and vanished from sight. I wasn't quite close enough behind to see what lay inside, and I slowed, my instincts crawling at the sight of the darkened doorway. Whatever was in there, they weren't using any lights.

Blinds were pulled closed over all the windows, with no hint of light behind them. So I'd be struggling to see when I stepped across the threshold. The perfect time for someone—or something—to attack.

Great.

Walk blind into what might very well be a demon's den or balk and get shot for my trouble. Not a great choice.

But apparently I'd reached the point where my body had accepted that fear was now normal and ascended into a sort of cool blankness focused on just getting through each next step. I reached the doorway and slowed my pace again, trying to give my eyes a chance to adjust.

It wasn't quite as dark as I'd feared. There were points of dim light flickering in the distance, though I wasn't sure what they were. The stench of rot and decay, the smell of imps, surrounded me, and for a moment, I had to fight off dizzy nausea. But again, that cool focus reasserted itself, and I swallowed hard and walked forward.

I'd expected to step into some sort of foyer, but instead, the house seemed to only have one large room. As though someone had knocked down as many of the interior walls as was possible while still keeping the second floor from collapsing. The pieces of walls that remained cast weird shadows, and I tried not to think what might lurk behind any of them.

No movement caught my attention, but that didn't mean we were alone. There was a staircase over to the right, but I couldn't see what it led to.

I followed Ted across the room, keeping an ear on what Ajax was doing. The front door closed with a final-sounding thud, and then footsteps echoed through the room, the floorboards and space making them too loud. I kept my eyes on Damon. There was nothing I could do if Ajax chose to shoot me in the back, but I might have a chance against a direct frontal attack.

Ted stopped halfway across the room. I kept walking, spine prickling. The wooden floor squeaked softly with every other step. Old. Hopefully not rotten. And thankfully, I could see no signs of circles painted onto the boards.

I knew circles could be used to amplify magic.

But Cassandra's book hadn't given me any details on how. That was apparently above the skill level of magical newbies. I'd never seen Sara actually use a circle, though I knew she did. She never let me watch, but she'd certainly been happy for me to scrub the remains of any chalk or wax off the floor when she'd finished. I was happy there were none here. Whoever had brought me here didn't need additional magical assistance.

I had almost reached the stretcher when Ajax said, "Stop."

I stopped. On the other side of the stretcher, Ted waited, hands clasped in front of his body, face arranged in the same sort of weirdly calm expression as Ajax's.

A spike of fear broke through. This place stank of imps, and that smell was enough to scare any sane human. It was probably *designed* to scare sane humans.

Yet these two were acting like we were standing in the middle of the Riley Arts campus, where nothing could hurt them and the most likely source of danger was some tech geek on a hoverboard bowling them over.

I let my sight flip over to see Ted's aura, expecting it to have that same jittery quality as Damon's, but instead it was a heavy dark gray. Rather than glowing, it was a band of smoked darkness around him. His face, viewed through it, looked corpse white. And odd, as though he wasn't quite real.

Right. Whatever was going on here, I didn't want Ted touching me. Something was definitely wrong with him. And he'd just cut Damon's wrist open. I almost stepped back but remembered Ajax.

My stomach rolled queasily. I swallowed. "Now what?"

Chapter Twenty-Five

"Now you wake him up, witch," said a voice that definitely wasn't Ajax's. It wasn't human at all.

I spun around, not caring about the gun.

The thing that stood next to Ajax wasn't an imp. At least I didn't think so. It looked more human than imp. Taller and less oddly bony. Not quite as human as the demon had looked though. It seemed unfinished somehow, the planes of its face and limbs wrong. As though someone had made the shape of a human with their eyes shut, then reached into their nightmares for ideas to finish it off.

"Well, witch?" it said. The words almost oozed and bubbled, as though there were too many teeth or tongues in its mouth. It made me feel like I was listening to something underwater.

"Why do you need him awake?"

It grinned then, and oh yes, there were definitely too many teeth. Gleaming black and spiked. Disconcerting against the almost human lips. Of course, any human with lips that shade of purplish gray would have been dead for quite some time.

A lesserkind, if I had to guess.

Damn it, I should have made Cassandra show me pictures of those as well as the imps. Though behind it stood an imp that looked remarkably like the one that had attacked us at my house. And several of its smaller friends, gleaming oily black, like the ones that'd first chased Damon and me through Dockside. From around me, chittering, rattling noises came from all angles, and more imps began to appear. I didn't waste time counting them. "A lot" was a near enough number. Too many for me to fry at once without a flamethrower.

"You are not here to ask questions," the lesserkind said.

"What am I here for?" I asked, stalling. Every second could be one second closer to help arriving. And I didn't think Ajax was going to shoot me for asking a question. Not without permission. Of course, the lesserkind probably didn't need to tell him to do it, it could probably just force him.

I snuck a peek at Ajax's aura. It swirled orange and yellow. Not jittery like Damon's, just agitated. That was better than dead gray like Ted's, I supposed.

"Keep your magic for the man, witch," the lesserkind said. Its gaze slid to one side, toward Ted. "Edward, step back and give the witch room."

Edward. Not Ted. Why was that name familiar? I moved to the stretcher, trying to remember. I laid my hands on Damon, knowing I couldn't stall too long. Not if the lesserkind could tell when I was using my magic.

Edward. Edward.

Then it sprang into my brain. Edward Greenstone was the last Archangel beta tester released from the hospital. It had to be him, surely? Did that mean he'd been the worst affected? And how in the hell had the healers let him go if his aura looked like that? Maybe it hadn't? It seemed hard to believe. But if a lesserkind could serve a demon, surely it could also corrupt humans. When that corruption had happened was less important than how far under its control Ted was. If I had to guess, I'd have said all the way. Which meant I needed to think of him as an extension of the lesserkind at this point.

"Do not waste time, witch." The lesserkind sounded annoyed, the bubbling quality intensified.

I stared down at Damon. Should I wake him up? *Could* I wake him up might be more the question. I actually had no idea what I was doing. I'd put him to sleep, but that had been half panic. Was he safer asleep?

Probably not. They had me now. Maybe they

didn't need him as leverage for much longer. In which case, I wanted him to have at least a chance of surviving this. If Mitch or the Cestis managed to find us, then awake, Damon might get out of here alive.

I closed my eyes and remembered what the book said. I needed to pull his energy field back up to where it should be.

Okay. So, if right now, my magic worked better when I was scared, then I would let myself be scared. Just for a minute. I opened my eyes and stared down at his face.

Let myself, just for a second, imagine what it would feel like if I never saw it again. If he never woke up. The fear that roared through me was torrential. I had to brace my knees to stay upright. But in its wake came a wave of fury.

No.

I wasn't having anything more taken from me. Not if I could help it. Not this man. Not my life.

Not without a fight.

I sent a pulse of power through Damon's aura, and his eyes snapped open, the blue unearthly bright in the weird half-light.

"Maggie?" he said.

"Stay still," I said. "We're not in Kansas any-more, Dorothy." He was a fan of retro culture, as Nat had been. A weird trait in people who em-braced the future and technology so enthusiastically, but there it was. I hoped he knew the reference.

He frowned but didn't ask anything else.

"Step back, witch," the lesserkind said. "Edward, untie him."

That made me scared all over again. Why was he happy to have Damon loose? Two humans against all of them wasn't great odds, but it was better than one. Unless it was counting Damon as being on his side. Another weapon. One who might just willingly put his hands around my throat again.

I stepped back, suddenly wary, angling my body so I could see the lesserkind, Damon, Ted, and Ajax. If Damon was under their control somehow, then it was three humans against one. That was without counting the lesserkind and its imp army.

In other words, I was screwed.

Ted released Damon, who sat up and swung his legs over the edge of the stretcher. Ted pulled a set of navy scrubs out of a bag tucked underneath and shoved them toward Damon. "Put those on."

Damon obeyed, face expressionless. That didn't ease my nerves. If you wanted to keep a human off balance, then keeping them mostly naked was a good tool. Giving him clothes gave him security. Did that mean they thought they had him under control?

While they were all distracted watching Damon

dress, I risked a quick glance at his aura. Still full of static.

And maybe, just maybe I could see a thread of energy extending out from his chest, the faintest glimmer of blue twisting in the air. But I couldn't turn to see exactly where it went. Not yet. I cut my power before the lesserkind could notice what I was doing and concentrated on Damon. If he came for me, then I would try to knock him out again. It was my only option.

"Now, witch," the lesserkind said. "Look at me."

I turned reluctantly. Demons could take over a human through sheer willpower if there was an opening. Could lesserkind do the same? I tried to remember what Cassandra had taught me about shields once upon a time. Something about pushing power out to strengthen your aura. It was worth a shot. I stared at the lesserkind, visualizing my aura turning solid. Nothing felt any different, but it snarled.

"Do you think that will save you?" it asked.

"Do you think your power will save you?" I spat back. "What do you want?"

"You hurt my master. You hurt us," it hissed. "We have slept, but we are awake now."

I hoped by "we" the thing meant it and its imps, not it and the demon. If the demon was already trying to find a way back to our dimension, then we had a bigger problem.

"So you took a nap." I tried to sound unconcerned. "If you were hoping for some beauty sleep, it doesn't seem to have worked."

It hissed at me. "Vanity is a human thing, witch."

Yeah, I didn't think so. The demons and their kind might be ugly, but they wanted to claim our world. That took ambition and greed, and vanity was an emotion wrapped up in that family.

"Edward doesn't look too hot either," I said. "What the hell have you done to him? Judging by his aura, he should be dead."

The lesserkind laughed. "He is useful but weak. He escaped us once. Now he is returned to us. His emotions twisted him. When the humans set him free, his despair called. And I found him again."

Found him and did what exactly? Drained his energy somehow to bolster whatever it was the lesserkind lost when I sent his boss back to the netherworld? That would explain the dullness of Edward's aura and his lack of independent action.

Come to think of it, I hadn't seen him do anything yet that Ajax or the lesserkind hadn't told him to do. So maybe he wasn't such a big threat after all. Sure, he would probably attack me if ordered, but I didn't think he would do anything at all, left to his own devices.

"Okay, so you got one of your demon's little toys back. Why do you need me?" I had a pretty good idea, but every word bought me time.

"Stop with the questions," Ajax snarled.

"Fuck you, Ajax," I said. "Shoot me if you want. But that won't change the fact that you're a piece of shit, selling humans out to these things." I waved my hand wildly, taking in the lesserkind and the crowd of imps. "I don't know what happened to you, but at this point, I don't care. Edward at least has the excuse of the Archangel glitch giving the demon access to him. And I'm sorry for him that he wasn't able to be cured. But you...you seem healthy enough."

For a moment his face twisted, his eyes going wide before his expression returned to calm. "We have an understanding," Ajax said, nodding at the lesserkind.

"What? Power? Revenge? Money?" I asked. "Trust me, Ajax, whatever it promised you, this can only end badly. My mother made a deal with a demon. She was dead weeks later."

His face twisted into a snarl. "You survived."

"I wasn't a volunteer. And you know what? When I found out about the demon, I kicked its ass back to hell. I wasn't stupid enough to join its team."

"Shut up," Ajax said. "You think you're so clever. But this demon came because of you. People got hurt. People died."

"And yet you teamed up with its little lapdog here? Slow learner, Ajax. I thought Riley was too smart to employ morons, but clearly I was wrong. I can't believe Nat thought you were cute."

"If I'm so stupid, how did I fool you all?" he snarled.

"Fuck off. You're going to regret this, loser." It wasn't the snappiest comeback ever, but somehow it hit home.

Fury flashed over his face, followed by something more like...regret? Was the old Ajax still under there somewhere? Could he be freed? Cured? Maybe. But at the moment, I had no sympathy to spare him. I would get myself out of this. And Damon. Then I'd worry about Ajax.

"Enough," said the lesserkind. "Wasting time is pointless." It stepped closer. "My master wants your power, witch."

"Your master can bite me," I said, baring my teeth at it.

"Brave words. But will you be less brave if I rip out the throat of the man? Or torture him until you comply?" It tilted its head at Damon, who hadn't so much as flinched at its words. "Do you value his life, witch?"

Fuck. My heart twisted. Tore a little. Did I want Damon to live? Yes. Did I want to live? Yes. Was I willing to rebind myself to a demon to do it? Hell no. Nor would Damon want me to.

Was I willing to give up just yet when there was

a chance that the cavalry might still be coming to save us?

No.

My hand strayed to the pendant at my throat.

"Your little stones are weak, witch," the lesserkind said. "They might give one of my children pause, but they will do nothing more than sting me for an instant should I choose to tear them from your throat."

"If human magic is so weak, why haven't you come for me before?"

"I was sleeping. When I woke, I was weakened. But I rebuilt my strength so I could find you. You were warded. Protected. But Ajax said the man would draw you out."

Fucking Ajax. But it made sense now. Someone with access to Riley's security and all its toys—someone computer savvy like Ajax—would be able to hack my system maybe. Or figure out how to set up a clone system that appeared to be mine. And Ajax had seen Damon and me together plenty of times at Riley. Nat might even have told him we were sleeping together.

"So much for company loyalty," I said, letting my disgust at him spill into the words.

"I don't owe Riley anything," Ajax said.

I wondered if he meant the company or the man. Close enough to the same thing in the end.

"He was right," the lesserkind interjected. "He will be rewarded."

Ajax smiled nastily.

I gave him the finger. In his place, I would have asked to read the fine print. A demon's reward for service from a human most often seemed to be death.

"You will be rewarded, too, if you take the bond," the lesserkind said. "Power beyond your weak human magic. Whatever you want."

If I took the bond? Interesting. The demon couldn't make the connection with me unless I agreed? Meaning they couldn't knock me out or hurt me enough to make me insensible. Good to know.

I risked another quick peek at Damon's aura. Or rather I looked for the glinting thread I'd seen emanating from it. I was expecting to see it join to the lesserkind, but instead the filament of light arrowed to the pale imp behind it. Apparently it was the one from my house. And it had somehow formed a connection when it hurt him. Maybe touch was enough for its contagion to work after all. Planting a seed of connection like a single bacteria. Something small enough that Radha had missed it. But now it had grown.

I needed to make sure it didn't grow more. A thicker thread, like a rope of smoke, ash gray and lifeless, stretched between Edward and the lesserkind. I wouldn't let that happen to Damon.

I had to free him. And given it was an imp, not the lesserkind controlling him, I thought I could.

Breaking this kind of link was something I knew how to do. I'd done it before. See the energy field, change the energy field. "Whatever I want?" I tried to sound tempted and took a step toward the lesserkind.

"My master is kind to those who serve," the lesserkind said. The corners of its mouth widened in some terrible parody of a smile.

I remembered standing by my mother's grave. They never let me see her body. Too shattered from the crash that sent her off a mountain road. I'd been shattered, too. With grief and loss, my whole world destroyed in an instant. And shattered again when I found out she'd sold my magic. That was a demon's kindness for you.

I took another step, then whirled and lunged for the stretcher, shoving it hard at Edward. He yelped and pulled his gun. I ignored him, taking advantage of the moment of chaos to reach for the link between Damon and the imp and sever it with a blaze of power that made my head swim for a second.

Damon blinked once before his expression snapped into focus, and then he seemed to take in the entire scene. He launched toward Edward, whirling into motion with a skill that told me Mitch had ensured his boss knew how to do more than just shoot. A gunshot, so loud it hurt, rang out. I ducked instinctively, not knowing where it came from. It was followed quickly by a second as I rolled back to my feet. Something hot tore across my arm.

"No!" shrieked the lesserkind.

I looked up to see it backhand Ajax with a furious blow. Ajax crumpled to the floor, his gun falling from a hand gone suddenly lifeless. Another shot sounded, and Edward also went down. Damon had the gun now. He aimed it at the lesserkind.

The lesserkind lifted a hand, face snarling.

"No!" This time it was me screaming, whether to warn Damon away or the lesserkind, I didn't know. I sent a bolt of fire in its direction, sending the imps scattering, but it dodged and gestured back at me. Magic rolled over me like a blow, followed by heat, as though my aura had caught fire. Pain shrieked through me for a moment before it faded, leaving me gasping for breath.

Fuck. I wasn't strong enough to beat that. It wasn't as though I could call lightning to strike it down like I had the demon. We were inside, for a start.

The lesserkind laughed. Lifted its other hand. I tried to call the shield back to life, to put something between me and Damon and it. My magic surged, then sputtered.

"Weak human magic, witch," the lesserkind hissed. "You will serve or—"

Behind it, the front door blew inward. I dove toward Damon, pulling him to the ground as more gunfire started. The lesserkind screeched and twisted toward the light. The pale imp from the garden fell to the ground, screaming as bullets tore through it.

I started to lift my hand, hoping to take advantage of the lesserkind's distraction as humans in black uniforms began to pour through the door. But the figure in the lead wasn't the sort of lean and muscular build I associated with Mitch's security team. No, it was short and curved. The one beside it was also short but slight. Another taller, curvy figure moved with them. Cassandra. Lizzie. Radha. The three of them moved faster than I would have thought possible. White light spewed from their fingers, though I wasn't sure if it was fire or magic. Wards sprang up around the lesserkind, and it twisted, screeching again, its own hands ablaze with magic pushing against the cage of wards.

"That won't save you," Cassandra said calmly. She looked over her shoulder, and Ian walked up to stand with them. He carried a complicated-looking bow. I knew immediately what the arrows it shot would be made from. Demon stone was too dangerous to put in a bullet. A bullet might go straight through a target and hit something beyond it. An arrow wouldn't. I'd been given demon stone-filled daggers to try against the demon, so an arrowhead made the same way made sense.

The lesserkind shrieked despairingly as though it knew what was about to happen, the sound ripping through my ears, making me want to curl into a ball and hide until the monster was gone. But I stayed put, made myself watch.

Ian's face was perfectly calm as he lifted the bow and sent the arrow arcing free.

He didn't miss. He could hardly miss from so close. The arrow took the lesserkind through the eye.

I'd never thought about what demon stone did to actual demonkind before now. It was almost anti-climactic to see the lesserkind fall forward, its skin turning silver. The thump it made as it hit the ground seemed to shake the building. The wards flared brilliant white around it, the four Cestis all sending more magic into them, until I couldn't see the lesserkind anymore.

It was no longer a problem. But we had another one.

The imps had gone crazy. More of them poured down the staircase and from every nook and cranny of the house. Damon and I pulled each other up, scrambling as one landed on Edward and bit a chunk out of his neck. I flung fire at it, and it caught like a candle's wick.

The next few minutes were a blur of flames and gunfire. Ian sprinted around the dead lesserkind and herded Damon and me back toward the door while Cassandra and Lizzie flambéed imps and the rest of Mitch's team rained bullets everywhere that wasn't our path. We stumbled out into the light, and the Cestis moved together like a well-oiled machine, bathing the house in a bright silver sheet of wards that hurt to look at.

Imps screamed at us from the destroyed doorway and from windows as they tore blinds down and smashed glass. I wasn't sure if their frenzy was their need to get free of the house or because of the lesserkind's death.

The Cestis watched them, deadly concentration in their combined gazes.

My attention snapped back to focus when Mitch strode up to me, a first aid kit swinging from the hand that wasn't holding the datapad he was barking orders into. Another of his team was already checking Damon over. From what I could see, he was in one piece.

"Let me look at your arm," Mitch said, shoving his datapad into his jacket. "You're bleeding."

"You found us," I said stupidly, still struggling to process the last few minutes.

"Well, you brought his datapad with you. Good thinking." He began to cut away at the arm of my jacket. Crap. I liked that jacket.

"Damon. They did something to his chip," I said.

"We know. It going offline set off an alarm. It was how we knew you were in trouble even before you didn't arrive at the hospital. Not smart of them, really." He grimaced, a flicker of grief crossing his face "Ajax...."

His voice cracked a little, full of disbelief. I knew how he felt.

"Demons twist people," I said softly. It was easier to believe that. Or at least to let Mitch, and the people who cared for Ajax, believe that. I wasn't convinced that he'd been under the lesserkind's control, but he had, at least, been seduced by its lies. Mitch would have to come to terms with that betrayal. I didn't need to add to that hurt if I could avoid it.

"That...thing. Was it the one who killed him?"

"Yes." I hissed in pain as Mitch dabbed at the bullet graze on my arm with antiseptic. "I'm not sure it meant to. Ajax tried to shoot me, and it hit him. Too hard." I didn't say more than that. Neither did Mitch. He just cleaned and dressed the wound before hitting my arm with a hypospray of painkiller.

"We should get Damon to the hospital," he said, packing everything back into his kit. "Dr. Barnard needs to replace his chip. My team can help with cleanup here." He suddenly had a lot more people on his team who knew about imps, I realized. That was going to prove interesting for the Cestis to handle. And Righteous.

"Thank you," I said to Mitch. My arm was comfortably numb. Pity he couldn't hypospray the rest of me.

"No. Thank you," he said. "Damon was right about you, and I was wrong." He looked me up and down, gave a satisfied nod.

That seemed to be as close as I was going to get to an apology. Before I could even start to think of a response, Mitch headed over to join the guy looking at Damon's wrist.

"We need to come up with Plan B for a panic button," I heard him say.

Damon laughed, the sound a little shaky but better than I would have expected.

Cassandra left the other three Cestis and walked over to me. "Are you all right?"

I looked back at the house and the imps, shrieking for freedom. "I'm alive," I said. "Other than that...." I shrugged. I was a long way from having any idea how I felt. Other than numbly exhausted.

"What do you think we should do?" Cassandra asked. "The wards will hold for a time, but that's a lot of imps for us to deal with. They'll be confused without the lesserkind, but they're still dangerous."

Ajax's body still lay within. And Edward's. At least, if anything remained of them. I shuddered at the memory of the imp tearing into Edward's neck. Should we try to bring them out? Or leave them?

That was what Cassandra was asking.

Presumably whatever cover story was going to be concocted could offer their families an explanation, just as one had been given to Nat's. And I had no sympathy left in me for Ajax, regardless of what I'd told Mitch. He hadn't been controlled like Edward. He'd chosen, and he'd paid for that choice. It was senseless to put anyone else in danger merely to make sure there was something left to bury. No doubt there'd be some spin, that he'd died saving Damon's life, perhaps. But that was as much as he got from me.

Edward was harder. I didn't know if he'd been willing. But he was dead, too. Which might be kinder in the end, given what I'd seen of his aura.

The rest of us were alive. There was no guarantee we'd stay that way if we went back in that house. I didn't want more families to lose someone today.

I turned my back on the house and nodded at Cassandra. "Burn it down." I looked across to Damon.

He nodded agreement. "Burn it down."

Mitch grimaced and bent his head, then straightened and gestured at his men. They backed away from the building.

"Do you want to do the honors?" Cassandra asked.

"I'm not sure how much magic I have left," I said.

"We'll help."

We walked to join Lizzie and Radha and Ian. Lizzie reached to squeeze my hand quickly, her eyes sympathetic. On Cassandra's word, we sent flames snaking along the ground. Five streams of fire to raze the evil within.

I watched just long enough to see the flames reach the house before I turned and walked away.

Chapter Twenty-Six

DR. BARNARD HAD TAKEN one look at Damon's wrist when we reached St. Isidore, muttered something that sounded suspiciously like "What the fuck?" and started issuing orders to prep him for surgery.

"Can Maggie stay?" Damon asked. He'd wrapped his good hand around mine after Mitch bundled us into a vehicle and had only let go when the doctor made him let the nurse take his blood pressure.

He'd asked me how we'd gotten to the house. I'd given him the short version but hadn't left out the part where he'd attacked me. He'd been horrified, even though I told him it wasn't his fault. The journey to the hospital had been very quiet.

But he hadn't let go of my hand.

"No," Dr. Barnard said. "This will take longer

than a standard installation. I'm going to put you under."

Damon grimaced but didn't argue. I'd just had time to tell him I'd see him when he woke up before Mitch and I were hustled out of the examination room.

At which point Radha and Cassandra pounced on me and hauled me off to another examination room to grill me about what exactly had happened.

I started to speak while Radha unwrapped Mitch's dressing to inspect my arm.

"You should go look at Damon before he goes into surgery," I said. "There was some sort of link between him and that imp. I broke it, but I didn't have time to do more than that."

Radha's eyes narrowed, and she made me describe the link and how I'd broken it. "Good girl," she said afterward. "The imp is dead, so that should be the end of it. But I'll go and check. Maybe Meredith is on duty, too." She marched out of the examination room, leaving me with Cassandra. Who made me tell her the whole story, including how the demon wanted me back.

"Well, it can't have you," she said shortly. "And now that its lesserkind is dead, I don't think we'll have to worry about it trying again any time soon."

She fussed with the hospital blanket, smoothing it over my legs. "So Ajax wasn't under its control?"

"I'm not sure," I said honestly, letting my head

drop back against the pillow. "His aura didn't look the same as Edward's. Agitated but it still glowed. And I didn't see a link between him and the lesser. I think maybe he made a deal. At this point, I don't think it matters, does it? He's dead." Another death to add to the demon's tally. And mine.

"Dead from his own choices," Cassandra said sharply. "This is not your fault. And you don't have time to wallow. You have power, young lady. You can do good with it. If you learn what you're doing." She started to ease the dressing on my arm back into place, her hands as sure and gentle as Mitch's and Radha's had been. I guess she'd dealt with her share of injuries over the years.

And her share of witches shaken by their experiences.

She was right. I'd seen a display of what real, practiced magic could do back at the house. Without the Cestis, I had no doubt that either Damon and I would both be dead, or he'd be dead and I'd be back in the demon's clutches. If learning magic would keep me—us—safe, then sign me up.

Cassandra finished redressing my arm. "There. You go wait for Damon. Plenty of time for us to talk about your training and what comes after that in a day or two."

What came after?

I was too tired to ask.

Which was why I was half asleep in a chair beside Damon's hospital bed when I heard him say my name.

My eyes flew open. I had no idea how long it had been since they'd wheeled him in from recovery. He'd been spaced out, giving me half a smile before falling asleep. I must have nodded off, too.

"Hey," I said. Happiness bloomed in my chest, tempered by wariness. The last time we'd been in this sort of situation, in the aftermath of fire and death and magic, he'd walked away from me. He could very well do it again. "How are you feeling?"

"I can't feel my arm, but otherwise okay," he said. He stretched his good hand toward me. "How are you?"

I curled my fingers through his, the warm weight of his skin making my heart lift. "I have no idea," I said.

He grinned. "Have I left you speechless?"

"I think that was everything else," I said, my mouth drying. That had been Damon in flirtatious mode. Surely he wouldn't flirt with me if he was about to tell me he was leaving again? But then again, he could also be hopped up on painkillers.

"Yeah, let's not do that again," he said. His expression turned serious.

I looked away, bracing myself.

"Hey," he said. "Look at me."

I lifted my eyes.

"I'm not a slow learner, Maggie. Well, maybe I

have *been* a slow learner, but I don't make the same mistake twice. And the biggest mistake I've made was walking away from you. I told myself I could do it. That it would be fine. I guess I should have known I was wrong about that when I kept drawing Archangel to look like you."

I held my breath, heart tumbling over. "That was you?"

He smiled. "Yes. I did her face about a hundred times. Each time she looked like you." He lifted one eyebrow. "I didn't think you'd seen it. You didn't say anything."

I waved that away. We could talk about all the dumb things we'd done later. "You were talking about mistakes."

He nodded, hand tightening around mine. "Letting you go was stupid. *I* was stupid. I hurt you. I'm sorry. And, if you can forgive me, I promise you I won't hurt you again."

"I'm still a witch."

"I know. I thought I could walk away from magic. But it's out there. That shit is out there. And you and the Cestis, you help people. And I can help you. If you'll let me."

I wanted to. Oh, I wanted to. But I had to know for sure. "Why? I've almost gotten you killed twice. Why do you want more of that?"

"Because I want *you*," he said simply. "I need you. I was miserable without you. You might be a witch, and magic might be scary, but not as scary as being without you again. You're a witch, Maggie Diana Lachlan. My witch. I love you. And your fight is my fight." He tugged at my hand, pulling me toward him. "I'm Team Maggie," he said. "Team Magic."

Magic was many things. I had no doubt it was going to bring more trouble with it in the future. But it had also brought me this man. This time I was going to hold on tight.

"Team Magic," I agreed. And leaned forward to kiss him.

THE END

Want more TechWitch?

Don't worry, Maggie and Damon's adventures continue in Wicked Nights - available now!

To keep up with news about them, sign up for M.J's newsletter at www.mjscott.net.

A note from M.J.

I hope you loved reading WICKED WORDS. This series is a lot of fun and I'm looking forward to writing more books in the series.

As an indie author, it really helps me when readers get the word out about my books, so if you enjoyed the book, please consider leaving a review at the store where you purchased it and tell your friends!

If you want to stay up to date with all my news, find out about new releases and sales, then please sign up to my newsletter at www.mjscott.net.

About the Author

M.J. Scott is an unrepentant bookworm who grew up in a family that fed her a properly varied diet of books. This cemented her story addiction and love of fantasy and romance. So it's not surprising she grew up to write books with both. When not wrestling with the magical worlds in her head, she can generally be found reading, doing something crafty, binge watching, and avoiding housework. She lives in Melbourne, Australia in a small house packed with books, cats, and craft supplies. She also writes romance as Melanie Scott.

You can keep in touch with M.J. on:
Instagram @melwrites
Facebook AuthorMJScott
Pinterest @mel_writes

Or email her at mel@mjscott.net

Also by M.J. Scott

Urban fantasy

The TechWitch series

Wicked Games

Wicked Words

Wicked Nights

Wicked Dreams

Wicked Ways

Wicked Deeds

Wicked Lies

The Wild Side series

The Wolf Within

The Dark Side

Bring On The Night

Romantic fantasy

The Four Arts series

The Shattered Court

The Forbidden Heir

The Unbound Queen

Courting The Witch (Prequel novella)

Acknowledgments

Thank you to all my family and friends for Zoom time, FaceTime, Messenger chats, phone calls, texts and general virtual communication that's kept us all sane this year. I'm lucky to have such a great bunch of people. Happy I can hug some of you in person again! Thank you to the internet, Red Frogs and Diet Coke because otherwise, there would be no book. Extra smooches to Sarah and Robyn for input along the way. Pats for the diva kitty for keeping me company this year. And thank you to all the readers who let me know you were enjoying my books during these crazy times!